"Squire Babcock's THE KING OF GAHEENA is a fascinating and complex novel which illuminates the most fundamental of human concerns: how to assess our purpose in the world and control our destiny. The characters are rich and vivid, and the prose is lush and evocative. Babcock is a splendid novelist who deserves a wide audience.

— **ROBERT OLEN BUTLER**, Pulitzer Prize-winning author of
A GOOD SCENT FROM A STRANGE MOUNTAIN

"*THE KING OF GAHEENA* is that rare thing: an absolutely original work that is by turns laugh-out-loud funny on one page and surprisingly moving on the next. Squire Babcock has created a living, breathing character in Calvin, whom I won't soon forget. He has also given us a fully imagined world populated by plenty of other memorable characters who are as endearing and as upsetting as your own family or neighbors. This novel is a wild ride, and I enjoyed every minute of it."

— **SILAS HOUSE**, author of *A PARCHMENT OF LEAVES*
and *CLAY'S QUILT*

"Squire Babcock's range is amazing. Not only does he write gorgeously about the country clubs of the Bluegrass and the brambles of the Arkansas swampgrass, but he elegantly shreds the thin veneer of civility that separates the two. His tale of discovery, peppered with shock and surprise, should come with a warning: Beware. Even the water is electric with sin and passion. *THE KING OF GAHEENA* will be hard to put down."

— **LYNN PRUETT**, author of *RUBY RIVER*

THE KING OF GAHEENA beautifully conjures the wild Arkansas landscape as the vast contested territory of family and individual identity. For 20-year-old Calvin Turtle, it is part of an inheritance freighted with entitlement and grief, violence and blind need, and surprising moments of wonder. Squire Babcock's compelling new novel brings the linked worlds of Gaheena and society Louisville vividly to life as Calvin reckons with irretrievable loss, misuses of power, and the vexed legacy of his father, to claim a life of his own.

— **NANCY REISMAN**, author of *THE FIRST DESIRE* and *HOUSE FIRES*

Rich in atmosphere and vibrating with suspen...
the work of a ma...
— **LEAH STEWAR**...
and 7

the KING of GAHEENA

For Patience —
My best Friend —
Thanks so much for
your support. All the best,
Squire
Paducah 10/20/09

SQUIRE BABCOCK

Motes
Books

THE KING OF GAHEENA

Squire Babcock

© 2008
All Rights Reserved.

ISBN 978-1-934894-02-6

FICTION

The publisher and the author wish to thank
the *U.S. PLAYING CARD COMPANY* for granting permission to use the image of
the King of Hearts (aka "the Suicide King") from their *BICYCLE* brand cards.

Design by EK LARKEN

Published by

PO Box 6034
Louisville KY 40206

WWW.MOTESBOOKS.COM

Acknowledgements

I am grateful to many whose support has led to publication
of this novel, especially to my mentor and friend, *George Cuomo,*
who believed in the book long before I did, and to
Lou Berney, Sarah Gutwirth, Arthur Kinney, David Milofsky,
Ann Neelon, Dale Ray Phillips, Lynn Pruett, Richard Steiger,
Lee Smith, and *John Wideman.* Thanks to *Margery Griffith*
and others at the U.S. Playing Card Co. for the tour
and all the playing-card information; to *Murray State University*
for the Presidential Research Fellowship; to *Kate Larken*
for believing; to *Dick Bruehl* for everything.
Finally, to *Melodie Cunningham,* angel, thanks for being there.

For Whitney and Meme

CHRISTMAS EVE, 1957

The earth spins, and darkness shrouds the House of God, one mansion at a time. On the surface of the spinning ball, in a fertile realm called Kentucky, soft black hills coil around the twinkling city of Louisville like sleeping serpents nested against the embers of a dying fire on this silent, star-bespeckled night.

At the eastern edge of the city, inside a mansion built on a limestone bluff overlooking a wide and polluted river, a seven-year-old girl slips downstairs in the pre-dawn stillness and tries to plug in the Christmas tree lights because she loves those primal reds and blues and yellows more than anything on this moonless night, but the old cord is frayed and her bare foot is in a puddle of liquid left there by her mother and father who stayed up last night fighting, though they did not understand why, and since the human body, by virtue of its water content, is an excellent conductor of electricity, which, like most forces on this spinning planet, travels the path with the least resistance, there is a sudden sparking and a small heart stops.

Because they drank all evening to intensify their angry little dance and then made love as they do after most marital conflagrations, the little girl's parents sleep the exhausted and dreamless sleep of spent warriors in their king-sized bed at the other end of the house, oblivious to the flicker and death of the nightlight in their marble bathroom.

Because he has come to expect a glorious mountain of presents under the tree on Christmas morning and is still curious enough about Santa Claus that he wants to see if the old fellow actually ate the milk and cookies on the coffee table, the girl's five-year-old brother gets out of bed and tiptoes down the carpeted stairs, where, the evening before, he sat listening to his parents argue, and yes, where he heard the drink spill and his father curse his mother, then his mother curse his father, and where he was still sitting when his crimson-faced mother came storming by the foot of the stairs, caught sight of him, halted abruptly, as if he were a deadly snake, screwed up her face in a horrible mask and screamed, "What the hell do you think *you're* doing? Get back in that bed!"

For a long time, the boy will not remember the acrid smell nor his sister's puzzled, sightless gaze. He will not remember screaming incoherently in his bed for two days, nor will he remember the psychiatrist who came into his room with nothing to offer but drugs. He will only remember a nuclear explosion, a world-shattering Christmas extravaganza in his head, and that's all.

THURSDAY, MAY 3ʳᵈ, 1962

On the way to Grandma and Grandpa's house, Calvin rides in the back seat of his father's "Woody," a lumbering old Ford station wagon with real wood panels down its sides and green seats that smell like piss when they get hot. Outside, it's spring, moist and warm, and the car windows are rolled down. People are mowing and raking their lawns.

At the traffic light on Lexington just before the turnoff to Grinstead Drive, Calvin's father lets out the clutch too fast and the Woody lurches and stalls. "Come on!" he growls, as the starter whirs and whirs.

"We look like white trash in this thing," his mother says.

The Woody's engine finally fires. His father smacks the dash. "Attababy."

Grandpa hugs Calvin's mother when they get there. "Hello, Punkin."

"Hi, Daddy," she croons into his neck.

Grandpa shakes Calvin's hand, then Grandma swoops him up in her flabby arms and gives him a wet one. She smells old and clean, like the house. This is the house where his mother grew up. His other grandparents died before he was born.

While the grownups have drinks, Calvin goes in the back room and gets out a deck of Turtle Cards for a game of Klondike. He works carefully to keep the free piles squared up and the tableau strings all in perfectly aligned, descending order. Soon he has built a succession from the King of Spades all the way down to the two of hearts, the cards in a highly disciplined line, each spaced the same, top to bottom.

For Calvin, solitaire is religion. The Church of Klondike, he calls it, referring to the most popular of all solitaire games and the only one Calvin ever plays. Klondike is life, life is Klondike; that's all you need to know. Calvin believes that God is the opponent in Klondike, and God's a crafty old Wizard. Calvin is convinced that if he can ever beat Klondike, God will have to give his sister, Jewel, back.

The *Official Rule Book for Card Games* says this: "It is a tribute to the Indomitable Human Spirit that this most popular of all solitaires (Klondike) is at the same time the most difficult to win."

Here's how it goes: First you deal out seven piles of cards left to right in increasing size from one to seven cards, top card face-up on each pile. This is your "tableau."

Then, one at a time, you turn over the remaining cards in the deck and either make plays with them or place them face-up in what's called the wastepile. You can also make plays with the face-up cards in the tableau, building strings of cards descending in rank, alternating in color. If you take one card or string of cards in the tableau and play it on another, then you turn face-up the next card on the vacated string. The ultimate object is to get each card in the deck face-up and ready for what is call the "liberation."

When you liberate a card, you remove it from the wastepile or from the tableau and play it by suit on one of four foundations, or "free piles." You may begin the "liberation" as soon as an ace turns up, then you build that suit's free pile in ascending order. You must liberate the two of hearts before you can liberate the three, and so forth, and you can't liberate a card unless it's the top card on the wastepile or happens to be the last card (or only card) on a string of cards in the tableau.

If the right cards don't turn up, you're dead; there's no going back in Klondike. One time through the deck and it's all over. But if the four aces come out early, and if you can make a lot of plays, build big strings, play strings on other strings, you might just liberate all 52 cards.

The odds are against you, of course, but Calvin is determined. Tonight, his determination pays off. When he's got all fifty-two cards neatly freed into the top four piles, he runs into Grandma's living room to tell his father.

"Dad! I did it! I beat Klondike!"

"You *didn't!*" his father says, making his eyes big and dropping his mouth open in mock disbelief. Cigarette smoke hangs above his head like fog.

"Did too. First game I played. Beat it fair and square."

"Attaboy," his father says, rubbing a hand in Calvin's hair.

"Cal, you know about running in this house, don't you dearie?" Grandma says. Lucky Strike smoke curls in a tiny curtain up her nose.

"Yes, ma'am."

"Ginny, let the boy be a boy," Grandpa says. He takes a long sip from his drink.

Smoke hisses from Grandma's mouth. "You've no respect for my things, Roy. Never have."

"For godsakes, the boy just beat solitaire. Can't he get excited about that?"

"Not in my house."

"Is dinner about ready, Daddy?" Calvin's mother asks.

"Comin' right up, Punkin."

They have dinner tonight the way they always do at Grandma and Grandpa's, rickety old lemon-smelling dining table, good silver, two forks, don't talk with your mouth full. Calvin keeps his eye on the doorway. He thinks his sister Jewel will suddenly just walk in that door and sit down as if she were never gone, and this makes him happy. But it's Grandpa who comes through the door carrying a steaming broccoli casserole. Grandpa always cooks, and he always does the dishes.

Grandma does the house. She is constantly redecorating and rearranging, keeping the antique furniture polished, the seat covers immaculate, bending down with a grunt to align the small oriental rugs just-so on the slick hardwood floors.

Grandma collects rare things, wonderful things: elephants carved from exotic wood, trees carved from ivory, a stampeding herd of crystal deer, exquisite seashells. She has a family of porcelain figurines with brown faces, another family of Scandinavian dolls dressed for Sunday dinner, and a delicate pair of stuffed shore birds mounted one atop the other, mating. She even has a tarnished old sword from Iraq, complete with inlaid royal seal and double blood-gutters.

In every room are her treasures, and on the walls hang large,

15

dark oil portraits, one of Grandma looking sadly into the distance, one of Grandpa in his World War I uniform, one of Calvin's mother and his Aunt Virgie as cherubic little girls in the flower garden, and one of brooding old John Wilhelm Board, the coal baron, Calvin's maternal great-grandfather, reposing in a deep chair, prized hunting dogs at his feet.

But Grandma's most cherished possession is her china hands. They're from an ancient land, she claims, made of hard, creamy-white, crystalline china, and small, about the size of Grandma's living ones, but fully muscled, not bony and thin like Grandma's. The two perfect china hands are cupped together to form a shallow bowl, both palms fully up and open in supplication, the fingertips smooth and rounded, the nails well-trimmed, the life-lines boldly asymmetrical. They seem so real and alive you almost believe you can see inside the creamy flesh to a faint blueish network of veins. One time Calvin's mother squashed a Lucky Strike in Grandma's china hands and Grandma ordered her to leave the house. They didn't speak to each other for a month.

Jewel doesn't reappear during dinner, but Calvin isn't worried. He shoves the cheesy broccoli around his gold-trimmed plate and imagines hugging and teasing his sister. Maybe she'll come back tonight when they are asleep. She has to come back. He beat Klondike tonight, didn't he, and that's the deal. God has to give her back.

After dinner, Grandma shows Calvin her latest acquisition, a set of frosted-glass wind chimes tinkling in the soothing breeze on the porch. "Aren't they pretty, Cal, darling? They're from New York. Don't touch." She gives Calvin a hug and another wet one. He can smell her whiskey.

Soon everyone is settled at the card table in Grandma's living room for a game of Hearts.

"Can I play?" Calvin asks.

"No," his father says.

"You don't know how to play, Cal, honey," his mother adds. She calls him "honey" when she drinks.

"I've been learning," Calvin argues. "I know how to play. Come on, *please* let me play. I'm almost ten."

"Maybe next time," his father says, shuffling the cards. "Why don't you go play some more solitaire? Wanna do that?"

"No, sir."

"Your father's too good for us anyway," Grandpa says. "He'll beat us all."

"You come sit next to me and watch, Cal, darling," Grandma says, patting the cushion of her chair.

So Calvin watches the Hearts game from his grandmother's side. He can easily fit next to her thin body in the big chair. Grandma is old, but her eyes are bright and sly. Calvin feels heat where their legs touch.

His father deals out the first hand, the cards landing in four chaotic piles of smiling Turtles. As he arranges and re-arranges his cards, he hums and smiles cunningly; that's part of his game. You always worry that he will shoot the moon.

Grandma has a lot of clubs in her hand, plus the dreaded Queen of Spades. Calvin whispers in her droopy ear: "You've got the Queen!"

She smiles and blows out a jet of smoke: "Shhh, darling. Don't give me away." Deception is the key in Hearts, of course. Grandma is good at it, but Calvin's father is the best.

"Who's got all the puppytoes?" he says, studying everyone's face. He's a big nicknamer: hearts are pumpers, diamonds are sparklers, spades are diggers, clubs are puppytoes. Calvin wonders what his father's nickname for him ought to be. *Champ,* maybe.

His dad takes the first trick. "I wish I knew who has the puppytoes, the pup pup puppytoes," he sings. "Is it you, Grandma? I bet it is. Cal, does your grandmother have all the pups?"

Grandma has most of the puppytoes, of course, but she doesn't let on.

"He's shooting the moon," Calvin's mother says through a stream of Lucky Strike smoke.

Grandpa rubs his whiskers and grunts his favorite word, "Oomska."

"Come on, I'm not shooting the moon. This is the worst hand I've ever had."

Calvin watches his father with intense admiration. It's risky to try and shoot the moon. Do or die. You either take complete control or you lose big. No in-between. His father tries to do it every hand he plays. Now he throws out his only club, the seven, and Grandma takes it.

Calvin's father says, "Better get rid of the Queenie, Grandma. Better send her on home before she decides to stay the night."

Calvin can't figure out how his father knows that Grandma

has the queen.

"Don't do it, mother," Calvin's mother says. "He's shooting the moon. Don't give him the Queen if you've got it. He's trying to talk you into it. Don't help him."

"What makes you think I've got the Queen?" Grandma says. "And what makes you think I'd take the points just to save you and your father?"

Grandma leads the Queen of Spades.

"Oh great, mother, now he's got the moon for sure." Calvin's mother tosses her cards on the table, grabs her drink and sits back in her chair. "I don't want to play. Sonny's just going to shoot the moon every time, and you're not doing a damn thing to stop him."

"Neither are you, dearie," says Grandma. "How do you know Sonny will take the Queen? Maybe your father will take it and save the day. Will you save the day, Roy?"

"Come on, Punkin, you mustn't quit," Grandpa says. "Pick your hand back up. I'll show you who can stop the mighty moonshooter." He throws out the ace of spades, topping the queen.

Now Calvin's mother picks up her cards and leans back over the table, smiling. "That's the way, Daddy. That'll fix his wagon."

"Ha!" his father says, as if everyone has done exactly what he wanted. "I wasn't shooting the moon."

"Sure, Sonny," his mother says, firing a blast of Lucky smoke at him, "and I'm Marilyn Monroe."

"I *wish*," his father says.

"Oomska," says Grandpa, rubbing his scratchy whiskers.

The grownups play more Hearts, and Calvin goes to the back room for a little more solitaire. They'll be going home soon. It's a school night.

All four aces show up early in the first game. Calvin begins to build neat piles of freed cards and deep down he already knows he's going to beat Klondike again, twice in a row. Soon he has all fifty-two cards in the free piles. He leaves the four immaculate stacks of sparklers, diggers, pumpers and puppytoes in the middle of the floor and runs to tell his father, but when he rounds the corner in Grandma's living room his right foot catches the little rug there and the rug slides forward on the slick wood. Calvin falls against a small table just inside the door, sending the herd of crystal deer and Grandma's precious china hands crashing to the floor. Calvin stands up as fast as he can, as if he can reverse time and put everything back in order, but he hears his Grandma saying, "Oh God. Oh Lord God!" Her mouth is open wide as Mammoth Cave.

Down at Calvin's feet in a chaos of sharded antlers and deer legs are Grandma's broken hands, nothing left of them but jagged chunks of palm and eerie, detached fingers. He expects to see blood, but none oozes from the dead chunks of milky china.

Grandma has fallen to her knees and is staring at the wreckage. She puts her own blue-veined, bony hands to her mouth and begins to bow and wail. "Oh God, oh Christ, he's broken my hands, oh my dear God, dear God, dear God..."

"Stop it, Ginny," Grandpa says, reaching for her. "Stand up here, now. The boy didn't mean to do it."

Grandma jerks away from him and shrieks, "He was running in *my* house. I've warned him a thousand times. You don't give a damn about my hands. You don't give a damn about *me*."

Calvin's mother remains at the card table, calmly smoking. His father puts his cards face-down on the table, pushes his chair back, stands up and comes toward Calvin, his jaw set. "Get in the back room," he says. "Right now!"

In the back room Calvin sits on the couch and stares at the four neat piles of freed cards in the middle of the floor. *I didn't mean to do it*, he tells himself. *It was an accident.* He can hear Grandma wailing in the other room. On the wall above him is a photograph of his mother in her wedding gown, a pure white angel suspended in a pure black world, her head turned to the side, as if she is expecting someone, a long flowing billowy white train pouring away behind her like a giant bucketful of milk. Calvin hears the tinkle of glass. Grandpa is sweeping up the wreckage.

Things are quiet for a time and Calvin is hopeful; then his whiskery old grandfather comes back to see him. "Calvin, your grandmother is very upset because you broke her things. I hope you are sorry about it and that you will never run in this house again."

Calvin begins to cry. "I didn't mean to."

Grandpa comes over to the couch and puts his big hand on Calvin's head, soft and warm, like a good cap. "That's all right, now. It's all right," he says, then he leaves.

Calvin's mother comes in, drink in hand, a nasty smirk on her face. "What're you bawling about? You broke my mother's priceless china hands running around like a wild man. *She's* the one who should cry. You've been told and told not to run in this house. They can never be replaced. I hope you know what you've done." She leaves.

Calvin's father comes in. "You're gonna get a whipping when we get home."

His father's belt is the worst thing Calvin knows. On the way home he sits on the smelly back seat of the Woody, windows up, thinking of nothing but the whipping. Every time he pictures the belt an explosion goes off in his head. He silently recites a little chant he has made up for life's emergencies: *Sparklers and Diggers, Pumpers and Puppytoes, into the Free Pile, here I goes.* In the front seat his mother and father are quiet and calm. Calvin prays that the Woody will stall and never start again.

When they get home he follows them to the front door. His father turns to him: "Go upstairs and take down your pants."

Upstairs in his room Calvin leaves the light off and closes the door. He pulls down his pants and gets down on his knees with his head to the far wall. He closes his eyes and waits, face in the carpet, naked butt pointed out and up into the darkness, ready. He thinks of those solitaire games. He beat it twice, didn't he? He whispers his chant again: "Sparklers and Diggers, Pumpers and Puppytoes, into the Free Pile, here I goes."

Now he hears his father coming up the carpeted steps, a heavy pumff, pumff, pumff. The door opens, his father flicks the switch, and the light hits Calvin's cold butt.

His father's buckle clinks. "This is for your own good," he says. The belt slides through its loops. Calvin is ashamed of his naked butt. His penis drips a little.

The belt strikes hotly and Calvin falls over and screams and scoots across the floor, hiding his stinging behind.

"Get back on your knees," his father orders, crimson face twisted into a strange mask, eyes hot, jaw muscles writhing like lovers under a blanket.

Calvin gets back on his knees and the belt bites him again, lower down, on the flabby part of the back of his legs, a new kind of pain. He screams and screams. He wants his mother to come in and stop it. Where the hell is she? When he reaches behind to cover himself, another blow strikes the back of his hand and he falls on his side and clamps his burning hand between his knees. His screams won't come out as noise any more.

The light goes out. Now his father is just a dark silhouette in the doorway, the belt dangling from his clenched fist like a dead snake.

"Get in bed," he says. Then he shuts the door and Calvin is blind.

Lying atop his bed in his Superman pajamas, Calvin cries for a long time, his hand and butt stinging every time his blood pumps. Life is stupid. Klondike is stupid.

His mother comes in, turns on the light, sits on the edge of the bed and kisses his wet cheek. He leans up and hugs her neck, melts into her. She is in her nightgown, but she still has her earrings on, the little diamond ones Grandpa gave her.

Sparklers.

She pulls away from his hug and says with hot whiskey breath, "I hope you have learned your lesson."

Calvin falls back into the pillow and starts to cry again.

"That's okay, honey," his mother says, thumbing away a tear. "He hits me too."

Calvin hiccups.

"Does it still hurt?"

"Yes, ma'am."

"Lemme see."

When he turns over, face in the pillow, his mother strokes the back of his head, then pulls his pajama pants and his underpants down a little way. "Lordy," she says. She pulls his pants and underpants down a little farther, past his butt. "Now you're shooting the moon," she jokes.

Calvin tries a feeble little laugh. His mother's cold hand touches the place on the back of his thigh. "Ouch," he says, trying not to move.

"Sorry, honey."

Now that cold hand slips under his shirt and smoothes rapidly up and down until it gets warmer, then it rubs his shoulder muscles, the long fingernails lightly stabbing his flesh.

Diggers.

The hand trails down each leg, then back to his naked butt, where it stops, resting warm and light, not heavy, on the place that stings. Calvin's blood pulses against the hand.

Pumpers.

His mother's hand is fleshy and smooth, with muscles, like Grandma's china hands. It slides slowly down to the back of his thigh and rests for a moment over the stinging place, then it pulls his pajama pants and his underpants to his ankles, then past his toes.

Puppytoes.

"Turn over," she says.

"Yes, ma'am." He rolls over and crosses a leg to hide his penis, then he searches her face, close above him. The skin is splotchy red and her eyes are sad, watery pools. He starts to panic. Whenever his mother cries, Calvin feels like he is going to die. A strand of her blond hair is loose and hangs down almost to his nose. Her hot whiskey breath is making him dizzy.

Trapping that wayward strand behind an ear with a motion of her hand, his mom leans down and kisses his forehead, then she strokes his face and Calvin closes his eyes and concentrates on the sound of her rapid, shallow breathing as that hand slides down the front of his pajama shirt over the big red *S* and jumps to his thighs, which she gently pulls apart and pushes down until he lies flat and his penis is cold and exposed to the whole world and underneath him his butt still stings as he holds his arms and his legs rigid and straight as a string of playing cards, but he doesn't open his eyes because his heart is blamming in his chest like a Fourth of July skybomb and her hand is on his penis now which is getting stiff and she leans down, that whiskey breath singeing his face, and coos, "Just relax, honey," so he tries to relax for her because he doesn't want to die.

GAHEENA

Gaheena, Arkansas, is a one-cop farmtown in the middle of a vast, dead-flat prairie where the highest hills are the levees curving around the rice fields. There are two churches in Gaheena, one white, one black, and a combination laundromat/grocery called The Washeteria, a filling station, an IGA, a pool hall, two cafés – one for blacks, one for whites – and a cotton gin. White folks live in small, one-story homes along paved, shady streets. Black folks live in shacks on gravel roads radiating like wheel spokes from the cotton gin.

When you round the third bend on Highway 79 out of Stutgart, the first thing you see is Gaheena's rusted Tin-Man water tank astraddle the railroad tracks that parallel the highway. *Population 383* says the sign as you enter town.

A few miles west of town, comprising nearly a thousand acres of woods, fields, ditches and swamp, is a hunting preserve known as the "Old Wilson Place." From the air you can see the shape of it, a giant diamond set like a billion-carat dream in the midst of a patchwork of rich Mississippi River Delta cropland. A narrow dirt road splits the Place down the middle, and halfway down this road, at the heart of the diamond, is the Old Reservoir, a vast, snaky dead-timber swamp so rich and teeming with life that you could easily mistake it for the Primal Soup. Rotting trunks, skeletons of a once-lively forest, jut out of the Old Reservoir like broken spines, their limbs long since fallen into the Soup, and every spring a heavy tangle of dark green stuff called Duck Moss grows beneath the surface, coiling around the fallen branches and trunks so that by duck season it's so thick you can hardly pull your leg through it. Ducks, apparently, can't get enough of it. You can shoot and shoot, but they keep spiraling down into the Old Reservoir, bent like addicts on one more hit of that Duck Moss.

A legendary man named Karl Buntingstrife is in charge of the Old Wilson Place. He maintains the levees around the Old Reservoir, hunts and traps in the woods, guards against poachers year around. He lives in a one-room wooden structure at the western edge of the Old Reservoir known simply as the Shack. There is no phone, no electricity, no running water, and only a propane stove for heat and cooking plus a little gas-operated refrigerator. If you want to talk to Karl, you park your car at the locked gate and walk half a mile down the narrow road to the Shack, or you call the whites-only café and leave a message.

SATURDAY, JUNE 27TH, 1964

Calvin turns twelve tomorrow. For his birthday, his father is taking him on his first trip to Arkansas. Sonny Turtle has just bought the Old Wilson Place and Calvin understands in a dimly disturbing way what this means: the Old Wilson Place is his now, too.

Calvin is playing a little Klondike on a pull-down tray in the back of a Kentucky Flying Service twin-engine Cessna. The pilot is "Sleepy Jim," a chubby, disheveled fellow with a quiet voice and a quick smile. Calvin's father calls him Sleepy Jim because he usually puts the plane on autopilot and sleeps, but right now Sleepy Jim is wide awake because Calvin's father is flying the plane. Headphones on, hands on the steering wheel, Sonny Turtle looks so cool. Everyone thinks he's a cool and funny guy, except Calvin's mother. Calvin pictures the plane suddenly dipping, nose-diving, crashing, Calvin the only survivor. His mother would wail and cry, but she wouldn't really miss his father.

The plane flies smooth and straight. Through the scratchy window the world below is a ragged skin of emerald woods and planted fields, with little towns and farm houses splotched here and there like ripened boils, all of it cut through the middle by a giant glistening river, the Ohio probably, or maybe the Mississippi, Calvin can't remember his geography. He spots the shadow of the plane speeding over fields and roads and houses and racing right past the giant shadows of clouds. He is Superman, faster than a speeding bullet. He will soar down and save all those people from evil, then he will make the earth spin backwards, reverse time itself, and bring Jewel back to life.

They land at the Stutgart Airport, which is just a small weedy runway and a tiny yellow-brick "terminal" building in the middle of an immense flatness. When the plane stops moving and Sleepy Jim kills the noisy engines, an old black man runs out to the plane and hollers, "Welcome to Arkansas, Land of Opportunity." They climb out of the cramped cockpit and down the wing of the Cessna. Calvin's father says, "Good to see you, Eli," and the old man says, "Yessuh," then he gets their stuff out of the storage compartment and hauls it all to a nearby rental car.

From the Mallard Motel in Stutgart it's a fifteen-minute drive past sprawling fields of soybeans, rice and cotton to Gaheena. They find Karl Buntingstrife sitting in one of the red vinyl booths at the café.

Built like an ancient statue with rippling, sculpted muscles, a hard chin and penetrating eyes set deep in a tanned, weathered face, Karl Buntingstrife is the most impressive man Calvin has ever seen. Karl offers his big hand to Calvin's father. "Hey," he croaks, his voice low as a bullfrog's, his powerful muscles bulging under the plain white t-shirt.

"Hi, Karl." Calvin's father sounds small.

Now Karl offers that rough, calloused hand to Calvin.

"Nice to meet you," Calvin squeaks as Karl crushes his little fingers.

"'Lo, son." Those dark eyes leave Calvin cold.

Later, Karl motors them around the Old Reservoir while they fish. There are hundreds, maybe thousands, of turtles sunning themselves on logs and stumps in this huge swamp, and Calvin can't believe it. That's the Turtle Company logo, after all, a smiling turtle perched on a log, sunning himself. Is Arkansas where that comes from?

The turtles slide off into the water when the boat gets too close, but then they climb right back out in the sun when the coast is clear. Calvin feels a surprising connection to these funny looking creatures, but he can't explain it. That's his last name, of course: Turtle. But why? Who came up with that name for his family? How long ago? How do families get names, anyway? He wants to ask his dad about all of this, but not now. Fishing is serious business, and he wants to prove to his dad and Karl Buntingstrife that he can do it.

Calvin's father catches a big shiny wiggling dripping bass with nearly every cast, but Calvin, sitting on the middle seat between Karl and his dad, struggles to keep his lure out of the trees along the edges of the Old Reservoir or out of the lily pads covering most of the surface of the water. Each time he gets hung up, Karl patiently helps him untangle his line or tie on another lure, but even when Calvin does manage a good cast and gets a bite, he lets the fish shake loose before he can stop slapping mosquitoes long enough to figure out how to reel the thing in.

"Boy, you're lettin' them fish git away!" Karl scolds.

Calvin's father says nothing. Despite the heavy summer heat, Calvin is shivering.

Now, seemingly out of nowhere, a large, dark snake slithers near the boat, its ominous head arched a few inches above the murky water's surface.

"Cottonmouth," Karl blurts, rocking the boat. "Let's git him. Pull in your bait." The long snake turns and winds away from the commotion.

"I hate snakes," Calvin says, staring at the thing.

"Don't' look at it, then," his father snaps, struggling to reel in his lure.

Karl fires up the motor and guides the boat through the muck, dodging stumps, humping over submerged logs, raising the howling motor to clear the propeller of duck moss, until they come right up alongside the darkly patterned snake.

"Kill it!" Karl says, handing a dripping paddle forward to Calvin's father, who hacks wildly at the curvy-thick body of the snake. The snake slithers like crazy now, racing over lily-pads and lurching around logs, desperate to escape but apparently unfazed by the clumsy paddle blows.

"Why do we have to kill it?" Calvin cries, unable to take his eyes off that pitted head, now even more upright and ominous, its long scaly body slicing a continuous "S" in the slime.

"Cause it'll kill *you* if we don't," Karl yells.

"That's right," Calvin's father says, as if in a trance.

The big cottonmouth makes it to the bank where it disappears underneath a fallen treetop. Karl guides the boat right into the middle of that treetop and Calvin is sure the snake's head will shoot out of there any second and bite them all to hell. Karl shuts off the motor, stands up, dangerously rocking the boat, steps past Calvin, past his

27

dad, then out onto the spindly trunk of the treetop where he pokes around with the paddle, trying to coax the snake out of hiding. The dark, diamond-shaped head suddenly rises from under the trunk and lunges at Karl's leg, but Karl deflects the attack with the paddle, pins the hideous head against the trunk, then reaches down and seizes the hissing cottonmouth just below the jaws, its thick body twisting in futile loops against Karl's arm.

"Get it *away!*" Calvin screams.

"It's jest a li'l old cottonmouth," Karl says, thrusting the writhing snake forward as if he's going to drop it on Calvin.

Calvin flinches and nearly falls out of the boat.

"Don't, Karl," his father says, pulling Calvin upright.

Calvin lets go of his father and whispers under his breath, "Sparklers and Diggers, Pumpers and Puppytoes, into the Free Pile, here I goes."

"What did you say?" his father asks threateningly.

"Nothing."

Karl is smiling, a thin line of teeth showing between his lips, his face full of menace, and for a moment Calvin thinks Karl might just throw that awful snake on his father, but then Karl lowers the writhing serpent to the trunk of the fallen tree, puts his foot just below the head to hold the snake in place, and pries open its mouth with a finger, exposing the cloudy white insides of the mouth and two small claw-like fangs curving down from the upper jaw. "See why it's called a cottonmouth?" Karl asks.

Calvin clutches the hard boat seat beneath him. "Yessir."

"Amazing," his father says.

Karl flicks one of the fangs with a fingernail. "Kill you in two minutes." The snake's slitted eyes bulge and its tail twists and writhes and thumps the side of the aluminum boat, but resistance is futile. Karl's got him.

"Okay, Karl, get that thing out of here," Calvin's father finally says.

Karl looks up. "You afraid too?" His expression is still menacing.

Calvin's father says, "No, I'm not," his voice wavering just a tiny bit.

"Well, you'd better be." Karl presses a thumb into the scaly head and liquid the color of semen drips from the fangs. "Two minutes," he says, glancing at Calvin. "That's all you get."

Now Karl lets the snake's mouth close and speaks gently to it: "Come on, Mister Cottonmouth, we're skeerin' these fellers." Holding the twisting snake by the head, Karl steps carefully down the fallen trunk, climbs the brushy bank, swings the snake around like a lariat and slams it against a tree, splitting the snake in two, the tail-half sailing a few yards into the woods, the head-half still writhing in Karl's hand.

"You won't kill nobody now," Karl says, flinging the head-half out into the Old Reservoir, where it twists as if to bite its own non-existent tail before it finally grows still and sinks into the slime.

INDEPENDENCE DAY, 1972

Because of the holiday, the Turtle Playing Card factory is closed. Calvin is sitting at the glass-topped table in the breakfast nook. A shower of watery sunlight pours through the window onto his untidy blond hair.

"We never do anything as a family," his mother says as she loads the breakfast dishes into the dishwasher. His father is still asleep at the other end of the mansion.

Calvin scans the front page of the *Courier Journal*. "And that's my fault?"

"Nothing's your fault, is it, Calvin?"

The *Courier* reports that Governor Ford is on the mend after his surgery, George Wallace's presidential campaign is faltering now that he's been shot, China is increasing its aid to Vietnam, and an Air Force nurse named Ann Hoefly has become the first woman general in the Armed Forces. In the picture, Air Force General Alonso Towner is kissing Nurse Hoefly on the lips; she has her eyes closed. Below the kiss, some South Vietnamese peasants are tending a rice paddy while tanks and trucks stir up dust in the background: *Man must eat as well as fight*, the caption says. Calvin wishes they would just drop a nuclear bomb on North Vietnam and get it over with.

"*Everything* is my fault," he says absently.

His mother smacks the Formica counter between them, her wedding ring causing a sudden *POW* like a starter's pistol. "I've had it with you!"

"Go to hell," Calvin mumbles, turning the page.

Now his mother is crying, her wails like the eerie song of a mourning dove: *down-up, dowwwn, dowwwn, dowwwn; down-up, dowwwn, dowwwn, dowwwn.* Calvin stands it as long as he can, then he throws down the newspaper, looks at her heaving back and says, "All right, I will go to the goddamned Country Club, but I'm driving my own car."

At the Club it's the usual scene: the same guy sitting on the same tractor mowing the same fairway in the hot sun, and another guy on another tractor dragging a rake over the piles of horseshit on the polo field while the bored and gorgeous lifeguard sprawls in her chair, all oily and smelling of butter and coconuts, the mothers laid out below her like caught fish, chatting each other up or oiling each other down, chair straps making parallel grooves like prison bars in their flabby backs while their kids play sharks-and-minnows in the glistening pool (the same ones always sharks, the same ones always minnows), and the men are at war on the golf course (no women, no children allowed).

By the end of dinner Calvin's mom and dad are fighting, so he leaves the table and goes out to the practice tee for the fireworks. Calvin used to love the Fourth of July fireworks, especially the sky-bombs. First the usual fireball shoots up and you think, *ahhhh,* a beautiful burst of color, but then there's a sudden lightning flash and a murderous *BLAM* instead. Kids get a thrill from a skybomb, but parents, the ones who aren't too drunk, jump like they've been shot.

Skybombs aren't all deadly, though. Every year one shoots up and explodes with the usual *BLAM,* then releases, magically, out of a chaos of sparks and smoke, a mysterious white parachute. Kids stand vigilant among the divots on the practice tee, focused only on the skybombs, ready after each blast for that dim apparition to appear. A shout goes up when the parachute materializes, and they race after it as it floats away on the night breeze. Whoever runs the fastest, climbs the quickest over rusting barbed-wire fences into the forbidden fields beyond Club grounds, captures it.

As a young kid, Calvin dreamed that if he ever captured the Fourth of July parachute he'd find a Wizard suspended from the silk and the Wizard would grant him a wish. Then one year he raced out ahead of the pack and grabbed the parachute before it ever hit the ground. There was no Wizard attached, of course, only a charred cyl-inder, but still, he strutted back to the practice tee swinging that cyl-inder like some duck he'd killed, hoping at least that his mom and dad would see, but they were nowhere around. Probably in the bar.

This Fourth of July there is no one Calvin's age on the practice tee, just the old people lined up in lawn chairs and the younger parents on blankets in the grass, their kids roaming in wary gangs of three or four, ready to chase the parachute, but there is no parachute this year, just the usual showers of color and a few sudden, cruel skybombs. To Calvin this seems about right; no more parachutes in this godforsaken world. Everything's gone to hell. He wants a drink, but he knows they won't serve him one in the men's grille. He's still only 20, and the bartenders know it. Who decided you're not a man until you're 21, anyway? Time moves so damned slowly.

When the hoopla is over, Calvin follows his mother and father back to Louisville in his Mustang, staying close the way a duckling might follow its mama. He knows they are still fighting in the car because against oncoming headlights he can see the outline of his mother's head, her permed hair shaking in angry staccato. The three of them have just passed the first *WATCH FOR FALLING ROCK* sign on Highway 42 when there's a frenzy of shadowy movement inside their car, as if his father is trying to hit his mother, or maybe, and this is crazy, he's *embracing* her, and their station wagon swerves, its taillights dancing little red circles in the night. Something lets go in Calvin and he tromps the gas pedal; his car smacks into the back of theirs.

Bumpers kissing, the family slams into the high rock wall alongside the highway and there is a fiery explosion, the last skybomb the three of them will ever see together.

HE IS NOT A CHILD!

Calvin **is taken** to Children's Hospital. That pisses him off.

"I'm twenty years old and they've got me in a goddamned children's hospital," he tells Nurse Crady. She's wearing pink makeup and her stockings chafe like sandpaper when she walks. She is about to give him a shot.

"I *know* where you're at, child."

"I am *not* a child." Calvin's bandaged right shoulder is killing him.

"Well, you're acting like a child. Now be a good boy and gimme here." She takes his good arm, polishes the muscle with damp cotton, sticks him with the needle and shoots in the juice.

Calvin winces. "What is it?"

"Something for your pain." She gathers up her equipment and raises a shiny metal rail into place at the edge of the bed.

"Can I have a deck of cards?" he asks. A little Klondike will help him think.

Nurse Crady's expression softens and she touches his chin. "Of course you can, hon." When she comes back with a worn deck of Turtle Cards, she says, "Want me to deal 'em out for you?"

"No, thanks." Calvin feels a heavy euphoria taking hold of him.

Nurse Crady hooks a little plastic table to the bedrail, sets the deck of cards down and eyes him carefully.

"You all right?"

"I feel like I'm swimming."

She smiles and nods. "Nighty-night, Mr. Turtle." She sandpapers out the door.

Calvin stares at the smiling turtle on the back of the top card, the famous company mascot perched on his log in the sun, grinning like he knows more than you do. "What's so funny?" Calvin asks, but the turtle, of course, says nothing, only grins from his permanent, sunny perch.

Tonight, unable to use his right hand, Calvin has trouble keeping the cards straight and quickly becomes frustrated. He smacks the little table and the cards scatter like fleeing quail, then he collapses into the hospital bed and lets the weight of the painkiller pull him *down down down* into sleep.

In His Dreams

Calvin stands at the edge of the Country Club pool, the water thick as liqueur and the color of a fresh bruise, his little round mouth opening and closing, sucking air in, pushing it out a little too fast because he knows there is a shark down there and that gorgeous lifeguard is nowhere in sight. He stares into the liquid bruise. All you have to do is get to the other side, he tells himself. The gang waves to him from across the pool. *Come on, Calvin. Go!*

Where is that damned lifeguard? How can she do this to him? The water is calm, but he knows that shark is down there, smiling, waiting. He stands at the pool's edge, arches his arms over his head and chants, "Sparklers and Diggers, Pumpers and Puppytoes, into the Free Pile, here I goes."

The water closes around him like a thousand hands, warm and smooth. He shuts his eyes and gives in to the gentle push and pull of voluptuous little currents kneading his temples, his shoulders, his buttocks, stroking the fear away. In the distance a dove cries, *down-up, dowwwn, dowwwn, dowwwn,* each note seeping into him like whiskey, the fire spreading with each refrain till his mind burns with a light so bright that he lets it all go and sinks into the slime.

The shark speeds through the darkness and bites him on the back of his thigh, those teeth like hot fingernails digging into his flesh. He tries to scream, but the in-rushing flood threatens to drown him. He flaps his arms and kicks at the blackness, touching neither bottom nor surface nor shore.

Calvin wakes. The hospital room is dark and silent. He feels heavy and sweetish, like cold, cheap syrup. His right shoulder seems remote, with only the potential for pain. A tiny red light beams at him from the bedside table. *Help button*, he surmises. Red usually means danger in this world: leaking blood, fire, anger. Calvin ponders this for a while. Can help be dangerous?

Now he hears something, a slight rustle, a long sigh. Someone is nearby. He lifts his eyes from the tiny red beam to a figure in a chair by the window. Long hair angles neatly along a slender face and falls across the faint outline of breasts. She is bent forward, looking out the window as if someone is coming, but is late, and might never come.

"Mom?" he says.

She gasps, jumps from the chair, puts her hand out to catch her balance. "Calvin!" she says, stepping forward. "You *scared* me."

It's Penelope George, Calvin's girlfriend. She moves toward the bed, lowers her face and nuzzles it next to his, cool cheek to his hot, her Shalimar making him feel a little sick.

"What are *you* doing here?"

"God, it's good to hear your voice." Penny scoots the chair nearer the bed. In the antiseptic darkness her face is only a dim, shifting oval, like the Fourth of July parachute. She takes his left hand between her thin, cold ones. "I've been so scared." She glances back toward the window and kneads his hands. "You were almost killed."

"How'd you get in here? What time is it?"

She lifts a hand and softly pats his lips. "We better keep it down. I snuck right past the nurses' station."

Calvin turns his head away and stares at the little red light. "You shouldn't have."

She squeezes his hand. "Why not?"

"You'll get me in trouble."

She drops his hand. "Oh, bull, Calvin. I came down here right away, soon as I heard."

"Maybe you should go, Pen. I don't feel very well."

After a period of cool silence, she takes his hand again. "I guess you know about your Mom and Dad."

He searches her dim face. "They're dead, right?"

She nods and squeezes. "Oh, Calvin, I'm so sorry." She leans forward to remove the little plastic card table and the scattered cards, then rests her head next to his on the pillow, her breath a warm fog massaging his temple. He closes his eyes and imagines he is drifting over the Country Club grounds, floating beyond the golf course, beyond the skybursts and skybombs and the screaming, beyond all knowing.

Penny's touch beckons him back to the hospital room. She has pulled the sheet off of him, climbed over the railing and eased into the bed, laying her body alongside the length of his. He feels her heat enter him and swirl around like a drug.

"I'm high," he says.

She smoothes her hand across his chest. "What did they give you?"

"I don't know."

"Does it hurt?"

Calvin opens his eyes and catches Penny's face suspended like a hazy moon just above his own. "Does what hurt?"

"Your shoulder. Dad said the bone popped out of its socket." She shudders. "Jeez, it hurts me just to think about it."

"I can't feel a thing."

Penny slides her hand through his hair and down the side of his face. Her breath comes in little gusts now, moist and sweet. "I've been waiting here to tell you something," she says, her voice low. "I think you need me now."

41

"Don't worry about me," Calvin murmurs.

She kisses him tenderly on the cheek. "I *am* worrying about you. I love you, Calvin Turtle, and you need me now more than ever. I want to be your wife."

He turns away from her and stares at the little red light again. *Danger*, he thinks. "Please go, Pen. I just wanna be alone."

Penny abruptly sits up and swings her feet over the railing, leaving a sudden icy void in the bed. "Be alone, then," she says.

Calvin imagines that he's sinking into the cold and murky pond at the Club. He tugs at Penny's shirttail. "Don't go," he says.

Penny yanks loose, hurtles the railing and pauses for a moment, her gaze on that window again, then she disappears into the darkest part of the room. The door opens suddenly, letting in light like fire, and she steps into the fire and vanishes.

WEDNESDAY, JULY 5TH, 1972

Groggy, his mind blank as a baby's, Calvin shields his eyes against blinding light. As his eyes adjust, his mind struggles to comprehend where he is and how he got here. The hospital. The crash on Highway 42. His mother and father dead. Gone. Heaven? Doubtful. No such place. Hell? Maybe. Or simply gone. Nowhere.

As Calvin closes his eyes and tries to imagine a void so vast and black that nothing ever touches anything else, a slow, cold terror seeps into his heart, so he opens his eyes and notices that on top of a low, egg-yellow dresser there are some flower arrangements. "Pretty," he says. Baby's first word.

There are cards wedged among the flower arrangements. Sympathy cards. Yes, he needs sympathy, an infinite river of it. He must read those cards.

When he tries to move, there is a sharp pain in his shoulder. "Jesus!" he whispers. *No crying, he tells himself. Don't be a baby.* He needs to see those sympathy cards.

Calvin feels a little woozy when he swings his feet over the shiny, four-inch railing, but *Hell*, he thinks, *I'm a man. I can do this*, so with a mighty lunge he lifts his butt over the railing and plants his bare feet on the cold white linoleum. Holding onto the rail, he stands up, wooziness turns to downright chaos in his head, and he throws up the gory remains of his Fourth of July dinner. On top of that, he suddenly has to pee.

Forget the flower arrangements. How is he going

to get across the Sea of Puke to the bathroom? He takes a small step, still holding the rail. *No sweat,* he thinks. On his second step toward the bathroom, he lets go of the rail and slips down into the cold and stinking Sea.

"SHIT!" he yells.

That brings Nurse Crady. "Holy Mother of God," she blurts. "What have you done, child?"

"I'm not a child. I threw up, that's all."

"That shoulder all right?"

"It's killing me. Would you pick me up, please? I have to go to the bathroom."

Nurse Crady sidesteps the mess, loads him under an arm and walks him to the bathroom where colorful clowns dance across the wallpaper and little fishies swim the sides of the bathtub. *Goddamn kids' hospital,* Calvin thinks. He stinks like a sewer, but he can still smell the cheap sweetness of Nurse Crady's makeup as they stand there, arms encircling each other, facing the toilet.

"Pee," she commands.

When he is done, Nurse Crady tells him to grab hold of the towel rack and, with a skilled jerk, pulls his damp, reeking pajama bottoms down to his ankles.

"What are you *doing*?"

"Mama's gonna give you a bath." Nurse Crady bends down and starts the water in the tub.

"I can do it myself."

"Can't let you. Hospital regulations." She takes his pants from his ankles, unbuttons his shirt, and with surprising gentleness lowers him into the filling bathtub, careful not to stress his shoulder.

Another nurse peeks around the partially closed bathroom door.

"Need any help in here?"

Calvin crosses his legs to hide himself.

"Naw," Nurse Crady says, her voice echoing against the tiled walls. "I got him in the water." She grins at Calvin. "Turtles like the water, don't they?"

"I'll get some clean sheets and a mop," the other nurse says, then she vanishes.

"It's too hot," Calvin whines.

"You'll get used to it."

Now Nurse Crady solemnly washes him, dabbing carefully

44

around the cuts and bruises. The water feels good, and her hands feel good too, on his back, his head. Calvin imagines he is a racehorse getting a steamy rubdown in the paddock after the Derby. He has just won the race, of course, and is the center of attention, head held high, muscles flexed.

"Ever been to the Derby?" he asks Nurse Crady.

"Naw, I ain't got time for that mess."

Calvin briefly wonders about her, where she lives, if she has a husband, kids, a house, a dog. He figures she probably lives in the West End, on the poorer side of things.

"Your Daddy was the one made them Turtle Cards, wasn't he?" she asks, soaping his hand.

"Yeah."

"Sorry I said 'Your mama's gonna give you a bath.' I know you lost your mama and daddy in that awful accident. I lost my daddy in a car accident too."

Her words send a sharp dagger of guilt through Calvin's heart. He closes his eyes and feels his foot hit the accelerator, feels the front of his car nudge the back of his dad's. He sees the crash, the explosion, the dancing flames, the dark silhouettes, hears the shouts, and there is an upwelling inside him, a dark flood of feelings threatening to wash over and drown him, as if a dam upstream of his life might break.

"That's all right," he says, his voice wobbly with the fight to yank his thoughts back to this tub with the little fishies and Nurse Crady's gentle soothing hands soaping his body. "I know you were just kidding around."

"When we play Tonk, we play with them Turtle Cards," she says. "I can't get over that smiling turtle on the back. Did your daddy dream that up?"

Calvin clears his throat. "No, my grandfather."

"Well, it sure is cute."

"Yeah."

"You gonna inherit the company?"

Calvin hasn't yet thought about it, but Nurse Crady is right. Now he will own the Turtle Playing Card Company. *Jesus*! And he will inherit the Old Wilson Place down in Arkansas, too, the finest hunting hole in the universe. Who wouldn't want to own that? But Karl Buntingstrife is down there, and Karl is dangerous. And on top of that, what about the Louisville Hunt Club? Those men would rather hunt than breathe, and now it's Calvin who owns their favorite hunting hole, not his father.

Calvin feels a malignant heaviness settling on him, the whole sorry burden of history. He thinks of Jewel. *Oh, God*, how he wishes she were still alive, but the truth closes around his heart like a cold hand. She's gone. They killed her.

He shuts his eyes as a fireball of rage mushrooms in his mind. The world is an inferno. *Burn, baby, burn,* he thinks. *Burn in hell. Burn to a crisp.*

He *will*, by God, take over the company and do it well, and he *will*, by God, take charge in Arkansas, too. Fuck Karl Buntingstrife and the Louisville Hunt Club. The world's going to change. Calvin Turtle is king now.

He opens his eyes. There are still little fishies on the sidewalls of the bathtub. Nurse Crady is soaping his balls.

THE INHERITANCE

Shortly after the first World War, Ishmael Turtle, a young, hot-blooded Welshman slaving six days a week over the oily machines in his father's Swansea print shop, told his parents he was tired of printing invitations to someone else's wedding, quit his job, purchased a ticket on a boat to America, and somehow ended up in Louisville, Kentucky, where he rented an apartment in old Germantown, bought out a small printing company on Washington Street, fired everyone but the design department, which consisted of one headstrong and talented Episcopalian named Oola McGraw, told her to draw a smiling turtle perched on a log in the sun, and then, when she'd done it, asked her to marry him, and together they printed, cut, packaged, sold and hand-delivered the first Turtle Playing Cards to the clubs and stores of Louisville at twenty-two cents a deck.

Soon Ish and Oola begat Sonny Turtle, their only child, and Sonny grew up and married a slim, golden-haired debutante, Anna Board Calvin, a few years after the second World War. The wedding was held at St. Mark's Episcopal down on Frankfort Avenue, where Sonny and his buddies, wearing black tuxedos with white bowties and trying not to laugh, marched like Canada geese in V-formation up the crimson-carpeted aisle past the cream of Louisville society to stand in a neat row before the church's new young minister, Reverend Cletis Bushrod. With her hand curled around the flabby arm of her father, young Anna, dazzling in her lavish white gown, seemed to flow up the aisle on a slow, inexorable river of love. The reception was held at the River Valley Club, of course, where, by the end of the evening, Sonny and his whiskey-besotted buddies were holding a contest to see who could sail the Club's silver serving trays the farthest out over the railing into the muddy Ohio.

Sonny and Anna begat two children: a girl, Jewel, born on Thanksgiving Day 1949, a beautiful seven-and-a half-pounder; then a boy, Calvin, born on a scorching 100-degree day in late June 1952. His mother stuck a rubber nipple in Calvin's mouth right away. His father stuck a tiny silver shotgun in his clutchy little hand.

The Louisville Hunt Club was the brainchild of Calvin's father and his best friend, Charlie Stanfull. In the fall of 1958, Charlie was a few years out of law school and working in his father's firm, *Stanfull, McElwen and Trites*, while Sonny had recently taken over for his dying father as the young new president of Turtle Manufacturing. Oh, yes, Sonny Turtle and Charlie Stanfull went to work, played with their kids and mowed the lawn, but what these young men really wanted to do was kill. Every weekend it was doves, ducks, deer, squirrels, rabbits, quail or bass, anything you could shoot or catch under the sanction of sport. To live was to kill; to kill was to live.

That fall, Sonny and Charlie decided to drive to Arkansas. They'd heard that the duck hunting down there was spectacular, and they were tired of paddling after a few lousy ducks on the treacherous Ohio, so they headed southwest in Sonny's Woody and in a few hours reached the bridge over the Mississippi River at Memphis. Smack in the middle of the massive steel structure an overhead sign straddled the road:

WELCOME TO ARKANSAS
LAND OF OPPORTUNITY

The bridge delivered the two men into a strange, flat vastness and their young hearts began to pound.

Eventually they came to a tiny prairie community called Gaheena, where they raised their eyes skyward and, Lo, the heavens were full of ducks! Sonny and Charlie followed the great flocks to an isolated, swampy realm where a rusty sign told them to **KEEP OUT**. Back in Gaheena, they asked around and found the owner, a bent old man named D. P. Wilson, having coffee at the shabby whites-only café, but Mr. Wilson, catching the strong scent of money, said no, he couldn't allow just anybody to hunt on his place, so the two Kentuck-ians left Gaheena and drove ten miles to the town of Stutgart where they booked a room at the Mallard Motel, broke out the whiskey and cooked up a plan to lease the hunting rights to Old Man Wilson's place.

D.P. Wilson thought he'd hit the jackpot, since he could still hunt on his own land anytime he wanted – that was in the contract – and now he was making a thousand times the money he used to make off a bunch of nickel-and-dime local boys who'd just as soon sneak out to his place and poach as pay him the two dollars he charged them for a day's hunt. The deal also stipulated that D.P.'s young pal, a dark-haired hotshot named Karl Buntingstrife, would be the perma-nent hunting guide and caretaker on the place.

When Sonny and Charlie got back to Louisville they called a powwow of their closest buddies, Jim George, Barn Kentlinger, and No-Knees Headmore, and decided to form a corporation called the Louisville Hunt Club, with Sonny as President and Charlie as Vice-President, through which they would lease the hunting rights to the Wilson place. Each member would pay dues equal to one-fifth of the annual lease, and the club would include the wives. They would hunt together, party together, and preserve the Wilson Place for future generations. Long live the Louisville Hunt Club!

Old Man Wilson enjoyed Easy Street for a little while, compli-ments of the rich boys from Louisville. Then cancer got him in the prostate; so much for the jackpot. His widow put the place up for sale and Sonny Turtle put up the cash. Now the Louisville/Arkansas con-nection was secure. Long live the Old Wilson Place!

A **red-headed** Jefferson County cop bristling with badges and bullets shows up at the Turtle mansion first thing in the morning, a big black pistol dangling at his hip.

"You Calvin Turtle?" he says, glancing at a sheet of paper in his hand.

"Yes sir." Calvin's arm is still in a sling, his wounded shoulder throbbing.

"You'll need to come downtown with me, Mr. Turtle. I have a warrant for your arrest."

"My arrest?"

"Vehicular homicide. You're charged in the deaths of Sonny and Anna Turtle."

A sudden wash of bitter guilt floods Calvin's body. "That's insane," he says, shaking his head. This must be a bad dream.

The cop urges the paper at Calvin, who stares at the blue and gold seal of the Commonwealth of Kentucky: *United We Stand, Divided We Fall,* the motto says. He feels weightless, as if it is he who has divided from the known world and is falling into a dark abyss.

Johnnie, long-time Turtle Family maid, eases up beside Calvin in the doorway, cups his elbow, pulls him back from the abyss. "What is it?" she says evenly, refusing to look at the cop.

Calvin hears himself announce, "I'm being arrested for killing Mom and Dad."

Johnnie's eyes are weary and sad. "Calm," she says, reaching up to straighten Calvin's collar. Her hand drops down and pats his chest. "Stay calm... remember you're my boy and it'll be all right." Her expression darkens as she tilts her head toward the cop, still not looking at him. "Just do what he says."

The cop says, "You want to change clothes, son?"

"Don't call me son."

A toothy smile breaks out on the officer's freckled face. "Okay, then. Let's go, big man."

On the way downtown, Calvin sits in the back seat of the police car behind a metal mesh partition. *Vehicular homicide,* he thinks. *Murder by vehicle.*

GUILTY, he hears the judge say. The gavel bangs.

A memory struggles to the surface of his mind: Jewel in her yellow pajamas, lying on the floor. Christmas Eve. The smell. Calvin shakes his head hard, as if to clear swimming-pool water from his ears. *No! Don't think of that,* he tells himself. *This is now, 1972, it's hot outside, and I'm in this goddamned air-conditioned police car.* He looks out the smudgy window. People in other cars are staring at him. He's a criminal. He's going to jail. Mr. Stanfull will get him out of this.

The cop turns his patrol car onto Zorn Avenue and starts down the big hill. In the distance is the Louisville Water Company with its distinctive tower, and beyond that, the dirty river. At the bottom of Zorn they will turn left and head into downtown Louisville past all the marinas and sand piles and rusting barges lining River Road. Calvin remembers coming down this hill a million times with his parents and now, sloping toward the Ohio, he thinks of that Biblical injunction, *Honor Thy Father and Mother,* and his heart constricts. He doesn't honor them. He doesn't even feel sad that they are gone. In fact, it's a relief.

That push on his father's bumper is what did it, too. He knows this. But he didn't plan it. No, this was not premeditated vehicular homicide. This was the Hand of God, no, the Foot of God, tromping on the accelerator, nudging them to their deaths. *Justice,* Calvin tells himself. They killed Jewel.

LIBERTY AND JUSTICE FOR ALL

The Jefferson County Jail is on Liberty Street in downtown Louisville, the city's idea of a little joke on the criminal element. First they book you, just like in the movies, a placard with numbers on it around your neck, your back to a wall-grid of height measurements, a sullen cop behind the camera who says "smile" when he takes your mug shot. You feel like a corpse, and you look like one too.

Then they make you strip and a guard tells you to bend over and spread your butt cheeks so he can look for weapons and contraband. Another guard says, "Hey, Al, I wonder if the rich boy wants a fuckin' in the butt." Al laughs and says, "That's some purty white meat, ain't it. Hey, rich boy, you want a fuckin' in the butt?" Both guards crack up laughing.

Each cellblock contains about a dozen grey steel cages with a walkway outside the doors. Everything is streaked with filth, and the whole place smells like sour milk and urine. Unshaven men pace the walkway like lions in a zoo, occasionally firing unintelligible streams of words at the guards, while other men slouch in their cell doorways smoking cigarettes down to the butts and still others crouch in their beds smoking the last quarter-inch of someone else's butt. Once in a while a guard shouts a name and one of the guests gets to leave. Gargantuan roaches scuttle across the floor. Rats skitter in the walls.

Your cellmate is a black dude. He sits on his bed

and watches the floor for rats. "I *hate* them motherfuckers," he says, gesturing violently and shaking his head like he just can't believe the rats are so close, right there in the walls. He has been waiting for a court date for four months, he says. He beat up his mother-in-law and burned her house, which, of course, was down in the West End.

When Mr. Stanfull comes to bail you out, you force a smile, tell your cellmate goodbye and good luck.

"Fuck you," he says.

Charles M. Stanfull III, Esquire

"They'll drop the charges," Mr. Stanfull says on the way back to the East End.

"How can you know that?" Calvin asks.

"The district attorney is an asshole. Fancies himself a man of the people. He loves to grandstand with a high-profile arrest like this one."

"But I *did* run into them."

Mr. Stanfull glances over at Calvin, his expression wary. "Let me do the arguing, okay? I'll get the charges dropped, don't worry. Would you like a beer? I've got some in the trunk."

"At eleven in the morning?"

Mr. Stanfull laughs. "That's drinking hours in the Hunt Club."

Calvin's face is hot. "I'm not *in* the Hunt Club."

Mr. Stanfull sniffs and turns his eyes to the road. "You are if you want to be."

He Killed Them!

Young Playing Card Heir Charged in Parents' Death, the Friday afternoon *Louisville Times* headline reads, but the article is on page seven, and brief. Calvin thinks it should be on page one with a giant headline: *HE KILLED THEM*! And why isn't there a mug shot in which Calvin looks like a corpse, plus a full-color picture of his father's burned-out station wagon?

He's in the den playing a little Klondike, drinking a little whiskey. After the first few hands, he calls Penny. "It's all over the country!" he says.

"Don't exaggerate, Calvin."

"Yeah? Well, what would you do if you were accused of being a murderer?"

"You're not accused of murder."

"Vehicular homicide. That's murder."

"No, it's not."

"It's hell, I'll tell you that."

Penny's tone is flat. "I'm sure it must be."

"Aren't you even gonna say *I'm sorry it happened, you poor bastard*?"

"Calvin, don't push me. I came to see you in the hospital, remember? And you told me to leave. I'm sorry this is all happening, okay?"

"I'm really weirded out over this. Can I come over?"

"No."

"Why not?"

"I want to break up. I'm going to U of L this fall."

Calvin's stomach is tight with panic. "Nice timing, Pen. I lose my parents, get accused of murdering them, and you want to break up with me. *Have a nice day, sir.*"

"I could've gone to Hollins, you know."

"Okay, here we go. It's my fault you didn't go to Hollins."

"Yes, it is. I stayed here because of you. And we are going *nowhere.*"

"And that's my fault too?"

"Yes, it is. I wanted to marry you, Calvin, I really did. I waited around and put my life on hold for you. You *were* my life. You have practically been my whole life the last few years, and that's why I have to break up with you now... I'm sorry. I know you're having a rough time, but I've got to move on. In the hospital you *told* me to leave you alone, remember? Well, that's what I'm going to do. But I wanna stay friends."

Calvin lets go a crazy laugh. "With a murderer?"

"Oh, God, Calvin. You are so melodramatic. You are *not* a murderer."

"He killed his parents! Stay away from him! Hide the kids!"

"Stop it."

"MURDERER! MURDERER!"

Penny hangs up.

THEY DRIVE EACH OTHER CRAZY

In the late, slow, hot and blurry afternoon, Calvin drives over to Penny's apartment. When she opens the door, he says, "I'm sorry," lowers his gaze to the porch mat like a forlorn puppy, and she lets him in. He sits on her flower-print couch, she on a giant purple pillow on the floor, her back against the bare plaster wall, her glass of beer on a nearby windowsill, untouched. Her eyes are puffy and red; she has been crying. She is wearing white tennis shorts, a t-shirt with a picture of James Taylor smiling like Jesus across her breasts, and nothing on her tanned slender feet. An air conditioner thrums in a window at the far end of the room.

"It's been a bad few days for you," Penny says as she fiddles with a strand of her hair. "You okay?"

"Yeah." Calvin takes a gulp of beer. "Sorry I was such a jerk in the hospital. I really do want to marry you." He looks down the dark hall toward her bedroom, up at the peeling paint on the high ceiling, down at the calluses on her feet, into his beer.

Penny twiddles a split end. "You are driving me crazy," she finally says, looking up at him. "One minute you're telling me to get out of your life, the next minute you're telling me you want me in your life." She pinches her nose, holds the pose. She is about to cry again. "It's been like this forever, Calvin, and I can't take it any more."

Calvin can't allow her to cry. "I'm an asshole," he says.

"No, baby, I don't mean that. Oh, I don't know..." Penny shuts her eyes and sways a little, then she slaps both hands on her knees as her eyes pop open. "Jesus, I hate this," she says. Then she shouts, "You are driving me *crazy*!"

One summer night about three years ago, Calvin was the one who cried. Still a virgin, he wanted worse than anything to go all the way with Penny, but she wanted to wait until they graduated and got engaged. This was driving Calvin crazy. It was the Sixties, after all, peace and love, sexual revolution, birth control, women's lib. What's the big deal? Sex isn't the Holy Grail, for God's sake. It's just sex, natural, beautiful, groovy and FUN. Come on, let's get with it!

Their habit on Saturdays was to go down in the cool basement of Penny's house and spend the evening watching TV, shooting pool, kissing, feeling each other up, dry humping on the couch and, finally, fighting. The fight was always about sex. Calvin would go home with a wet spot on the front of his pants and vow that he was done with Penny, this was it, forget it, but by the next Saturday he was back with her again.

On this particular Saturday night Penny was acting strange, a little loopy, though they'd had nothing to drink. For some reason, seeing her this way made Calvin sad.

"I don't wanna watch TV," she said, and she didn't want to play pool either. Her parents were out of town and both of her big brothers had moved to Colorado, so the house was quiet overhead. The George's maid, Sally Fosterman, who stayed in the little converted pantry at the back of the house when Penny's parents were out of town, had already gone to bed.

Calvin sat beside Penny on the couch. "Well," he said gently, "what *do* you want to do?"

Penny stared at the floor, her shiny brown hair spilling down the front of her shirt, hiding her eyes. She was wearing a man's cotton shirt, Oxford blue with button-down pockets and collar, its tail untucked and loose over a pair of stringy cutoffs, her tanned legs together and folded up under her like the closed blades of a pocketknife. One slender hand fiddled with the ends of her hair, while the other lay dormant and hidden between her knees.

Calvin reached to tuck some hair behind her ear. "What's the matter, Pen?"

The hidden hand came free and searched for his own, then she began to unfold, first placing her bare feet on the floor, then rocking forward to stand, then pulling Calvin up, her Shalimar cloud enveloping him like a great benevolent fog, those eyes warm brown wide-open beseeching pools holding his gaze, her warm lips holding his lips while her long arms pulled him to her, leg to leg hips to hips belly to belly breast to breasts cheek to cheek, the warmest softest most wonderful hug he'd ever had, and he began to tremble, damn it, *What's wrong with me?*

"Let's go upstairs and take off our clothes," she whispered.

Calvin's mind exploded in a Fourth-of-July colorburst. This was it, what he wanted, what he needed, but for some reason he was trembling like an alcoholic on Sunday morning.

She stroked his hair. "It's all right, baby. Just relax."

Calvin let her lead him up the basement stairs, through the immaculate, dimly-lit kitchen into the dining room, across the living room into the tiled foyer, then up the thickly carpeted stairs, where on the middle step she paused, turned, kissed his lips and smiled. "I love you," she whispered.

"Sally will hear us," he answered.

Her eyes sparked with conspiracy. "She won't tell." Penny turned and tugged him lightly behind her until they were in her bedroom, where she hugged him again and kissed him long and open and wet, then pushed away and began to unbutton that manly shirt.

Naked, eyes closed, holding her warm smooth hard curvy moundy hairy lovely body beneath the cool, smooth covers, Calvin ejaculated immediately, before he could even enter her, shooting all over her belly. "Shit," he said, but she put two fingers to his lips and said, "No, no, my love, it doesn't matter, I don't care about that, I want to make love *this* way, just holding you, I don't ever want to stop holding you. Here, please, just hold me right here like this and never let me go."

For Calvin, all time fell away and he held her just as she wanted, just as he wanted, who cares about penetration this is fine just holding her here like this, she me we, there's no difference, and in her arms he let go entirely and began to cry like a baby. He had no idea why.

"Come here," he says now, rising fearfully from her couch.

Penny stands, sniffs, wipes her nose, pads over to him. She takes the sweating beer glass out of his hand, sets it on a table, pulls Calvin up and in that wonderful way of hers applies her soft body to his, careful not to jolt his sore shoulder, her Shalimar cloud closing over him.

"I'm not a murderer," he says into her hair, voice wobbling.

"I know, baby. I know. I am so sorry everybody's treating you that way."

Calvin is trembling. It's that flood again, welling up inside of him as if the dam upstream of his life is about to bust.

"What's wrong, baby?" she whispers, squeezing harder.

Calvin's shoulder is killing him. "I gotta go," he says, wrenching himself free. "I love you. I'll call you. I promise."

Penny's face is scarlet. "I hate you!" she screams as Calvin hightails it out the door.

LOST ON THE MIDWAY

Calvin pulls away from the broken curb in front of Penny's Crescent Hill apartment house intending to head home, but he finds himself turning west toward Our Lady of Peace, the mental hospital, instead. *Maybe I should check myself in*, he muses as he turns into the parking lot. He has come to see Aunt Virgie, his only remaining relative, who's been here longer than he can remember. Calvin can't stand this place, but sometimes he just ends up here. The residents of OLAP's are sad and even downright scary sometimes, but not Aunt Virgie. She is sarcastic and tough and one hell of a lot of fun.

The first thing they do, as usual, is get out the Turtle Cards.

"Gin," Calvin says, after not very long.

"You evil dog," Aunt Virgie says, slamming down her cards. "I've got forty points this time, but I'm gonna beat you today, sonny boy."

"You're never gonna beat me."

"Deal, you arrogant brat."

Calvin deals out a few cards and stops. "You know about Mom and Dad, don't you?"

Aunt Virgie studies him. She is around 60, but looks more like 70, with dry brownish-yellow skin and short thick grey hair that droops down the sides of her head like the puny falls of the Ohio. She always wears the same faded-pink nightgown, which quite often droops so wide open you can see her old fried-egg breasts, and her shriveled, purplish hands are usually darting around from place to place like hummingbirds, never quite resting, but now those hands are still. "My sister is dead," she says, her wrinkled face colorless.

"I'm sorry," he says, wondering if she knows that he's accused of killing them.

The hands come alive now, flitting to her hair, the cards, her lap. "Hell, we're all sorry, sonny boy, don't you know that? But what about you? You lost your mother and father."

"I'll survive."

Aunt Virgie studies him again, her yellowed eyes cutting right through him. "You hated them, didn't you?"

"No."

"And you killed 'em."

Calvin's face burns with shame. She knows. Aunt Virgie is fiddling with her nightgown, eyes downcast, but she knows. It seems like she always understands things in a way that he cannot. She's the one person is this world he can't outsmart, except in gin rummy, of course. How ironic that *she's* the one in the hospital. He finishes dealing and they play another hand in silence.

"Gin," Calvin says, laying down his cards.

Aunt Virgie is staring at him again. "You gonna join the Hunt Club?"

The question makes Calvin's skin rise in a million bumps. "They want me to. Penny wants to get married, too."

Aunt Virgie spreads her cards face-down on the little TV tray and aims a long, bony forefinger at all the smiling turtles. "Look at 'em," she says. "They're laughing at you, sonny boy." She stirs the cards around and cackles, "You're in the Hunt Club now."

"I won't join," Calvin says angrily. He remembers Charlie Stanfull offering him a beer at 11:00 in the morning and saying, *You are if you want to be.*

"You will, too," Aunt Virgie says. She circles her hands again and again through the smiling, spinning turtles. "Can't shake the Hunt Club. Never changed in a million years."

"I will not, you sicko!"

"Sicko?" she shrieks. "*You're* the sicko. You're gonna go to the Country Club and play golf with the Hunt Club fat asses, that's what you're gonna do."

Just then Mrs. Bonson, the supervisor of the long-termer floor, strides in. Dressed in the standard OLAP's pale-green uniform, she always reminds Calvin of a giant bottle of Phisohex. "Pipe down in here," she says.

Aunt Virgie lowers her eyes to the cards. "Yes, Ma'am."

When Mrs. Bonson leaves, Aunt Virgie and Calvin both give the empty doorway a silent, middle-finger salute.

"You heard the woman. Keep it quiet, sicko," Calvin whispers.

Aunt Virgie grins. "Deal the cards, sonny boy."

Calvin begins another hand of gin, then stops. "I've gotta go to the john. Don't cheat."

"Ha!"

In the hospital bathroom, Calvin catches his face in the mirror: pale, scared, stupid, a wretched kid lost on the midway at the Kentucky State Fair.

SATURDAY, JULY 8TH, 1972

Calvin eases himself into a dark suit and drives his Mother's car through the shimmering heat to St. Mark's Episcopal. People are milling out front next to the fountain and looking his way, so he ducks through a side door. In the air-conditioned waiting room he runs into Reverend Cletis Bushrod and the four remaining charter members of the Louisville Hunt Club.

Reverend Bushrod is pale and tense, and the others are all a bit red in the clean-shaven face, as if there has been a confrontation. Calvin notices someone else, far end of the room, posed stiffly on one of the armless chairs, brown woolen pants, white shirt, no tie, hands fisted atop his knee, eyes to the floor. Karl Buntingstrife. How very strange to see this legendary man in Louisville; it doesn't seem possible that he even exists outside of the treacherous state of Arkansas. In fact, Karl Buntingstrife has never seemed quite possible to Calvin, not even in Arkansas, yet there he is right now, sitting in that chair. Calvin turns back to the impeccably dressed and very possible men standing before him.

"Hello, son," says Reverend Bushrod, a tall old softie of a man, who, dressed in his white robes and red undergarments, reminds Calvin of a barber pole. The stress drains from the Reverend's lumpy face as he steps forward, lands a wide, soothing hand on Calvin's good shoulder, cocks his head, and pours a comforting gaze right into Calvin's soul.

"Uh, Reverend, one more thing," Charlie Stanfull says, one polished shoe a-squeaking as he buttons his tapered gray suitcoat. "When the service is over, do we take them out first, or wait till everyone's in their cars?"

"After," snaps the Reverend as he spins out the door.

Calvin glances back to the far end of the room: Karl is up and moving toward him now. Calvin sticks out his hand and Karl crushes it. "Mighty sorry about your Mama and Daddy," he says, those dark eyes zeroing in on Calvin.

Calvin retracts his hand, flexes the throbbing fingers and glances at the dull carpet. "Thanks, Karl. And thanks for coming all the way up here."

"Had to. I thought the world of your Daddy."

A hot jolt shoots up Calvin's spine. "Yeah, well me too."

Karl is already retreating to the far end of the room.

Now his father's hunting buddies stand before Calvin in a semi-circle, but not too close, as if Calvin is a coiled and dangerous snake.

"How's the shoulder?" asks Dr. George, whom his father nicknamed "Sweetness." Dr. George really is a sweet guy, all things considered. He's the nicest of the men in the Hunt Club and a good doctor too. He lights a Salem and clinks shut his lighter.

"Much better," Calvin chirps. The sling is gone but his shoulder still throbs inside the suit.

Dr. George hisses out a thin stream of bluish smoke and looks around for an ash tray. "Good," he says.

"No smoking in the House of God," says Mr. Headmore, dubbed "No Knees" by Calvin's father, breaking up the nervous little semi-circle by limping to the couch against the wall. Calvin expects to hear his metal knees clank when he bends down to sit; he lost his real ones on a Philippine island in the War.

"There *is* no God," huffs Mr. Kentlinger, the 300-pound president of Kentucky Trust Bank, whose nickname is "Barn."

Mr. Headmore sighs like a weary schoolteacher. "Right."

Dr. George smiles, urges another cigarette out of his pack and offers it to Mr. Headmore. "God loves you."

Mr. Headmore snatches the cigarette. "God's a fag."

"I need a drink," Dr. George announces. "Anybody got a flask?"

"Surprised *you* don't." Mr. Stanfull winks at Calvin. Calvin's father had no nickname for Mr. Stanfull.

"Fuck you, Charlie," Dr. George says, plopping down next to Mr. Headmore on the couch.

Calvin looks over at Karl, who is gazing out a window as if he can't wait to get the hell out of this church.

"I'll second that," Barn Kentlinger says as he lands his huge carcass at the end of the couch, forcing a short and violent wind from the cushions. Small droplets of sweat bead beneath his thinning red hair. He closes and opens his eyes, exhales deeply as if to make sure he's still alive, then produces a silver flask from inside his billowy coat and swigs down a long shot of its contents.

"I knew it!" Dr. George cried. "Pass that baby around."

The flask goes from Mr. Kentlinger at one end of the couch to Dr. George at the other, who takes a swig and passes it up to Mr. Stanfull, still standing, who takes a gulp and offers the flask to Calvin.

"No thanks," he mumbles, his cheeks burning.

Calvin can feel Mr. Stanfull watching him as the shiny contoured flask makes its way back along the lineup of men on the couch. Mr. Kentlinger takes another long pull, then slips the flask back inside his voluminous coat. As a wispy pall of cigarette smoke and bourbon fumes gathers, Calvin can sense his father's absence in this room. No amount of whiskey or cigarette smoke is going to conceal what has happened. Mr. Stanfull still stands to his left, arms folded. Calvin tries to get past him to leave.

"Wait!" Mr. Stanfull demands, tugging on Calvin's sleeve.

Calvin halts and steals another glance at Karl, who is still staring out the window.

"Gentlemen," Mr. Stanfull proclaims, "this young man is a Turtle. Sonny's boy. I propose that we elect him to full membership in the Hunt Club."

"Let's do this later, Charlie," Dr. George says.

"No, it's okay," Calvin says. "I won't be joining."

"The Hunt Club is dead," Barn Kentlinger declares.

"Shut up, Barn," Mr. Stanfull says.

"Fuck you, counselor. You're not the boss."

"No one said I was."

"Oh, you think you are, now that Sonny's gone. You always wanted to be the big cheese of the Hunt Club, and now you've got your chance, don't you, pal? Well, you'll never replace Sonny Turtle."

"Sonny and I founded this Club, asshole, and that's how you

got to be in it. Don't forget that."

"Gentlemen, *gentlemen*," Dr. George says, rising from the couch to stand between his two friends.

Calvin notices that Karl is now watching these men. Mr. Kentlinger is right: Charlie Stanfull wants to be in charge. Karl sees it too.

Mr. Stanfull turns his flushed face to Calvin and tries to recover. "I'm sorry, son. Don't pay any attention to all of this. I'm upset and Barn's upset. Everyone is upset, as I know you are. We're like family, and we've lost one of our own. You'll change your mind about joining the Hunt Club, after you've had time to grieve."

"He's making me sick," Mr. Kentlinger says.

"You puke on my suit, you big bastard, and I'll kill you," Mr. Headmore says.

Reverend Bushrod pokes his graying head in the door. "They're here."

EPISCOPALIANS LIKE IT DARK

St. Mark's Episcopal is a small stone church with tall stained-glass windows that don't let in much light. *Episcopalians like it dark*, Calvin thinks. At the very front of the church, high over the altar, berobed and somber, Jesus hovers, His head tilted slightly, arms outstretched, punctured hands beckoning, ready to embrace all who cometh to Him.

Calvin sits alone in the front pew. *Jewel should be here*, he tells himself, a little tide of anger pushing its way into his fluttering heart. Under his breath he asks Jesus, "How about it, Fella? Can you bring my sister back?"

Jesus just hovers.

"Didn't think so." Calvin swivels around and scans the crowd: Penny isn't here, dammit. The church is so full that a few people have to stand in the back, including a tight little cluster of folks from Turtle Manufacturing: Fornton Bruhall, company vice-president, Orville, the plant superintendent, Betty, his father's longtime secretary, plus Nelle Brown, Zephyl Purdy, and a few others from the factory floor. Johnnie stands in the back, too, as if this is the old days and they are all on a big cross-shaped city bus.

Maybe three rows back, by himself at the outside end of a pew, sits Karl Buntingstrife. Calvin catches his eye and Karl nods slightly, the way a King might nod at a lowly subject. *Asshole*, Calvin thinks.

Now three pasty-faced elderly funeral-home men

help Dr. George, Mr. Stanfull, Barn Kentlinger and No-Knees Head-more carry in Calvin's mother's casket, then they go back and get his father. With their fallen comrade in place, the four men slide into the front pew beside Calvin. Directly behind them sit the women, Sags Kentlinger, Kitsie Stanfull, Nancy Headmore, and Dee Dee George. Penny is still not here.

After some opening mumbo jumbo from Reverend Bushrod, all of the wives rise and form a half-moon behind the caskets, each grasping a piece of paper. "Sags" Kentlinger, second from the left, nicknamed by Calvin's father for the permanent pink pouches of skin under her eyes, is spokeswoman for the plain-but-smartly-dressed and somber-faced group.

"We would like to remember Anna with a poem we put to-gether, because she was always writing bad poetry for our birthdays and every other occasion." Mrs. Kentlinger smiles thinly, then nods to the other ladies and raises her hand like a band leader. They begin in unison, weakly at first, then bolder:

> *Oh, Anna, we are the Quails,*
> *It's for you that our heart ails.*
> *We already miss you,*
> *Wanna hug and kiss you,*
> *In sorrow our words do fail.*

Each of the four wives has also written a personalized stanza. Penny's mother, Dee Dee (Dianne Delaney) George, is first. Dark like Penny, with chestnut hair, smooth skin, and a nice bust even at fifty-something, Mrs. George is the most pleasant of all the wives. Calvin's father called her "Ducky," because, he said, everything seemed to slide right off of her. Her stanza:

> *As a cook, you wrote the book.*
> *I can see you in your kitchen nook,*
> *Making that garlicky hollandaise or venison divine.*
> *Some even said it was better than mine.*
> *When you chopped a salad, you chattered so merry,*
> *Lettuce and 'maters and a dash of tarry,*
> *You kept us laughing with jokes so hairy,*
> *And under the counter that bottle of sherry.*

Next is Kitsie Stanfull, about a head shorter than Calvin's mother and thin as a page from the Bible. "Slim," his father called her.

> *Fore! That's the score,*
> *Golf with Anna, never a bore,*
> *Tee to green in a hundred and four.*
> *But laugh as we may,*
> *She would gamely play,*
> *And that's for shore!*

Calvin's mother and Mrs. Stanfull were not close. Oh yes, they had each other over for lunch, played tennis together, shot doves side-by-side in Elizabethtown and laughed together at Hunt Club parties, but they never really liked each other. In fact, it seems to Calvin that, deep down, no one in the Hunt Club was ever really all that close to anyone else. All the buddy-buddy stuff is the way they conceal themselves from each other and stay friends.

Nancy Headmore couldn't take it. She dropped out of the Hunt Club, rented an apartment down on Bardstown Road and filed for divorce. According to the rumors, she even started burning incense, smoking pot and listening to rock and roll. "Think of it," everyone said. "In her fifties, and living like a hippie!" Calvin's father called her "Nasty Nancy" behind her back.

Calvin is surprised to see Mrs. Headmore at the funeral in a black dress instead of threadbare jeans and a tie-dyed shirt. Her stanza:

> *Roses are red, violets are blue,*
> *No one had legs better than you.*
> *Sugar and spice and everything nice,*
> *For the men we were just a vice.*
> *But fee, fi, fo, fun,*
> *You had the blood of an Amazon.*
> *Insolence, Defiance, Appetite, Glee,*
> *You were an inspiration to me.*

Next to Calvin in the pew, all four men of the Hunt Club have frozen stares on their faces, and there is nary a sound in the church. Did this woman just bad-mouth the Louisville Hunt Club? The heavy silence dissipates into coughing and people shifting positions as Mrs. Headmore folds her paper, closes her eyes and nods her head to his mother's gleaming casket. Calvin has never thought of his mother as inspirational, particularly not to an independent woman like Mrs.

Headmore. At least this much is true: his mother was no duck.

Finally it's Sags Kentlinger's turn. She is crying before she ever gets out a word, her puddled, baggy eyes staring down at the two shiny caskets before her. She manages only one line:

You were my friend, whenever I'd call....

Then she breaks down entirely and the other women swarm around her.

When the wives have settled back in their pew, Mr. Stanfull rises and paces back and forth behind the coffins for a few seconds as if he is about to deliver a critical closing argument, then he halts suddenly, raises his head and his hands theatrically, as if he is going to speak directly to the Lord, but instead lets his hands slap to his sides and speaks directly to Calvin.

"Son, I just want you to know that no loss of mine can ever touch what has happened to you. My thoughts and prayers are with you."

Calvin feels the weight of every gaze in the church on him. *Murderer!* they're probably thinking. Bile comes up in his throat. *Go on*, he pleads silently, staring at the blood red carpet. *Go on, asshole. Go on!*

Mr. Stanfull finally goes on. "Last night I sat down to write a eulogy," he tells the crowded church, "but the words wouldn't come. All I could think of was the time Sonny and I wrecked his father's 1939 Cadillac. I know this is a horribly inappropriate time to be telling this story, but, well...." He lowers his head and lets a few moments pass, then the head comes back up. "Please forgive me. Sonny was driving, and we came to the curve on River Road down near the River Valley Club. Sonny took it too fast, we flipped, and ended up against the River Valley Club wall. The impact knocked me out. When I woke up, I was on my head inside the flipped car.

"I got out and started looking around for Sonny. I didn't know till then how much I loved the guy. I was so scared I couldn't think straight. I looked everywhere, even in the river, but I couldn't find him. He had just disappeared, and it felt as if the world had ended. That's how I feel now. Sonny's been in another car accident and I can't find him."

Mr. Stanfull puts his hands in his pockets and moves a step closer to the caskets. There is sniffling behind Calvin, one of the wives. He concentrates on the rise of his chest against the pew and wonders how many of the people in this church have ever even heard of the River Valley Club. He thinks he can feel Karl Buntingstrife's menacing gaze on the back of his head.

"I finally found him," Mr. Stanfull continues, his voice wobbling a tad. "Sonny was inside the River Valley Club having a highball. I told him he was a selfish so and so for walking off and leaving me in the car, but I forgave him because there's no way you could stay mad at Sonny Turtle for long. He was a hell of a man, that's all I can say. I keep hoping now that he's just down at the River Valley Club having another highball."

Calvin turns around and glances past the wives to Karl, who solemnly nods as if to agree that, yes, Calvin's father was one hell of a man. Calvin swivels back to face the caskets, thinking that Karl Buntingstrife is an ignorant brute and he doesn't give a shit about anything but fishing and hunting. He thinks he's King of Gaheena. Calvin realizes that he's always hated Karl Buntingstrife, and he hates Charlie Stanfull too. They'll try to take over down in Arkansas now. Calvin will be damned if he'll let that happen.

Hands still in his pockets, head lowered, Mr. Stanfull slides back into the pew and his shoulders begin to heave. Dr. George pats him on the knee and Mrs. Stanfull leans up from behind and gives him a quiet little peck on the cheek. *What a phony*, Calvin thinks.

Unearthly, Unending Love

While the solemn funeral home attendants shove his mother and father back into the hearses, Calvin stands in the shade of a giant oak near the water fountain. At the center of the fountain is a serene Mother Mary with little Baby Jesus cradled in her loving, concrete arms. She gazes down at her little Cherub with unearthly, unending love, while gentle sprays of water disturb the shallow pool at her divine ankles. Overhead, one grey squirrel chases another along the branches of the tall oak.

One of the first people to offer condolences is Little Barn Kentlinger. For a while, Little Barn and Calvin were best buddies. They were always in school together, of course, at Louisville Country Day, but Calvin was in the habit of going home after school, doing his homework and playing Klondike until bedtime. When they were around 13 or 14, Little Barn finally coaxed Calvin into hanging around out at the Country Club. They played sharks and minnows and golf together and stared at the bulging bikinis of the girls in the Snack Shack, and with their fathers went dove hunting in Elizabethtown and duck hunting down in Arkansas. When he got his license, Little Barn even talked Calvin into asking Penny out on a double date with Little Barn and Amantha Stanfull. They became a famous foursome, going out nearly every weekend. Most of those evenings ended in the line of darkened cars at Seneca Park, Little Barn and Amantha clenching in the front seat, Calvin and Penny in the back, lots of lip smacking and clothes rustling, the windows so fogged up you couldn't see in and you couldn't see out.

But something happened. By the end of high school Little Barn and Calvin weren't speaking. Little Barn had stopped hunting and Calvin had stopped going to the Country Club. Little Barn spent his evenings fattening up with his future wife Amantha, while Calvin spent his playing solitaire or fighting with Penny. The other Hunt Club offspring were doing their own things too: Little Barn's sister, Mary, had moved to New York where she was singing folk songs in a Greenwich Village bar. Charlie Stanfull Jr., already a rabid environmentalist and mortal enemy of his father, was filling out law school applications while his crazy little brother Tommy smoked dope and listened to Hendrix in the next room. Cyrus and Henry George, Penny's older twin brothers, had found Eastern spirituality and moved west to Colorado. One of the Headmore girls was living in a commune in Tennessee, another married and already a mother, the youngest disappeared altogether.

The Vietnam draft was the last thing Little Barn and Calvin had in common. Little Barn had gone to the University of Kentucky and copped a deferment. Calvin had shown up for his freshman year at the University of Virginia but couldn't stand the dingy dorm, pimply roommate, what's-your-student-number three-meal plan, bend-over-and-spread- 'em health check, pre-law, pre-med, pre-MBA, pre-CPA, pre-CIA, pre-NBA, gorgeous hordes of now-you've-got-me-now-you-don't girls, and the constant beer bash Frisbee dash on the immaculate lawn of good old Thomas Jefferson, so he dropped out, came back to Louisville and went to work for his father at Turtle Manufacturing. When the draft lottery came around, Calvin's birthday drew a high, safe number. Just blind luck, he told people, but Calvin has never believed in luck. He believes only in Klondike.

Little Barn, nearly as big as his father now and wearing a rumpled grey suit vast as Freedom Hall, sticks out a swollen hand for a vigorous, puffy, sweaty shake. "Hey, old buddy," he says, his face screwed up into a cheeky, pep-rally smile. "Good to see you. Can't tell you how sorry I am."

Amantha Kentlinger gives Calvin a squishy hug, her flowery perfume nearly suffocating him. "I thought the world of your mom and dad."

As Little Barn and Amantha step away, Little Barn says, "We'll have to play golf. I'll call you."

Now, as if out of thin air, Karl Buntingstrife appears in front of Calvin. No handshake this time.

"Hey, Karl," Calvin says cautiously.

"Sorry I can't go to the cemetery. Gotta git back."

"I understand. Thanks again for coming."

Karl scans the branches overhead as if he is looking for a squirrel to shoot, then those penetrating eyes land back on Calvin. "What are you plannin' on doin' with the Place?"

"You mean the Old Wilson Place?"

"Uh huh."

"Well, nothing. I mean, I don't know. I haven't thought about it. Why?"

"You need to come on down to Gaheena soon as you git the chance."

Calvin feels a queasy, rising excitement. "What for?"

"Me and you gotta talk."

"About what?"

"Just come on down." Karl pivots and heads to the parking lot, just like that.

Calvin wants to shout *You're not the boss!* as he watches the broad white shirt recede through the crowd. *I'll fight you*, he thinks. *You are not the King of me.*

Last to offer condolences is Johnnie. "You're my boy," she says as she hugs Calvin's neck. Johnnie is about the same age as Aunt Virgie, with grey hair pinned around her soft, wide, chocolate face, and nearly as tall as Calvin. On days when Calvin's Mom was still in bed or sashaying around with the Junior League or hacking her way around the golf course with the other wives, Johnnie took care of Calvin. She was the one who got him out of the rabbit cage when the neighborhood bully, Ray Moorehead, thought he'd see if Calvin would fit inside it. Johnnie told Ray she'd "whup" him if he ever hurt Calvin again, and Ray didn't come around after that.

"They're gone," Calvin tells Johnnie as they stare together at the idling hearses. Calvin closes his eyes and feels again the front of his Mustang smack the back of his father's station wagon. The whole thing seems inevitable to him now, as if they had all been locked in some horrible dance right from the start.

Johnnie takes Calvin's hands, the yellowish corners of her eyes tinged with red. "C'mon now," she says, studying his face. "You hold on, and I'll look out for ya." She tightens her grip on both of his hands and shakes them a little. "We'll be awright, you hear me? We'll be awright."

They hug again, and for a moment Calvin allows his weary head to rest on her shoulder.

THE MOST BEAUTIFUL PLACE ON EARTH

When you come through the tall wrought-iron gates of Cave Hill Cemetery, it's as if you're suddenly on the narrow, windy road to Oz. Giant blossomy trees shelter you from the sun, their cool fragrance a sweet seduction. Luscious manicured grass blankets the gentle hills that cradle smooth marble monuments, which always seem to have fresh flowers leaning against them. Fat squirrels feed lazily everywhere, cardinals serenade you, and mockingbirds hide in the magnolias, pretending to be cardinals. A peacock struts by, indifferent, you think, then suddenly he stops, fans a blue-green mandala at you, and you believe in God.

The curvy-smooth road leads gradually downhill to the narrow teeming lake at the heart of the place. The Cave is nearby, and out of its cool darkness the water flows, filling the lake for the ducks and the geese and the magisterial swans. Somewhere deep in the Cave, you think, there just might be a Wizard.

The Turtle plot overlooks the lake, 40 yards from the water, maybe 45. Ducks nest all around in the thick grass. Calvin's father always joked that it would be so easy to limit out.

"You better not shoot *these* ducks," his mother would warn.

His father would grin weirdly and say, "I'll shoot anything I damn well please."

The dirt from the two big holes is covered with a green tarp and flowers, and to one side are some folding chairs. Jewel's little grave is on the far side of the two holes, impossible to see over the two gleaming caskets at rest in their lowering cradles. Calvin sits down and the four Hunt Club men fan out beside him, sliding their unsheathed shotguns beneath their chairs. That's what the argument with Reverend Bushrod was about, gunfire at graveside. Down on the lake, ducks quack, geese honk and children squeal. Calvin wishes that Jewel could have seen this beautiful day, all these people, the gaping holes in the ground where their parents will be buried.

After Reverend Bushrod's gloomy incantations about ashes and dust, Mr. Stanfull gives the signal and the men of the Hunt Club stand up, raise their guns to the wispy sky, and, on command from Mr. Stanfull, let go with three tremendous, deafening *BLAMs*, more or less in unison. Spent shells fly everywhere.

Now every duck and goose on the lake rises in desperate flight. Panicked parents are gathering up their screaming children and the swans, residents of the pond so long that they can no longer fly, screech and flutter in a chaos of feathers toward the mouth of the Cave.

While everyone at graveside is shaken by all the blasting, no one is surprised. You can expect this kind of thing from the Louisville Hunt Club. Reverend Bushrod simply shuts his Bible, touches Calvin on his good shoulder, pours one last compassionate look into Calvin's soul, and walks back to his car. He is finished with the whole business.

The bitter smell of spent gunpowder lingers as Mr. Stanfull heads over to the cemetery office to explain things to the nervous Cave Hill security people and the rest of the Hunt Club men beat a retreat to the limo with their shotguns. Calvin remains seated as people file by to give him a final pat on the hand and his mother and father a final pat on the casket until at last he is the only one left beside the graves. He gets up and walks around his mother and father. Jewel's grave is covered by that green tarp; he can't even see her headstone. *Just as well*, he thinks. She is cold and dead down there and soon his mother and father will be under all that dirt too, no light, no love, nothing but worms and water and rotten stench. Calvin is done with all of them.

He returns to his folding chair and sits down. *I hate this god-forsaken world*, he thinks as he looks around at everything but those two damned bulky, shiny boxes with his scorched mother and father inside.

The hearses pull slowly away, leaving only the black limo now, idling quietly, the men of the Hunt Club no doubt passing the flask inside. The lake is calm again. Too calm. No quacking or splashing, no children frolicking along its edges. Broad pink streaks have begun to form across the afternoon sky.

Dr. George gets out of the limo and hustles back down the hillside, sits next to Calvin. They both rest their feet on the brass railing of the casket-lowering device and together they stare at the coffins.

"Penny wasn't here," Calvin says.

Dr. George turns his palms up. "We tried to get her to come, but she's really mad at you."

"I'm such an asshole."

"No you're not, Calvin. You just lost your parents, for Christsake."

The streaks in the sky are deepening to a fiery orange.

"Dad would've loved that shotgun salute," Calvin says.

"That *was* a fine thing, wasn't it?"

"The wives didn't like it."

"Fuck 'em."

"Reverend Bushrod didn't like it either."

"Fuck him, too."

All is silent for a time, then Calvin hears them, a pair of masked Canada geese gliding over the opening in the canopy of trees, penetrating everything with their shrill honks. They fly by once, circle back, ease down, huge wings cupped, floating *down down down* until their dangling feet skim gentle V's in the water and they come to rest with a decisive flutter.

Johnnie is singing her favorite hymn, "Sweet Surrender," prolonging the word *Sw-ee-ee-ee-ee-eet* in her lilting soprano until Calvin wants to climb the walls. She seems to float about the Turtle mansion as she cleans. Of course she has eliminated reminders of Calvin's parents' last day alive, the mussed bed, his father's faded boxer shorts on the bedroom floor, his mother's pink nightgown tossed on the back of the dressing-room chair, the half-read *Courier-Journal*, dishes in the sink, but you can't get rid of people that easily. His father's golf clubs are still in the garage, the once-coveted Bullseye putter bent, dented, sticking out of the bag as if his father recently tried to re-live the glory days before it failed him; his mother's aromatic arsenal of makeup in her bathroom: *Magic Mud, Wrinkle Away, Young and Soft, Love After Dark, Healing Essence, Wonder Girl,* bottles and tubes promising more than they can ever deliver; his father's guns, worn to grey dullness from all the blasting, at rest on the rack in the den above his favorite reclining chair; his mother's vodka stash, hidden like a loaded gun in a kitchen drawer; the family checkbook, his father's hurried scratchings a harsh contradiction to her full, rounded script. Their old bank statements contain canceled checks to Byck's Department Store for clothes and to Taylor's Drugstore for "misc.," meaning booze. There are dues checks to the Country Club, monthly checks to the water company, checks to the Fire and Sanitation District, to Louisville Gas and Electric, to Winn Dixie for groceries, and to Sanders Cleaners for "Sonny's shirts." There are checks to Stock Yards Bank for loan payments, checks for donations to the Louisville Ballet, the Crusade for Children and St. Mark's Episcopal Church, checks to Johnnie Katherine Clay for "services," checks to "Cash," and checks to Calvin for "allowance."

You can tell a lot about people by looking at where the money goes, but you can't learn everything. From the den Calvin calls Johnnie.

"Yoo hoo," she sings from the kitchen.

"Could you come here a minute, please?"

She appears in the doorway.

"Can I ask you a question?"

Her posture stiffens, but there is still gentleness in her eyes. "What is it?"

"What did you think of my mother and father?"

She grimaces and shakes her head. "What kinda question is that?"

"I just want to know what you thought about them, what you *really* thought, the honest-to-God truth. They fought all the time; you saw it. They must've seemed ... I don't know, crazy to you."

Johnnie shifts her weight. "What I think is none of your business."

"It's important to me..."

She turns away. "Enough of this nonsense. I got work to do."

MONDAY, JULY 24TH, 1972

Calvin sits on a hard leather chair in Mr. Stanfull's paneled office high atop the Citizens Tower downtown. Two ducks – mallards, a drake and a hen – are suspended in flight across the polished wall near a tall window, forever trying to escape.

Calvin has vaguely expected his father's Will to be hundreds, perhaps thousands of pages long, but there it is, dwarfed by the huge wooden desk on which it sits, just a puny little stack of pages, double-spaced. When Mr. Stanfull settles in behind the desk and hands him a copy, Calvin says, "What do I do?"

"I'd like to read it to you, okay? Are you ready?"

Calvin nods.

Mr. Stanfull dons a pair of brown half-glasses, fires a glance at Calvin over the top of them, clears his throat and starts to read: "*I, Sonny Turtle, domiciled in Jefferson County, Kentucky, being of sound mind and disposing memory, do make, publish, and declare this to be my Last Will And Testament, hereby revoking all wills and codicils heretofore made by me...*"

Calvin stops following along and stares out the window toward East Louisville. A flock of pigeons is circling around and around in the hazy summer sky. He watches them for a time, wondering if they are just playing or if the constant circling is some important pigeon ritual. He wonders what happens if one of the pigeons suddenly decides to fly its own way.

Beyond the pigeons it's easy to spot the giant turtle on top of the factory at Turtle Playing Card Co. Yes, there is a replica of the famous Turtle perched atop the factory, looking as if he's just crawled out of the Ohio to sun himself. He's fifteen feet tall, green and smiling, his eyes lily white with hollow black pupils. The Turtle's head bobs when a rope that drops through a pipe into the factory is pulled. Kids come by all the time: "Pull his head!" they say. "Pull his head!" Who can resist that? At night there are spotlights on the Turtle and red beacons shoot from his eyes. It's a famous Louisville landmark.

Calvin turns back to the Will: *All the rest, residue, and remainder of the property which I may own at the time of my death, real, personal, tangible, and intangible, which shall include all capital stock in the Turtle Manufacturing Company of Louisville, Kentucky, and the aforementioned real estate in Gaheena, Arkansas, I bequeath in fee and in total to my son, Calvin McGraw Turtle, herein known as Beneficiary. If, however, at the time of my death, Beneficiary has not yet reached the age of twenty-one, said assets shall be held in Trust until his twenty-first birthday, at which time all rights, privileges and obligations pertaining to said assets shall transfer to him. Charles Milton Stanfull, III, of Louisville, Kentucky, herein appointed sole Trustee, shall assume all rights and responsibilities appertaining to said Trust until the twenty-first birthday of the Beneficiary.*

Mr. Stanfull takes off his reading glasses and leans back in his tall leather chair, causing a long, low farting sound.

Calvin's head is spinning with legal mumbo jumbo. "Does that mean I don't own the company?"

"No, it just means that you don't take full control until you turn twenty-one."

Calvin forces his voice lower, calmer. "Explain a Trust, please."

Mr. Stanfull probes the inside of his mouth with one wing of his glasses. "It just means that until you're twenty-one years old... what's that, a few months?"

"June 28th."

Mr. Stanfull leans forward, flips through his desk calendar, makes a note, leans back, causing another fart. "Right. When something's in a Trust, it means that the Beneficiary of the Trust, that's you, has to work with the Trustee, that's me, and the Trustee reports to the Board of Directors.

"Who's on the Board of Directors?"

"Barn, No-Knees, Jim and myself. The Hunt Club. You'll be on it now, too, of course."

"So the Hunt Club is in charge of my company?"

"It's not uncommon, an arrangement like this in a family business. It's done so that... no offense now, but you're still pretty young, and this is commonly done so that a young heir has time to learn the ropes. It's really for your own good. You can understand that, can't you?"

"How can I inherit the family business but not control it?"

"That's the way the world works, son."

"Don't call me son."

Mr. Stanfull chews on his glasses wing and gawks at Calvin for a moment, as if he is puzzled by some deep mystery, then he dons the glasses and rocks forward, arms on the desk. "Look, I know this has all been pretty rough for you, Calvin, and I want to help, I honestly do, but it wouldn't hurt if you acquired a little more of your dad's sense of humor. He was a great guy. I miss the hell out of him, as I'm sure you do, too."

Yeah, right, Calvin thinks. "What about my mother? Did she have a Will?"

"No, she died intestate. No Will. She had some coal stock, I believe, which will come directly to you as soon as her estate can be probated. Usually takes about six months."

Calvin looks at those stuffed ducks trying to get the hell out of that office. "What about Arkansas? Do I control that?"

Mr. Stanfull lowers his eyes to the papers on his desk, a smug look on his face. "No. Not until you're 21."

"Shit!"

The smugness drains from Mr. Stanfull's face. "I beg your pardon?"

"You are in charge of the Old Wilson Place until I'm 21?"

"That's right." Mr. Stanfull shuffles the papers, lifts them, bangs them against the desktop, a phony sincerity in his eyes. "But I'll consult with you on everything, okay?"

Calvin stands, starts for the door, stops, wheels, paces the plush carpet toward the wall with the ducks, turns, paces back. Behind the desk, Mr. Stanfull watches. *That's the way the world works, son.* The words eat at Calvin like poison. God, he hates this arrogant bastard, his father's so-called best friend. Come to think of it, Calvin's father was drawn to assholes like Charlie Stanfull and Karl Buntingstrife. Why? *That's the way the world works, son.* Well, all right. In this world, you have to deal with men like Charlie Stanfull and Karl Buntingstrife.

Though Calvin is raging inside, he knows that blowing up at Mr. Stanfull right now is not going to help. He needs a strategy. He needs time to think. He'll play some Klondike when he gets home. He stops pacing and turns to Mr. Stanfull. "Can I have that drink now?"

Mr. Stanfull breaks into a smile. "Attaboy."

While Calvin waits for the drink and pretends to be all buddy buddy with Mr. Stanfull, he gets a killer pain in his chest. Later, when he calls Dr. George about it, the doctor says it's "referred pain," not to worry, you can have gas pressure in your gut but feel it in your chest. What you think you're feeling is not what you're really feeling.

KING OF THE MISBEGOTTEN

The Washington Street area of Louisville is a shabby collection of shotgun houses, red-brick factories, parking lots, oil tanks and sand piles. Some Turtle Company employees live in the closely packed shotgun houses stretching like loaves of Wonder Bread behind their little fingernail lawns and combination storm doors with the family initial twisted into the grille. When Calvin first started at Turtle Cards, he worked right beside those shotgun-house people. His father had given him the lowest job in the place, sweeping up all the misbegotten kings and queens from the floor of the stamping room for $2.10 an hour, but everyone knew it was a sham.

On his way home from Mr. Stanfull's office, Calvin stops by the factory, pulls his mother's car into his father's space, number one in the office lot. It feels weird to park here, as if he is violating some profound and unalterable order, but he's determined. This is his company now. He is his own man.

Violet, the receptionist and switchboard operator, is gnawing a hangnail as he comes through the doors. She spits out a fleck of skin and says, "Why, if it ain't Calvin! Dang my hide it's nice to see you, boy."

"Thanks, Vi." Calvin gets a whiff of the patchouli and cigarette cloud that always envelopes her. "You smell delicious."

"Well, what're you gonna do about it?" Violet's phone console begins its electronic blither, she pushes the blinking button and her eyes glaze as she says into her little headset, "Good Morning, Turtle Cards, how may I help you?"

Calvin heads straight up to the noisy stamping room, figuring that Orville, the plant superintendent, will be there. He isn't, but some of Calvin's old buddies, Zephyl Purdy, Nelle Brown, people he worked with in his first days at Turtle, holler his name, give him quick smiles and waves. They seem different somehow, on their guard perhaps. Calvin waves back and shouts *Hey* to them.

He finds Orville on the third floor inspecting newly printed sheets of bridge cards as they fall from the mouth of one of the giant printing machines. Orville is around fifty and thin as a conveyor belt; he started at Turtle Cards before Calvin was born. Orville has never been the most popular guy in the plant, but he knows how to make a good playing card. As he turns to Calvin this morning there is a sudden hesitation in his motion, as if he's spotted a big cottonmouth in the weeds, then he recovers.

"Hey, Calvin, how ya doin'?" he says, his rough hand landing lightly, stiffly on Calvin's shoulder.

"Can I talk to you a minute?"

"Sure thing. Just lemme finish this batch."

They meet on the first floor in Orville's cramped little office near the shipping dock. Orville shakes Calvin's hand loosely.

"Coffee?" he says.

"Black, thanks." Calvin still feels a little high from the booze at Mr. Stanfull's.

Orville pulls up a chair and hands Calvin a steaming mug of coffee. From outside the office Calvin can hear the subdued voices of the shipping crew.

"How ya been?" Orville says.

"Fine."

"How's that shoulder?"

"Good as new."

"Guess I haven't seen you since the funeral. That sure is a beautiful cemetery, what do they call it? Cave Hill? They keep it like a dang park, don't they?"

"I don't really want to talk about that."

"Sorry. I reckon I got a big mouth. It must be right awful for you to think about it."

Calvin sets his coffee cup on the cluttered desk. "I'm coming back to work soon."

Orville holds Calvin's gaze for a moment, then looks away. "Well, that's good, ain't it?"

Calvin winces. This is so awkward. Orville is old enough to be his father, yet Calvin is now the boss. "Will you teach me how to run this place?" Calvin says.

When he looks back at Calvin, Orville seems to have shrunk a little bit. "I worked hard for your daddy, and I'll keep a'doin that for you."

Calvin nods, takes up his coffee, tips back in his chair. "So how are things going?"

Orville stands up and shuts the door.

"Must be top secret stuff." Calvin feels a little thrill at being on the inside of things.

"Naw, I just don't want nobody hearing nothing they shouldn't."

"Like what?"

Orville sits down again, his expression grim. "Well, things has got pretty rough around here."

"Why?"

"Well, for one thing, we got new competition out in California, and they're makin' a pretty good card. 'Sides that, maybe the economy's not so good."

"What's Forny doing about it?"

Orville shakes his head. "He's about got this place scared half to death, is what he's doin' about it. Says he's gonna lay off a bunch."

"Do we have any choice?"

Orville's eyebrows shoot up like little warning flags. "It'll kill this company."

Calvin feels blood thrumming at his temples. "How's that?"

Orville speaks to the floor. "Well, I think these folks are likely to try something, maybe a strike, I don't know. They haven't had a raise in more'n a year, and now these layoffs."

"There's been a freeze on wages all over the country, Orville. It's not just us."

Orville is defiant. "Nixon lifted it."

Calvin thinks, *United We Stand, Divided We Fall.* He feels divided: Orville has him over one barrel, his father's Will over another. "I'll talk to Forny," he says.

Orville shifts in his chair, leans toward Calvin, his voice quiet, warmer: "Last night I stayed up thinking about how we might cut this thing off at the pass."

"How?"

"Well, you comin' back to work is the main thing I thought of. That's gonna make a big difference around here. These people trusted your daddy because he wouldn't lay 'em off just to save a little money here and there, and they trust you too. I know they do. Forny will have to listen to you."

Orville doesn't know about the Trust arrangement. Calvin wonders what else they know or don't know around here. He tries to make this sound like a little joke: "Don't people think I'm a murderer?"

Orville leans away, doesn't laugh. "Aw, don't nobody believe that mess."

"I didn't kill them, Orville. I want everybody to know that. It was an accident."

"I know that, son, and I'm mighty sorry they're on you about it. It ain't right."

"Please don't call me son, okay?"

Orville smiles weakly. "I don't mean nothin' by it. It's just the way we talk down home."

From Orville's office Calvin heads to the breakroom. Tacked to the wall is one of the promotional posters featuring the ever-smiling company Turtle. Mr. Stanfull's whiskey has given him a headache. He pours another cup of coffee and says *Go to hell* to the grinning poster-turtle just as Betty Sykes, his father's longtime secretary, comes banging out of the ladies room. Betty is a soft-hearted woman with too much flab and too little hair for someone not yet sixty. She has obviously been crying.

"Betty, are you okay?" Calvin says, his face hot. Did she hear him say *Go to hell*?

She wipes her nose with a hankie, locks her eyes on Calvin for a long, indignant moment, then her expression softens and she says, "Oh, Calvin, I'm sorry to blubber so, but I miss him, you know? When I saw you walk down the hall this morning, I thought it was him coming in like he always did. Late!" Betty forces a shy smile.

"I miss him, too," Calvin says, hoping it doesn't sound like a lie.

"Of course you do, honey." She wipes her nose again and starts to leave.

"I'm coming back to work," he blurts.

Betty pauses, glances back at him. "Oh, that's wonderful." He senses guardedness in her, too.

Calvin's gut winds tighter as he follows Betty down the narrow office hallway, at the far end of which is his father's office, the brass nameplate still on the door:

SONNY TURTLE
President

Calvin chats with Betty for a moment in the outer office, then, holding himself tall, inhaling, summoning as much bravado as he can muster, steps through the inner door into his father's office and sits behind the big oaken desk, where a tidal wave of panic catches up with him. He puts both hands on the glass desk cover to steady things. Orville's words echo in his head: *It'll kill this company.*

Calvin mutters: "Sparklers and Diggers, Pumpers and Puppytoes, into the Free Pile, here I goes." This is it, his chance to be his own man. A thrilling, electric energy shoots up and down his spine. He will turn things around at Turtle Cards. The employees will love him.

On the desk sits the latest issue of *Shuffling About,* the trade magazine for the playing card industry. **NEW CALIFORNIA VENTURE SUCCEEDING**, the top headline blares.

Calvin gets out a deck of Turtle Cards and deals a hand of Klondike. *I can handle this,* he thinks. He'll come up with clever strategies to stomp this new competitor in California. Sales will boom. Everyone will get a raise for Christmas. Halfway through the solitaire game, Forny pops his misshapen head in the door: "Heard you were here. Got a minute?"

Fornton Bruhall, vice-president of Turtle Playing Cards, dubbed "Forny," with obvious sexual overtones, by Calvin's father, is a pudgy, yellow-skinned, perverted-looking bachelor with a head like a sideways three-wood and an all-business manner. "Just the kind of disagreeable toad a business needs," Calvin's father always said. Now Forny stands rigidly before the desk and, with a rapid drop of his overly large Adam's apple, swallows as a man must when confronted with the limits of his own future. Here Calvin is, leapfrogged right over him into the President's chair.

Forny plops some papers in front of Calvin: "Sales report for the first three weeks of July. We've got to lay off ten percent of the workforce."

"Orville says that will cause trouble in the plant."

"Got to be done. Charlie Stanfull agrees."

A chilly pain shoots up Calvin's spine. "How does Mr. Stanfull know about it?"

"I called him. He *told* me to call him. I believe he's in charge of your father's estate now, isn't that correct?"

FRIDAY, AUGUST 4TH, 1972

It's been a month since his parents died and Calvin has not gone back to work. Every day he plays solitaire and watches soap operas in the den. He *will* jump into the fray at Turtle Manufacturing and turn things around. He just needs something to get him going. But what? Every morning he springs out of bed boldly, but by the time he's eaten breakfast, read the *Courier-Journal* and gotten dressed, he finds himself back at the card table trying to beat Klondike or sprawled on the TV couch, where he daydreams about saving some gorgeous soap-opera heroine from the sordid affairs of her world. Johnnie just cleans around him, singing that infernal song, *Sweet Surrender.*

"Still grieving," he says when Forny calls midmorning, "but I'll be back to work soon. Monday, maybe. How's business?"

"Not so good."

"I'm sure it'll turn around if Nixon doesn't screw things up again."

"Right. We're going ahead with the layoffs."

In the afternoon, while Calvin is watching *The Edge of Night*, Karl calls from the Café down in Gaheena.

"Thought I told you to come on down here," he says.

Goosebumps rise on Calvin's skin. "Yes, you did."

Karl is silent.

"You don't tell me what to do, Karl."

"Just git down here," Karl growls. The line goes

dead.

Calvin nests the curved receiver in its cradle. Suddenly it's clear what he needs to do. "All right, I'm coming, asshole."

Calvin hasn't been to Arkansas in the summertime since the cottonmouth episode. On the plane he plays a little Klondike and agonizes. What if Karl beats him up, or worse, kills him? *Silly*, Calvin tells himself. He bunches the cards and taps the deck solid, ready to shuffle again.

Up front, Sleepy Jim is, what else, asleep, their lives in the hands of the automatic pilot. *Like believing in God*, Calvin thinks. He imagines them suddenly pitching into a crash dive, Sleepy Jim still sawing 'em off up there in the pilot's seat, Calvin screaming bloody murder as they hurtle to the hard green earth below, the Automatic Pilot oblivious to his cries. But the plane just drones on, level as she goes. *In God We Trust*, Calvin thinks.

Half an hour past Memphis, Sleepy Jim, now upright and alert, breaks the droning monotony.

"This is Seven Six Padre, Stutgart, hello Stutgart."

No response.

Out the scratched window Calvin spots the grain elevators of downtown Stutgart. On a clear day and from a long way off, those concrete towers look like giant skyscrapers, but Arkansas is famous for illusions. The people of Stutgart have dubbed their town **THE RICE AND DUCK CAPITOL OF THE WORLD**, but it's just a run-down collection of houses and concrete silos in the middle of an ocean of rice.

"This is Seven Six Padre, Stutgart, Seven Six Padre,

hello Stutgart," Jim repeats.

"All right, S'em Six Pod-Ray, I gotcha."

"There's old Eli," Calvin says to Jim.

Jim says, "Afternoon, Stutgart. Seven Six Padre permission to land."

"All right, Se'm Six Pod-Ray. Wind one-niner outta the southwest. Y'all the plane from Kentucky?"

"Affirmative, we are the plane from Kentucky."

"Come on, then."

Eli hustles out to meet them on the oven-hot runway. He is wrapped in sweaty blue coveralls, and his flared nostrils leak mucous. "Welcome to Arkansas, Land of Opportunity!" he hollers, his bloodshot eyes, for a moment, bright as the sun.

"How're you getting along, Eli?" Calvin says, catching a strong whiff of motor oil and rancid sweat.

Eli's face contorts as he shoves his hands in the pockets of his faded coveralls. "I heard 'bout yo mama and daddy. Mighty sorry."

"'Preciate it," Calvin says.

"Yassuh, mighty sorry."

As soon as Calvin's bags are on the blazing, weedy concrete, Sleepy Jim climbs back into the cockpit of the Cessna.

"Pick me up tomorrow around noon?" Calvin asks.

"Will do," Jim says, pulling the door shut.

Eli wipes his nose on his sleeve and hefts off with Calvin's bags. "Gonna put 'em in that Foad yonder," he huffs.

Calvin follows him to the rental car. The Cessna's engines rev and growl as Jim pulls the plane away.

"I remember when you first started comin' down wit your daddy," Eli says, sweat beading in the grey fuzz at his temples. "You wadn't hardly big as that gun you wus totin'." He peals off a laugh and winks a bloodshot eye. "You a big man now, though, ain't ye?"

"Yes," Calvin says, proud that somebody thinks so.

As the Cessna hurtles down the runway and rises into the heavy, hazy sky, Calvin feels a rising excitement in his belly, too.

WHAT ARE YOU PLANNING ON DOING WITH THAT PISTOL?

The Café is full of weathered men in worn clothes. On the wall between two dusty deer heads is a shiny new poster of the 1972 Arkansas Razorbacks. *GO HOGS*, says the caption. Karl sits at a long table in the middle of the room, a court of admirers around him. He stands up and crushes Calvin's hand. "Hey," he croaks.

"Hey," Calvin says.

A couple of the local men, ones Calvin recognizes from November mornings at the Café, mumble something about how sorry they are about Calvin's mom and dad, etc., and a young waitress brings him coffee. Karl is back in his chair and silent. One of the locals, a pulpy, wrinkled fellow named Red, finishes telling a story that Calvin has interrupted:

"So, anyway, they wus five of us in deer camp that year, maybe six, and we was stayin' in the Shack on Old Man Wilson's Place..." Red picks up his coffee cup, takes a sip and shoots a glance Calvin's way.

Calvin smiles. "Must've been before my father owned it."

"Yessir, that's right," Red says, nodding emphatically. "Shore wus." He puts down his coffee. "So, anyway, we went to camp the week before Thanksgivin'. Karl had everything set up, and he'd done been out in the woods checkin' things over. *Be a big'un through early t'morrow mornin*,' he says. A ten, twelve pointer, he figgered. Sure enough, about seven the next mornin' we wus on our stands, just past sun-up, and *POWWWWWW*, you heard a shot down on the old buffalo slough and you know'd it wus Karl. About a hour later here he come, draggin' that fourteen point buck, biggest 'un I ever seen, all by hisself. Shot him right in the ear, then dragged him a mile, maybe two mile. Now, when Karl got that deer to the middle'a camp – and I ain't lyin', this buck was *big*, bigger'n Karl – well, when he got it to the middle'a camp, ole Karl bent down on one knee, shouldered that damn bloody thing in one heave, then throwed it maybe thirty feet through the air, maybe thirty-five, right into the back of his pickup like it wasn't no more'n a bag a cotton."

The men around Karl howl, but he remains regal, indifferent.

"Red, you're the biggest liar in Arkansas," the waitress says, refilling his coffee cup.

"Hit's the truth, I swear," Red pleads. "Happened just like I told it. Throwed that buck forty feet in the air!"

Now Karl swats Red with his hunting cap. "You old coot. You wouldn't know the truth if it rammed you in the ass."

Red fakes a swing at Karl. "I'm gonna ram *you* in the ass, son."

"Boys," Karl says, shoving back his chair, "I gotta go."

Calvin gulps his coffee and follows Karl out the door to Karl's muddy green pickup. "Get in," Karl says.

Karl and Calvin head out Highway 79 in Karl's pickup to a gravel road the locals call the W.P.A. Road, then down the W.P.A. Road to the southeast corner of the Old Wilson Place, where they park on the shoulder, engine off. Karl rolls down his window, letting in the hot, skeening drone of summer, and the air inside the truck quickly turns heavy with a faint sulfurous smell; there's a paper mill in Pine Bluff maybe 20 miles west of Gaheena, and when the wind's just right the stink is strong.

A blinding sun drains the green out of the vast rice fields across the road from the Place as mosquitoes whine and flit against the inside of Karl's cracked windshield. The back of Calvin's shirt sticks to the vinyl truck seat. Karl reaches across Calvin, takes a big black pistol out of the glove compartment and lays it on the seat between them. Calvin stares out the window. Nailed to a nearby hickory tree is an old, bullet-riddled sign:

POSTED
THIS IS MY LAND
I DON'T WANT YOU ON IT
D.P. Wilson

Calvin imagines that if he says the wrong thing, Karl will grab that pistol and shoot him right in the ear.

"What're you plannin' on doin' with this Place?" Karl finally says.

Calvin lets out a little nervous laugh. "What are you planning on doing with that pistol?"

Karl smirks. "You never know what'll crawl outta the woods around here."

"Like snakes?"

Karl nods his head and says, "Snakes," as if he is talking to the biggest coward in history.

"I'm not planning on doing anything different with the Place. What do you mean?"

Karl's narrowed eyes penetrate the filmy windshield into some dimension beyond Calvin's grasp. "This Place is in trouble."

"What do you mean?"

Karl starts the truck. "I'll show you." He drives up to the turn-off that leads into the Place. "Git the gate," he says, handing Calvin the key.

Calvin eases out of the truck, carefully scanning the dry roadside ditch for cottonmouths, unlocks the gate, and Karl drives through. Calvin re-locks the gate, then they ride on back through the dense summer woods toward the Shack.

MONEY

A woman sits on the crooked porch of the Shack. She looks around 30, maybe 35, with long whitish-blond hair, a face tanned the color of oiled oak and a body right out of your dreams. *The Queen of Gaheena*, Calvin thinks. She is sitting in a battered old rocking chair, her bare feet tucked under her thighs, her quiet gaze enough to make you crawl out of your skin.

"Who's that?" Calvin blurts.

"Money," Karl says.

"Money?"

"That's her name."

"Not Moan-ee?"

Karl aims a hard look at Calvin. "What did I say?"

"I didn't know you had a girlfriend."

Karl's eyes dart past him out toward the Old Reservoir. "There's a lot you don't know."

Karl parks right in front of the Shack and they get out. Money is wearing a man's button-down white shirt with the tails tied at the bottom, leaving a patch of bare belly smooth as a strip of butter-brickle ice cream. Her high breasts push that shirt way out in front, and she fills up those shorts, too, not with cheeseburger and a Coke hips, but prime-cut hips. And her lips – big, wet and glossy with silvery pink lipstick – spread out beneath a sculpted nose sleek as the prow of a luxurious watercraft. There is an intoxicating smell about her too, not perfumy, but a musky, animal scent.

"Hey there," she says, striking Calvin dumb.

"Meet my woman," Karl says.

Money frowns. "I'm not your woman. I'm nobody's *woman.*"

Karl snorts. "Well, then, what're you settin' out here in the skeeters for?" He opens the screen door to the Shack and steps inside, the big black pistol in his left hand, the door smacking shut behind him. Calvin stands in the hot dust at the bottom of the porch steps and inhales that unfamiliar scent, unable to even look at this creature before him. *Only in Arkansas*, he thinks. Everything seems almost Biblical down here, too full of the quivering and dangerous plasma of life.

He glances up and Money is staring at him with melancholy curiosity, her head cocked slightly to one side, the hair on that side falling down the front of her shirt like a pretty little waterfall. *She probably thinks I'm just a spoiled rich kid*, he tells himself, but she just sits there gazing at him like some Renaissance painting.

"Hello," he says, inhaling another whiff of that exotic odor.

"Hello yourself." She has begun to rock a little bit now, and her fingers play lightly on either arm of the chair. "My name's Edmonia, but people call me Money." Her voice is a bit lower than you'd expect, with just a hint of a rasp, like a mourning dove's.

A mosquito whines near Calvin's ear. He slaps at it and says, "Calvin Turtle."

She smiles and holds out a hand, the fingers long and slender, the nails painted the same pink as her lips. "It's nice to meet you, Calvin."

As Calvin steps onto the Shack porch to take that hand, Karl bangs back out of the screen door, that pistol now in a worn leather holster at his hip. "Come on."

Calvin retracts his hand. "Where we goin'?"

"You, too, baby."

Money rises from the rocker and they follow Karl down the path to the boat dock at the edge of the Old Reservoir.

A Cozy Little Dance Troupe

It's not as Calvin remembers. Oh, it's swampy all right, and full of rotting tree trunks and duck moss, but the water seems more open now, a dull greenish-grey expanse unbroken by even a small patch of lily pads, the sun glinting off the water in sharp knives of heat. The old tree trunks seem thinner too, weaker, more ready to collapse into the Soup.

Karl dodges the boat around fallen trunks and guns it over hidden stumps. Money rides the middle seat while Calvin sits in front and watches for snakes, but there don't seem to be any out in this heat. He can feel Money's eyes on his sweaty back.

When the boat gets hung on a submerged stump, the three of them hunch to the rear like a cozy little dance troupe until the boat comes back off the stump and Karl can swing the boat around it. Mosquitoes cloud around them in evil swarms kicked up by their motion through the still water. Calvin slaps and swats until his arms are a bloody mess. The outboard motor drags through the heavy duck moss. Every minute or so Karl has to raise it entirely out of the water to free the propeller, creating a sudden guttural howl.

Calvin turns to look at Karl, Money a hazy angel at the fore-edge of his vision. "Where are we *going*?"

"Keep your shirt on."

Money laughs. "You'd better keep it on, or you'll get eaten alive." The skeeters don't seem to bother those two much, but Calvin is ready to dive into the Soup to get away from them, to hell with the snakes.

Finally they stop, just stop, right in the middle of the Old Reservoir, motor off, the world suddenly reduced to the whine of skeeters and the raw smell of organic muck. There are no cottonmouths in sight, no fish jumping, no birds singing, no breeze, just the hot sun, the murky water, the skeeters, the coots, and them.

"I love this place," Money sighs. She crawls into the bottom of the aluminum boat and arranges herself as if she were in a hammock under a shade tree at the Country Club. She looks uncomfortable cramped up like that, but Calvin could crawl right down there with her. Instead, he scans the oaks and hickories and willows along the perimeter of the Old Reservoir, pretending that he's not thinking of her. The dense wall of trees makes it seem as if they have come to a place separate from all other places, a place not even of this earth. The sun's softening light casts shadows across the water. Afternoon clouds pile up in a pillowy bank to the west and Money's scent wafts to him with new intensity, enhanced, he imagines, by the heat. She lies with her eyes closed in the bottom of the boat like a caught fish, a *keeper,* he thinks. Calvin imagines he is a mosquito buzzing right down onto that buttery patch of skin below her shirt to suck for a while.

"You see it?" Karl says.

"See what?" Calvin yanks his surreptitious eyes off of Money.

"Duck moss."

Calvin leans over the dented edge of the boat to peer at the coils of dark green moss just under the water's surface. "Yeah, I see it. What about it?"

"There's too much of it."

The boat rocks as Calvin turns around to look at Karl. "Is that why there are no lily pads?"

"Uh huh. You git too much moss, it chokes off everything else. *Everything.*" Karl points to a place in the water just beside Calvin where the duck moss looks like a heavy wall of intestines. "You see how thick that is, yonder? It's that thick all over this Reservoir."

"The Reservoir is dying from too much of a good thing," Money says without opening her eyes. "Karl is tore up about it." Calvin has never seen such a look on Karl's face, not fear exactly, but something else intense.

"Won't it just die back and then the balance will be restored?" Calvin says. "It's a natural process, a cycle."

Karl says, "You're not hearin' me, son. If this Reservoir gits choked out with moss, *everything* will die, the moss too."

"And the ducks will be gone," Money adds, her eyes open now and watching Calvin.

"If this moss is gone, them ducks is gone too. It'll take..." Karl swallows the next word and turns his head.

Now Money raises herself, dangerously rocking the boat as she climbs back to the seat beside Karl and puts a hand on his knee. "Baby," she says, then she swings around and looks at Calvin. "It's his whole life. Duck huntin' means *more* to him than life itself." She turns back to Karl. "Ain't that right, baby?"

Karl stares at the bottom of the boat, his eyes watery now, no mistaking it, the holstered pistol at an awkward angle against the boat seat. Several mosquitoes on Karl's arm are filling up with his blood, but either he hasn't noticed or doesn't care.

Calvin says, "So, what do we have to do?"

Karl clears his throat. "We have to quit huntin' this Reservoir for a spell. If these ducks is allowed to rest without gittin' shot at, they'll eat this moss back outta here." He runs a hand over his face and his voice takes on its familiar, aggressive energy. "There's gotta be no duck huntin' this year, next year either, and maybe the year after that til they git this moss eat back." He reclines against the motor housing and scans the sky. Case closed.

Calvin imagines himself telling the Hunt Club there will be no duck hunting in Arkansas for three years. *Karl can go to hell*, they will say.

Money is sprawled across Karl's lap now.

"What if we just cut back on the number of hunting days?" Calvin says.

Karl jerks his body upright, nearly knocking Money off his lap. "You'll ruin it if you hunt even once."

"I don't buy that. One hunt won't scare all those ducks away for good."

Karl's face is an angry, threatening mask. "You better listen to me, boy."

Money puts her hand on Karl's knee again and he falls back against the motor, an ominous tightness on his face. Calvin releases a long breath and stares into the dark water full of duck moss, wishing that hand was on his own knee.

"You boys shouldn't argue," Money finally says. "How 'bout I fix you some supper?"

Money catches Calvin's eyes for a moment and he suppresses a little shiver. He looks down and slaps a mosquito on his arm, then wishes he hadn't. If Karl can let 'em go ahead and suck, so can he.

While Money cooks dinner, Karl and Calvin sit on the Shack steps, the sound and smell of frying chicken drifting through the screen door. On one side of the porch are Karl's deer horns, thirty racks, maybe forty, cut off and nailed to the Shack wall, many of the oldest so bleached by the relentless sun that they've turned white. Calvin wonders if Karl shot each one of those bucks right in the ear, then hauled 'em back to the Shack on his mighty shoulders. Perched on a wooden stand on the other side of the porch is the forlorn frame of an outboard motor, its parts scattered everywhere.

Karl produces a bottle of whiskey and takes a drink, then offers it to Calvin. The whiskey, some cheap unfamiliar brand, makes Calvin's skin pop out in a rash and burns his stomach. Over the Old Reservoir the sky has turned a sickly greyish-yellow, and the skeeters are getting really bad. Calvin takes another swig of whiskey and hands the bottle back to Karl, who sets it on the porch next to his rusty chair.

"One hunt this year," Calvin says, watching Karl's whiskery face. "Opening day. That's all I want. Then we'll shut it down for the season."

Karl shakes his head. "You'll ruin this place."

"The Hunt Club won't stand for it."

"They can hunt somewhere else, cain't they?" Karl's voice is full of contempt for rich people.

"There *is* nowhere else like this, and you know it." Calvin slaps a mosquito, leaving yet another bloody spot on his forearm.

They watch the changing sky for a few minutes, then Karl suddenly rises, causing Calvin to flinch.

"Let's get outta these skeeters," he says, his broad back already disappearing through the door.

Inside the Shack the light is dim, *like an Episcopal church*, Calvin thinks. A stale human pungency hangs underneath the mouthwatering smell of frying chicken. Along one windowless wall there is a mussed double bed and a dark dresser spilling clothes. Calvin sees no women's things and feels a secret twinge of pleasure in concluding that Money does not live here. *I'm nobody's woman*, she said. On the far wall of the Shack, under a smudged, unpainted window, is a narrow vinyl couch, the cushions torn and patched with tape, and in the center of the bare wooden floor is a white metal table, three plates set atop it along with napkins, forks, knives and three battered old chrome chairs pulled up as if Karl, Money and Calvin have lived here forever.

Karl and Money sit at either end of the small table and Calvin in the middle, his back to the door. Dinner is fried chicken, mashed potatoes, ham-cooked green beans, creamed corn, sliced tomatoes, biscuits: delicious.

Karl shoves food to his fork with a biscuit, forks food into his mouth, says nothing, nor does he look at Money or Calvin. You can't always tell what Karl Buntingstrife is thinking, but Calvin is pretty sure that right now he's contemplating some brutal way to make Calvin and the men of the Hunt Club go away.

"I bet you miss your mama and daddy," Money says, her sky-blue eyes locking on Calvin.

"Yeah," he answers through a bite of chicken. "This is a fine meal. Thank you very much."

"You're most welcome."

Later, on the way back from the outhouse, Calvin detours down the path to the Old Reservoir, watching for snakes until he comes up over the levee and down onto the dock. The cloud bank in the west is a stunning pink now, and Calvin feels himself beginning to soften. Karl really cares about this Place, it's obvious, and well, maybe he's still a bully, but he did give Calvin a drink of whiskey and let him stay for dinner. There really is too much duck moss in the Old Reservoir, anybody can see that, but Calvin wants to hunt, too. It's in his blood. In a few months this vast, swampy Reservoir will fill with a quacking, peeping multitude, nothing else like it in this world. Right now, even in the mosquito-infested heat of summer, just thinking about all those ducks makes Calvin's heart pound. When he turns to leave the dock, he is determined. He *will* hunt here in November. One day of shooting, just two guns, Calvin and Karl. That will *not* run all those ducks out of this Reservoir. That's just bullshit. Karl wants to take over this Place completely, but it's not going to happen. And the Hunt Club? Well, they can wait a year or two until the duck moss diminishes. Calvin watches the path for cottonmouths. This Place is his now.

When he comes back inside the Shack, the kerosene lanterns are lit and Karl is already in bed, half under a sheet and turned to the wall, his bare, powerful back pale except for the darkly weathered neck.

LET'S PLAY CARDS

"**S**tay with us," Money says when Calvin tells her he needs to get back to the motel in Stutgart.

Calvin glances over at Karl in the bed, turned so you can't tell if he's asleep. Calvin has to get back to his rental car at the Café, and Karl's truck is the only vehicle out here. He feels vaguely trapped. "No, I've already got the motel room in Stutgart, but thanks anyway. And thanks for such a great dinner. Could you drive me back to the café?"

Money wipes her hands on a thin dishtowel and gives him that unnerving stare again. "Stay a while. Please."

Calvin helps Money finish the dishes and put away the food. There is nothing now but the flickering light of two kerosene lanterns. The room seems smaller, constricted, womb-like, in the weak, nervous light. Over against the far wall, Karl is apparently asleep, his snoring like the low growl of a dangerous animal.

"I gotta go," Calvin says.

Money pulls a worn deck of Turtle Cards from a drawer and settles into her chair at one end of the table. "Let's play cards."

"I really can't."

"One game," she pleads. "Then I'll take you back to the Café."

Calvin cannot resist. "You're on." He sits in Karl's chair. "What game do you like to play?"

"Poker."

"Deal 'em," Calvin says, thinking *She's no card player.*

Money shuffles the deck, looking up at Calvin each time she snaps the card edges together with her thumbs. "What do you want to play for?"

"I don't know, matches or something. How about pennies?" He shuffles in his pocket for change, thinking *She doesn't have any money.*

"Strip poker," she says as she deals, one and one, two and two, three and three, so many turtles smiling up at them.

Calvin watches the cards land in disheveled piles and feels his insides begin to unravel the way a high-compression golf ball does when you cut the cover off, jumping and skipping as the long rubber band leaps in relief from the tightly bound ball of its existence, the result a relaxed pile of windings thick as duck moss, free at last.

"*Strip* poker?" he says.

Money's icy blue eyes are wild, inviting pools. "Five card draw." She picks up her hand.

Calvin looks over at Karl, who is snoring louder now.

Money says, "Once he's asleep, he don't know nothing."

Calvin shakes his head and laughs. "I can't do this. He'll kill me."

Money pats his arm. "He scares me too, honey. I promise he won't wake up."

"Are you his wife?"

Money averts her eyes. "Do you wanna play or not?"

Calvin shakes his head again. "I can't believe this."

"It's just cards." There is irritation in her voice.

Calvin cannot stand to disappoint her. "Can I have some more whiskey?"

Money gets the bottle, pours some of the light brown stuff in a fruit jar and they both take a good swig. The whiskey scorches Calvin's throat and they sit quietly for a time, not looking at each other. Karl's beastly snoring is the only sound, burnt kerosene the only smell.

"He beats me," Money suddenly says. She is looking at the little pile of Turtle Cards in front of her, the poker hand she has dealt herself. Her chin is quivering.

"At cards?"

Moncy shakes her head. Any second now she is going to cry.

Calvin feels a familiar panic. He glances over at the sleeping beast and imagines Karl striking Money's beautiful face with one of those powerful hands. *You brutal bastard*, he thinks. "Let's play cards," he says.

Calvin's first hand is a bust: a pair of twos and three trash cards. He draws three more trash cards. Money's hand is even worse, a ten-high bunch of trash. She removes one slender canvas shoe, dropping it with a lively clonk to the floor. Calvin's hands tremble as he deals out the next round.

"Relax," Money says, her hand on his arm again, lightly patting. She pours some more whiskey, takes a sip, hands him the fruit jar, and Calvin tips it up. Now the whiskey burns more like kerosene, low and soft. *How old is this woman?* he asks himself. Her skin seems a little drier, a tad more wrinkled than it did before. And is that hair naturally white?

The second hand: two pairs for Calvin, a pair of kings for her. She takes off another shoe and smiles. Clonk. Karl is snoring. In the low kerosene light, Money's shirt glows like the Fourth of July parachute.

Third hand: a pair of eights for Calvin, two twos for her. Money stands up and takes off her shorts. Her panties are silky white and lacy, a faint dark patch at the crotch, curls of hair spilling out the sides. "This is exciting," she says. She leans over and gives him a little hug, her musky odor and the whiskey fumes a heavy fog around him, then she sits down and he can only see the top of her again, still clothed. Calvin's head reels with the whiskey and the image of those panties.

Fourth hand: jack high for Calvin, three threes for her. Calvin takes off a shoe. Clonk. As she deals the fifth hand, Money sings a little tune, low and jaunty, "A'hunting we will go, a'hunting we will go, hi ho the dairy-oh, a'hunting we will go."

Fifth hand: a pair of fours for Calvin, a pair of kings for her. He takes off another shoe. Clonk.

Money scoops up the cards and smiles. "I'll git you naked as a baby."

And then what? Calvin wonders.

Sixth hand: three queens for her, a full house for Calvin.

"You lucky so and so!" Money hollers.

She'll wake him up! Calvin thinks, but Karl keeps on emitting that nice slow rhythmic growl, just as she said he would.

Money stands up and there are those hips again, barely contained in the silky panties with the faint patch of delta forest at the center of things. Breathing short and fast, Money yanks at the tied-together tails of her manly shirt. Out come those breasts, lively full-house breasts with big nipples like little finger sausages.

"He'll kill us," Calvin whispers, glancing over at Karl's prone, snoring body.

She is grinning and leaning toward him, her hands on the table. "He won't never know." She winks. "Unless you tell him." She sits back down, those finger sausages now rising and falling just above the smiling turtles spread out on the table before them. Calvin's gut has come completely unwound, the strands of whatever held fast his desire all loose and easy and relaxed.

Seventh hand: a pair of aces for her, nothing for Calvin. He starts to pull off a sock.

"Naw, take off them pants," Money insists, so he does, his erection pushing out the front of his underpants like the barrel of a hidden gun. *What the hell*, he tells his drunken self, and he yanks the underpants clear of the gun barrel and drops them to his ankles. Standing like that, jutting at her, he feels like a little boy showing off to his mommy.

Money says, "You're bigger than he is." She gets up and cups her warm hands around him. "Mmmm," she murmurs. "Let's go swimming."

Calvin lets her lead him down the dark path to the Old Reservoir.

ANOTHER KIND OF MOURNING

The smell is organic, of dirt and slimy protoplasm rising in bubbles through the thick mossy coils, those bubbles playing like little fingers around his legs as they rise and erupt between them, joining her musky swooning foggy whiskey breath in his mouth, her mouth on his mouth, then his mouth on those sausage nipples sucking, sweet sugar juice, her *ooh ooh ooh'ing* like the mourning dove's *down, down, down* where those long full fingers guide him into the hot cave, his moans another kind of mourning altogether.

HOW COULD SHE
DO THIS TO HIM?

Calvin lies alone and naked on the dock, a spent skybomb in the darkness under a whining, invisible cloud of mosquitoes. *Let them bite*, he thinks, but they don't, as if he no longer has anything they want. He feels nothing but the cold uneven boards beneath him and the darkness, hard and ineffable, above him.

After an indeterminate time, Calvin rises and steals back down the path to the Shack. The kerosene lamps are out and all is darkness. How long was he lying on the dock? Has she already gone to sleep?

His clothes are in a heap at the top of the porch steps. How can that be? He thought he was supposed to sleep on the couch. He tiptoes up the steps and across the creaky porch. There is movement inside, but he can see nothing through the screen door. The springs of the bed screech under them. She is moaning.

A Different Kind of Bliss

Mysterious chirps, peeps and shrieks accompany the beat of his shoes on the dirt road out of the Old Wilson Place. *Karl did this*, Calvin concludes. Threw his clothes on the porch, beat Money, then dragged her to his bed and had his way with her. Calvin imagines a hunting accident: Karl is killed and Calvin takes Money for himself. They'll live together for the rest of time.

He sings to the shuffle of the night: "A'hunting we will go, a'hunting we will go, hi ho the dairy oh, a'hunting we will go." He can still smell the organic slime all over him as he marches ahead in the darkness, barely able to see the road, much less a snake, but not caring. He feels a kind of empty bliss, but it isn't ignorance. Ignorance isn't bliss, anyway. Vengeance is bliss. He makes it to the W.P.A. Road, then to the highway, then all the way to the Café and the safety of his rental car without encountering a single cottonmouth. Karl and Money don't come after him either.

MONDAY, AUGUST 14ᵀᴴ, 1972

Calvin is raring to take on the company now. It's all about Money. Since his visit to Arkansas, everything has felt different. It's Money he wants, and Money he'll have. She's not Karl's wife, after all. She doesn't even live with him. And he beats her.

The plan is simple. Bide his time until he can get back down to Arkansas and see her somewhere away from Karl. That's all it will take. Calvin loves her, and he believes that she loves him too. Needs him. The way she made love to him? Oh God. And when she told him about Karl beating her? It breaks his heart. He will take her away from that godforsaken Place and that awful monster, but first he's got to get his ducks in a row at Turtle. Money will be so impressed with him, the owner of his own company. He will show her around the factory, his office, his house. She'll move up here and live with him forevermore, amen.

Today is Calvin's first day back at work, and even though the impending layoffs have the whole factory in a dismal mood, he's ready to take the Turtle Playing Card Company to the Promised Land. He's got clever plans for promotions and sales, and he's already asked Forny to create an ad campaign to counter the new competitor out in California. He'll boost sales so fast they'll be able to hire the laid-off workers back in no time. This morning, he walked every floor of the factory, shaking hands and smiling like a returning hero. Orville gave him a fakey thumbs-up. Nelle Brown wouldn't even look at him.

Late in the afternoon, Mr. Stanfull calls and tells Calvin to dress "in mourning" for the arraignment tomorrow, so Calvin leaves the office and heads for the Mall in St. Matthews, where he buys a new suit, Episcopalian blue, with stripes, barely perceptible, of another, lighter denomination. Mr. Stanfull told him that the judge is a "mean old bastard," especially if his hemorrhoids are acting up. "Let me do the talking, Calvin," Mr. Stanfull insisted.

"What if he asks me something?"

"He won't. The District Attorney will drop the charges."

"How do you know this?"

"Don't worry about that. Just don't say *anything.*"

HE DIDN'T KILL THEM

The drab, fluorescent courtroom is full of Cub Scouts, a flotilla of pale little faces bobbing on a sea of blue uniforms, there apparently on a field trip to see how the justice system works. On the way in, Calvin feels like he's swimming in boys. Smartly-dressed lawyers and dazed-looking defendants occupy the seats on either side of him and Mr. Stanfull, all waiting for their turn before the judge. A bunch of cops, some in uniform, some in coat and tie, sits across the aisle behind the prosecutor's table. Calvin looks around for the buck-toothed cop who arrested him but can't spot the guy. Shouldn't he be here?

Calvin is sure of one thing: he's innocent. He's thought it all over and decided that the accident was in the cards, meant to happen, God punishing the wicked. He's played game after game after game of Klondike since his parents died, and this is what he believes the cards are telling him: *Not guilty.* Yes, he tapped their bumper, pushed them into the wall. No, he did not kill them. God killed them. If they had not been drinking and fighting fighting fighting all the time, Calvin (agent of God) would not have had to ram his car into them to make them stop. For that matter, if they had not been drunk and fighting all those years ago, Jewel would be alive today. They would *all* be alive today, and happy. The Turtle Family.

Jesus Christ, Calvin says to himself, shutting his eyes and wiping a sweaty hand down his oily face. He is so bone weary dead goddamned tired of thinking about his family. The Wizard of Klondike killed his parents, period. Jewel is avenged. Calvin is avenged. That's the truth, the justice and the American way of it, and that's what he's going to tell the judge today, then the judge will bang his gavel, *Not guilty*, and it will all finally be over. He can get on with life. With Money. God's Will be done.

When his case is called, Calvin and Mr. Stanfull come through the little gate to sit at the defendant's table. *Free*, he silently prays to the judge. *Just set me free.* At the other table the Assistant District Attorney rises and casts an unpleasant look at Calvin.

"Your honor?" he says.

The judge, gaunt, curly-haired, bushy white eyebrows, tortoise shell glasses, does not respond. He is reading some papers and shifting in his chair. *Hemorrhoids*, Calvin thinks. *I'm fucked.* Now the judge raises his eyes and points a bent finger at Calvin while he addresses the Cub Scouts: "Here, boys, is a young man who has had every advantage, yet he's in court today because of his reckless behavior on the highway, resulting in the death of his parents."

Calvin feels his face go red as something sharp moves through his heart.

"Your honor, what is the point of this?" Mr. Stanfull asks.

"The point, counselor..."

"I didn't kill them, your honor," Calvin blurts, sensing all those innocent little Cub Scout eyes on him. Mr. Stanfull grabs his arm, leans in and whispers, "Shut up!"

There is fire in the Judge's old eyes. "Mr. Turtle, you speak out in my courtroom again and I'll lock you up."

Calvin lowers his head and swallows. "Yes, sir."

"Now." The judge eases back in his chair with a fierce, tight-lipped look on his face, daring Calvin to say anything else.

The Assistant District Attorney starts again: "Your honor, the investigating officer in this case, Detective O'Donnell, is not present."

The judge lurches forward. "What?"

"The state will drop the charges against Mr. Turtle."

The judge picks up the papers and throws them back down. "*Where* is Detective O'Donnell, Mr. Swintner?"

"I don't know, your honor."

The judge hisses, shakes his head, rubs his hands together for several moments, as if he is trying to remove all the impossible dirtiness of this world, then finally he takes up his gavel and glowers at

Calvin. "Mr. Turtle, you are getting away with murder, in my opinion, but that happens sometimes in this world."

You know it all, don't you? Calvin thinks, glaring back at him. There is another hard squeeze on his arm.

"Shut the fuck up," Mr. Stanfull whispers.

Calvin continues to glare at the judge, but keeps his mouth shut.

"Very well, then, case dismissed," the judge says wearily. His gavel comes down with a decisive smack.

As they head back through the gates toward the rear of the room, Calvin catches one fuzzy-headed Cub Scout gaping at him, little mouth open slightly, cherubic eyes full of worry and excitement, as if he's just seen his first *real murderer.*

"I didn't kill them," Calvin whispers as they pass by.

The freckled face turns red and the boy quickly drops his eyes.

Outside the courthouse in the bright sweltering din of downtown Louisville, Calvin feels light as a feather. Not guilty or case dismissed, it's all the same: he's free. As they stroll down the stained sidewalk toward the towering Citizens building, he asks Mr. Stanfull how he arranged for the charges to be dropped.

"The arresting officer didn't show up, that's all there is to it. Things work out that way sometimes."

"Yeah, right."

Mr. Stanfull sighs. "Let it go, Calvin. It's over, and we've got a company to run."

"*I've* got a company to run."

Mr. Stanfull aims a finger at Calvin and laughs. "*You've* got a company to run."

Back in his office, Mr. Stanfull fixes them both a drink. "I hear you went to Arkansas," he says, handing Calvin the small glass of bourbon.

Here it comes, Calvin thinks, the big confrontation over Arkansas, but he's feeling easy and brave just now, he can handle anything, even Charlie Stanfull. He'll just announce it outright: No hunting in the Old Reservoir this year. Or next. He leans back into his leather chair, smug, powerful, smooth bourbon warming his gut. "Yeah," he says.

Mr. Stanfull settles in the big chair behind his desk. "How's Karl?"

"Same as always. Thinks he's King of Gaheena."

"What's he up to now?"

"Oh, he wants us to stop hunting down there for a few years."

Mr. Stanfull rocks forward and puts his drink down. "Why?"

"He says there's too much duck moss, and it's killing everything in the Old Reservoir, and if we don't stop hunting and let the ducks eat that moss out of there, it's all over, no more ducks."

"Oh, bullshit. That's not going to happen. He doesn't know a thing about it." Mr. Stanfull picks his drink up, takes a swallow, puts the sweaty glass down and casts a hard stare at Calvin. "So what did you say?"

Calvin turns his eyes to the darkly paneled wall where those two mallards are still trying to fly the hell out of that office. He closes his eyes and pictures Karl and Money in the Shack, bedsprings screeching. A skybomb goes off in his head. He opens his eyes: Mr. Stanfull is still staring, still waiting for an answer. Calvin feels his courage leaking away. He takes a sip of his own drink and meets Mr. Stanfull's cold stare. "I told the son of a bitch we would duck hunt this year, just like always."

"Attaboy."

FRIDAY, AUGUST 18ᵀᴴ, 1972

Pink notices are included with paychecks at Turtle Playing Cards. Ten percent of the workforce is laid off according to what's called the "L.I.F.O." system, Last one In, First one Out. When Calvin goes to Orville's office and tries to explain that businesses must cut expenses when they're losing money, Orville calls him "a little Judas."

At quitting time a long-haired forklift driver from the paper department barges into Calvin's office, throws his wadded pink slip at Calvin, and shouts: "You can keep your fucking job!" Then he storms into the reception area, spits on the stately portrait of Ish Turtle, Calvin's grandfather, and bangs out the front door.

That's L.I.F.O.

The first bad decks turn up in a batch sent to a Vegas casino. On the back of each Ace of Spades is a tiny imperfection in the casino logo, a nick off the edge of one of the letters, something only the keenest eye could spot, but something nevertheless that the plant's closed-circuit inspection system should never miss. Dishonesty is the one thing the inspection screens can't pick up. Someone can sabotage a printing plate and look the other way when the flaw shows up on his screen. Bango, you've got ten thousand flawed decks of cards, and in the playing card business, a flaw in a deck of cards which might enable a sharp-eyed card player to have an advantage is the equivalent of a splotch of cancer in the corporate chest. If word spreads that your cards are imperfect, you're dead.

The Vegas casino returns its entire supply of cards and demands free replacements. Calvin watches over the new batch like a mother watching her child the first time it waddles near the Country Club pool. Later, in Calvin's office, Orville claims that the bad run of Casino decks must've been an accident. "We been making good cards for so long," he says, not quite meeting Calvin's eyes, "it was bound to happen. Wasn't nothing but a tiny nick on the plate. Coulda happened when we set it on the printer. I seen it happen before."

"How did it get by the inspection line, Orville?"

"Wasn't no inspector on line that day. You laid him off."

FRIDAY, SEPTEMBER 1ST, 1972

A delegation of employees – Orville, Zephyl Purdy and Nelle Brown – has asked for a meeting. Nelle, a thin chain-smoking middle-aged black woman, long an employee at Turtle, is spokesperson. The three of them look so odd sitting in the leather chairs and staid surroundings of the boardroom: ducks out of water. The air in the room is cold and smoky.

"We have two demands," Nelle says, jamming her cigarette into a glass ashtray. "We want a pay raise first. After that you promise no more layoffs."

Calvin sits at the head of the table, Mr. Stanfull at the foot, his blocky chin resting in a hand, his age-spotted forehead beading up sweat, those keen brown eyes moving from one person to the next.

"How can we come up with the money for raises?" Calvin pleads, "when we can't even afford the payroll we've got now."

"We ain't had no raise in more'n a year and a half," Nelle shoots back, "and inflation ain't gonna stop like a city bus while we catch up to it. We got families to feed."

Orville, Zephyl and Nelle are all looking at Calvin, and he feels a little blanket of something wrapping around his heart. Guilt, yes, fear too, maybe, but not exactly fear. Excitement? This is his first real test as the new owner of Turtle Playing Cards. "The company's losing money, Nelle," he says. "How can we keep people working and give out raises when there isn't even enough business to pay the light bill?"

"You ain't having no trouble paying no light bill, and I don't see you and Mr. Stanfull here going on welfare, neither."

"Look, Miss Brown," Mr. Stanfull says, dropping his hands to the table, "Calvin and I are concerned about you folks, but we have to do what's best for the whole company. You can understand that, can't you? You don't want Turtle Playing Cards to go out of business, do you?"

"Whaddayou know about *folks*?" Nelle sneers.

"Come on, Nelle," Orville says.

"Naw, I won't come on, neither. He don't care about no *folks*. We need a strike to make him do for us."

Mr. Stanfull stabs a finger at Nelle. "If you go on strike, we'll hire people to take your place."

She jumps up and stalks toward him, then stops, hands on her big hips. "We'll fight you, Mister!"

Mr. Stanfull stands up and towers over her. "You will lose."

Nelle's nostrils flare, her eyes narrow and her jaw muscles bulge and twist under the wrinkles and faint sideburns on her brown face. Zephyl Purdy, a quiet, sturdy soul from Indiana, takes her arm, tries to pull her out of Mr. Stanfull's face.

"Get offa me!" Nelle screams as she wheels around to Orville. "I told you that's what they'd do. These motherfuckers ain't gonna give us nothing, and you're just gonna sit there and take it in the ass." She storms out of the room and slams the door.

Now Orville and Zephyl are staring at Calvin again. "Well?" Orville finally says.

Calvin glances down the long slick table at Mr. Stanfull, who is still standing, ready to fight. Something about that posture of his – tensed shoulders, arms dangling, fingers twitching, sleek jaw set, eyebrows raised – causes a little skybomb to go off in Calvin's head, blinding him for a moment. When he can see again, Orville and Zephyl are looking at Mr. Stanfull, who is shaking his head. The meeting is over.

THEY'RE SWEATING LIKE BEASTS

Calvin has lunch in his office. He is so agitated after that meeting, he's got to get out of this place. It's a clear, hot afternoon. Something in his mind says, *Golf*.

He tells Betty he's taking the afternoon off and heads out Highway 42 for the first time since the accident, the charred place on the rock wall still visible as he speeds by. He parks in the shade near the polo field and heads toward the pro shop. Two of the Hunt Club wives, Sags Kentlinger and Kitsie Stanfull, are squared off on the tennis courts, their white outfits a'flashing, aging bodies a'glistening. Mrs. Stanfull sees him first: "Well, if it isn't Calvin Turtle."

"Hi," he answers, walking along the chain-link fence. They stop their game and move toward him.

"Gonna play some golf?" Mrs. Kentlinger asks, her breathing labored.

Calvin nods.

"Sure is hot," Mrs. Stanfull says, wiping her small forehead with a plush wristband.

"We're sweating like beasts out here," Mrs. Kentlinger says, her face splotchy red, the bags under her eyes swollen even larger, a few damp strands of blond hair matted to her temples.

"Well, see you," Calvin says, and starts to walk off.

"You gonna hunt with us on Sunday?" Mrs. Stanfull hollers.

Calvin remembers. This is Labor Day Weekend,

and that means dove season. Mrs. Stanfull is inviting him to the big hunt out at the Kentlinger's farm, and he feels a familiar little jolt of desire, the desire to kill. He turns around: "Well, I'd like to."

"We insist," Mrs. Kentlinger says, swinging her racquet to and fro, to and fro.

In My Name, Please

Calvin hasn't played golf in more than four years, but his clubs are right where they've always been, in the cubbyhole marked *C. Turtle*, shiny and dust free. The caddies clean them once a week whether you play or not. Frank Smythe, the club pro, is behind the counter in the pro shop. The place reeks of new leather and Frank's awful cologne.

"Well, I'll be damned," Frank says.

"Hi, Frank. I need some balls and tees, please."

Frank hands him a sleeve of Tru-Flight balls. "These the ones you like?"

"Better make it two sleeves. I haven't played in a while."

Frank gives him a second sleeve of balls and a little packet of white tees. "What've you been up to, son? We haven't seen you around here in a long time."

"Charge them, will you?" Calvin says, adding quickly, "In my name, please."

"No problem. We've missed you around here. You're one of the best golfers we got."

"Once upon a time, maybe."

"Shit, son, you've got one of the best swings I ever saw. It's a crime you don't play any more."

"Please don't call me son, Frank. I hate it."

"Hey buddy, don't mind me, it's just something I say, you know? Listen, I'm mighty sorry 'bout you losing your Mama and Daddy like that. I would've come to the funeral, but I never know what to say at those things, know what I mean? Real sorry 'bout it, though. I thought the world of them."

"Thanks," Calvin says, thinking, *You don't think the world of anybody but yourself.*

CHAMPIONSHIP
OF THE UNIVERSE

Kentucky is a sauna bath in August. Before Calvin hits the first shot he, too, is sweating like a beast. Cicadas keen like high-tension electric wires as he sticks his tee in the hard ground. The strong odor of cowshit wafts over from some nearby field as he smacks his first drive well over the hill. "Whoa!" Calvin says. He catches himself wishing his father had been here to see that.

A couple of weeks before Calvin's sixteenth birthday, he and his father had a match with the Stanfulls, Charlie and Little Charlie, two of the best golfers at the Club and two of the biggest cheaters. Little Charlie was already sixteen and driving a new Camaro. The girls at the Country Club thought he was a big stud, and he seemed to agree. Calvin thought he was a big prick.

Calvin's father dubbed it the Championship of the Universe whenever they played golf with the Stanfulls. The bet was always just five-dollar Nassau, but the stakes seemed much higher.

On that June day in 1968 it was hot too, the grass in the fairways dry and starting to brown, the electric song of cicadas, the occasional shout of "Fore," or the thwock of a golf ball against the solid wood of a tree trunk the only sounds. By the third hole, it was all-out war. Mr. Stanfull and his hotshot son had already started improving their lies when they thought the Turtles weren't looking. When

Calvin lost his ball in the rough behind the third green, his father came over and said in a low conspiratorial whisper, "Just throw down another one, and don't say anything." Calvin slipped another ball out of his pocket and let it drop into the long grass. "Here it is!" he shouted.

When Little Charlie scuffed a fairway wood on number four, he threw the club so hard it spun through the air like some ancient weapon and hit a startled robin trying to take off. The robin dropped dead to the ground and the club landed a few yards away, undamaged.

"Great shot!" Calvin's father yelled.

Mr. Stanfull, who sat in their cart just ahead of Calvin and his father, turned around and said, "Fuck you."

Calvin's father leaned over to Calvin and whispered, "We got 'em now."

Little Charlie picked up his three-wood, came back to their cart and slammed the club into his bag. "It's all right, son," Mr. Stanfull said, patting Little Charlie on the sweaty back. "Shake it off." Little Charlie climbed in the cart and they zoomed off down the cart path.

Calvin's father gunned their cart and, as they breezed by, Calvin gazed at the robin, a small grey heap lying immeasurably still in the hard, dry fairway.

"No blood," Calvin's father announced as he tallied up the scorecard after nine holes. They all ordered a sandwich from the grille and ate without talking much.

On the eleventh hole Calvin hit his tee shot in the water, putting them down by a stroke. On the twelfth he had to hit two shots to get his ball out of the trap in front of the green. "Come on, Calvin, keep your goddamned head down," his father said, beating the ground with his putter.

"It's just a game," Calvin said.

"The hell it is. Now keep your goddamned head *down!*"

On the thirteenth Calvin stood at the tee and repeated to himself, *Keep your goddamned head down,* but when he swung, his head came up so fast he missed the ball entirely. There it was, still perched on the tee, a stinging little indictment.

"Shit," his father mumbled.

That asshole Little Charlie was laughing, so Calvin wheeled and started toward him, intending to crush his big fat head.

"Whoa, here comes tough man," Little Charlie said. He was

maybe an inch taller than Calvin, and much stockier. They had never fought, but Calvin had always wanted to smack that arrogant bastard, so he got right in front of Little Charlie, cocked his shoulders, raised the driver skyward and told Little Charlie to shut the fuck up or he'd send his head rolling up the fairway.

"*Whoa*, I'm scared," Little Charlie said, shaking his hands in mock alarm, his lips twisted up in a sneer.

Calvin cocked the driver even higher, and despite himself, Little Charlie raised a hand against the blow.

"*BOYS!*" Calvin's father shouted, moving between them.

"Let 'em fight," said Mr. Stanfull.

"Don't be stupid, Charlie."

"Don't patronize me, Sonny Turtle. They're big boys, let 'em fight it out."

"Grow up, Charlie."

"Fuck you, Sonny."

Calvin pictured Little Charlie's head exploding like a sky-bomb, but he didn't swing. Little Charlie was clearly cringing. That was enough. Calvin lowered his driver, snorting his disgust when Little Charlie flinched again.

"Let's play golf," Calvin's father said. "Calvin, hit your drive."

Calvin stood up to his ball again and swung as hard as he could, not caring whether he kept his head down or not, and the ball flew out of sight right down the middle of the fairway.

"Hell of a drive," his father said sadly.

"You lie two," Mr. Stanfull declared.

They lost another stroke on the thirteenth, even though Calvin's father had a birdie. The Stanfulls parked their cart in the shade and strode onto the fourteenth tee. His father pulled Calvin aside: "Okay, we're two strokes down with five holes to go. We gotta get going. Now, keep your head down and swing easy."

"Stop telling me what to do."

Jaw muscles bulged under his father's reddening cheeks. "Don't get smart with me."

"I don't care if we lose."

"Why don't you quit, then. Be a little quitter."

"I will." Calvin dropped his driver and started walking toward the clubhouse.

"Calvin, come back here," his father said, a smidgen of apology in his voice.

Calvin kept walking.

"Where's he going?" Mr. Stanfull asked.

"He's quitting," Calvin's father said.

"Quitter!" Little Charlie yelled.

Calvin turned around and gave them all the finger, then he walked all the way back to the clubhouse, through the parking lot, past the polo field and headed down the long Country Club drive to Highway 42. He had walked nearly halfway back to Louisville before his father came by in the station wagon and pulled off the road ahead of him. Calvin halted. His father watched him in the rear-view mirror as cars whizzed by. Calvin didn't budge. More cars whizzed by. Finally Calvin's father started the car and drove off. Calvin walked the rest of the way home, not getting there till well after dark.

His mother studied him carefully when Calvin came into the kitchen. "Are you hungry?"

"No."

"Are you all right?"

"Yes."

"Did you and your father have a fight?"

"Something like that." The television was on in the den, his father watching a baseball game. Calvin went the long way around to the stairs and up to his room.

Two years later Little Charlie and his father got in a fight over politics and stopped speaking for good. Calvin never played golf with his own father again.

SO WHAT'S THE PROBLEM?

On number five tee, back by the river, a couple in a cart catches up with Calvin. It's Jim and Dee Dee George, avid hackers. Dr. George comes around the cart to shake, his grip strong and dry, his eyes genuine and direct. He looks like an exotic bird in those white shoes, black socks, blue seersucker shorts and crisp red golf shirt. "How you hittin' em?" he says.

"Not bad," Calvin answers.

"May we join you?" says Mrs. George. "You've got to promise not to laugh." She is wearing the perfect golf outfit, pastel polo shirt with rounded collar, khaki shorts and little white half-socks peeping over her spotless two-tone golf shoes.

Calvin goes first, stroking a great drive, long and straight.

"Tremendous whack!" Dr. George says. "God, I'd love to be able to do that just once in my life."

"You will, dear," Mrs. George says, winking at Calvin.

Now it's Dr. George's turn. He has a manic golf swing, only about a half-swing actually, with a short, hurried takeoff, then a stiff, all-out retaliatory thrust.

"Nice shot, Doc," Calvin says.

"That's a lie, Calvin, but I forgive you. I can't play this goddamned game." He slams his driver into his bag, climbs in the cart, lights a cigarette and reaches into a small cooler full of beer.

They drive forward to the ladies' tee and Calvin follows on foot. After a couple of measured, slow practice swings, Mrs. George now stands up to her ball. Calvin can tell she's had lessons from the lecherous Frank Smythe: wiggle the butt to establish balance, hold the club shaft six inches from your body, find your rhythm, turn the hips into the ball, breathe, keep the club high on the follow-through. Mrs. George does all that and virtually nothing happens. Her ball dribbles fifty yards, maybe fifty-five, and halts, gleaming back at her under the hot, insulting sun, but she just quietly slides her driver back into her bag. "Calvin, I'm so glad we ran into you," she says.

They insist that Calvin drink a beer and put his clubs in their cart, then they jounce down the fairway and he follows on foot. *This is nice*, he tells himself. Golf. Beer. Freedom. He's forgotten about the mess at Turtle Cards.

Dr. George drinks and drinks. On every tee he cracks open another beer, and by the time they get to the green it's gone. His swing gets weaker, his putting more erratic, and a couple of times Mrs. George has to reach out and stop him from toppling over after one of his manic swings.

Calvin drinks more beer too, and his head begins to ache. When they get to number fourteen tee back against the woods, they form a drunken little triangle in the soft shade under some pines, as if they are about to have a game of cards. Calvin's head swims from the heat and the alcohol. There is just a slight breeze. Someone yells "*Fore!*" in the distance.

"Calvin, how you doin', old buck?" Dr. George says.

"Great."

"Betcha miss Penny, don'tcha?"

Calvin's stomach muscles tighten. "I guess so."

"You *guess* so? Goddammit, you'd better *know* so." Dr. George beams at his wife. "Hell, we could be your mother and father-in-law some day. Howsabout that?"

Blood rushes to Calvin's face. "That would be nice," he says, thinking that, well, it might be nice. Dr. and Mrs. George are great, after all, and Penny is great too, if you have to be honest about it. Her brothers would be his brothers. He could visit them out in Colorado. Instant family. It all sounds pretty good to Calvin this hot afternoon. *So what's the problem?* he asks himself.

Mrs. George is swaying slightly, as if she can hear music no one else hears. "Why don't you come over for dinner tonight, Calvin?

Penny will be there. I know she would love to see you. I'm making pot roast."

"Thanks, but I can't." Calvin is not sure why he says this. All he knows for sure is that he will end up playing Klondike in the den tonight.

"You can so, goddammit!" Dr. George yells, then he lies down in the grass and goes to sleep.

Calvin is not going to sit here alone with Mrs. George. He gets up and hefts his golf bag from the cart. "I'd better go," he says politely. "I enjoyed it, thank you very much, and thanks for the invitation. Please tell Penny hello for me."

"Okay, honey," Mrs. George says, still swaying and smiling.

Back home, sore and hungover, Calvin sits at the card table in the den, a lousy Klondike tableau before him. Every face-up card is red, no plays possible, no chance he'll win this game. Sometimes you're doomed before you even start.

He leans back, closes his eyes, rubs his face with both hands, thinks about the scene at the Club today. Why did he even go out there? He hates the Country Club scene: raked polo field, fancy tennis outfits, manicured fairways, people being so courteous, all that civilized pretense. In fact, tonight he hates his whole life: this immaculate, empty mansion; Charlie Stanfull and all the problems at Turtle Manufacturing; his fucked-up relationship with Penny; and Karl Buntingstrife. It's all catching up to him, crashing down on him.

Calvin needs Money.

In the kitchen, he looks up the number and calls the Café down in Gaheena. A woman answers. Calvin's heart is blamming; he asks for Edmonia.

"Not here," the woman says.

"Could you please have her call Calvin Turtle?" He gives her the number.

Calvin knows this is suicide; Karl will find out. In a small place like Gaheena, everybody knows everything, but Calvin doesn't care. He needs Money and that's all there is to it.

Saturday, September 2ᴺᴰ, 1972

Calvin wakes in the motionless black night. The phone is ringing.

A woman says, "Oh, I'm so glad you're there." It's Money, her low voice faint and wobbly. She's crying, but it's still her voice, right out of his dreams.

"Money!" he says.

She sniffs. "Can you come down here right away?"

"What's wrong?"

"He beat me again."

"Karl?"

"Uh huh."

"Because of me calling?"

"No, no, honey."

"Well, why then?"

"Just please come down here. I need you."

"Where are you?"

"My trailer. You know where you cross over the Bayou Meto bridge just before you come into town? Well, right after the bridge, turn left off the highway, go over the railroad tracks, and follow the bayou road. I'm two miles on the left. A white trailer."

"Perfect. I'll find it."

"Please hurry."

REVIVAL

Bayou Meto, a wide depression shaded by giant cypress trees growing in muddy, slow-moving water, slithers around the eastern perimeter of Gaheena, a narrow paved road snaking right along with it. A few houses hunch along the strip of land between the water and the road, many accompanied by at least one old car sitting like some rotting beast in the high grass.

After two bumpy miles of winding bayou road, Calvin comes to a dull-white, plain-looking trailer. There are no cars, just an old aluminum boat turned bottoms-up in some high weeds. *One of Karl's boats*, Calvin thinks.

He pulls into the dirt driveway and kills the motor. A bullfrog bellows somewhere in the wide, cypress-shaded expanse behind the trailer. Watching the grass for snakes, Calvin climbs the steps and knocks. No answer. A typed note is taped to the handle of the screen door:

> *Calvin. I'm at church.*
> *Gaheena Baptist. Please come.*

"Church?" Calvin says, looking around the weedy yard. She wants him to meet her in church, for Christsake. What's that about? It's not even Sunday. Calvin tells himself that she has gone to church to hide from Karl. Yes. That's got to be it. *He beat me again*, she said.

REVIVAL TONITE says the crudely painted sign in front of the boxy brick building. Battered cars and pickups are parked everywhere. The air is heavy, hazy, and smells

141

of sulphur. The paper mill in Pine Bluff.

Calvin's shirt sticks to his sweaty back; he can hear singing as he approaches. He does *not* want to go in there, but Money said, *Please come.* Who could resist that? But what if Karl is in there? *No chance*, he tells himself. Karl Buntingstrife would never set foot in a church. Calvin will go in, get Money, then they can go back to her trailer.

He opens the heavy door just as the singing stops. A few faces turn to stare at him, hands fanning little white programs like so many hovering doves of peace. The place smells like flowers and old, sweet wood. Money is nowhere in sight.

The preacher's voice cuts into the silence. "Come in, Brother. God's house is your house."

Now he sees her. Wearing a simple white cotton dress, Money emerges from a pew near the front and comes back to get him. Her hair is tied up in a bun, and the full, billowy dress hides those breasts. Smiling radiantly, she takes Calvin's hand, leads him back to her pew. Two frowning women let them by and he sits down between a little girl clad in a blue dress and Money, who leans over and whispers in his ear, "Glad you're here."

Calvin nods, looking for bruises on her smooth skin. *Where did he hit her*? he wonders, and a furious wave of anger fills him. There is a shotgun and some shells in the trunk of his car. He will kill that bastard. He leans into Money, catching a good whiff of that musky smell of hers, and whispers, "Are you okay?"

She nods, but doesn't look at him.

"Let's get out of here," he whispers.

Money shakes her head.

"Shhh," says the little girl on the other side of him.

Money leans around Calvin, smiles warmly and nods at the girl, who seems to glow like a little sky-blue candle. A wheezing, heavily wrinkled old man with a beak for a nose sits on the other side of the little girl, clearly not her father. Her grandfather, maybe? The old man's head hangs forward, his eyes on the back of the pew in front of him, giving no sign that he's here with the little girl. Is she here alone? Calvin decides it's none of his business.

He turns and whispers into Money's lovely ear again. "Why are you here? Why can't we leave?"

"Shhh!" the little girl insists.

Money will not look at him, will not answer. This is starting to piss Calvin off. She *invited* him here!

"Welcome, sir, to the house of the Lord," the preacher says, looking at Calvin. "Would you stand and tell us your name, please."

Calvin shrinks into the pew under the regal gaze of this preacher. "Me?" he mumbles, pointing a finger at himself.

The preacher nods.

A hot rush of blood rises to his face as Calvin halfway stands. "Uh...Calvin Turtle."

A chorus of voices says, *Welcome, Brother Turtle,* and he quickly sits down. The little girl pokes him in the arm. "Welcome, Brother Turtle," she says, a solemn look on her face, such a pretty round face, vaguely familiar.

"Brother Turtle," booms the preacher, a stocky, sweating man wearing a dark suit with a thin little tie. He wipes his forehead with a handkerchief. "I am Brother Doorock, and we" – he sweeps his hand out over the congregation – "are gathered here tonight in the name of our Lord and Savior, Jesus Christ."

Amen, the voices say. Money says it too.

"Amen," Calvin mumbles, barely moving his lips.

"We are the children of God," Brother Doorock says, his voice taking on a lilting, musical quality now.

Praise the lord, the congregation says.

"We... are the famlee... of God... here today."

Yes we are.

Money takes up Calvin's hand and moves it into her lap. *That's more like it,* he thinks. "Amen," he whispers, watching her beautiful face. She turns slightly and smiles shyly at him, flashing a perfect row of teeth, sending a rapturous shiver down his spine. He smiles back, but her eyes have already left him.

"The world... is an atom," Brother Doorock says, his voice slowing, and a notch louder.

Yes, Lord.

"And the famlee unit... is the Nucleus... of the atom."

Amen.

"So-ci-ah-tee..."

Uh huh.

"So-ci-ah-tee... consists... of people... who rotate around... the famlee nucleus... like *protons*."

Yes, that's right.

"Protons!"

Yes, Lord, a-men.

"Close orbit!"

Hallelujah.

Calvin's never been to a church like this, much less a Revival, and he is feeling something, a revival of sorts, no doubt about it, though it's not spiritual, but rather a gathering storm of desire overtaking him like the onrush of a double shot of whiskey or a heavy drug. He wants out of this crazy church. He wants Money. He inches closer to the heat and smell of her.

"The famlee unit," Brother Doorock says, his voice climbing, "is the *heart*... of the system... the gravitational center... of the *WORLD*... and the very force... that binds the famlee... together... is *Love*."

Oh sweet Jesus, a-men.

"A deep and abiding Love... holding us together... through the *HELL* of disappointment... and cruelty... and betrayal... and physical suffering."

Praise Jesus.

And this Love... can *NOT* be pierced... by the strongest bullets... of the Devil."

Amen. Hallelujah.

Some people are standing now, waving their arms. *This guy is good,* Calvin thinks. Despite himself, he is hanging on every word. The preacher's voice is mesmerizing, his words undeniably powerful. Calvin doesn't really believe this stuff, but this preacher's sure got a way.

Money's right there, so close, so luscious, even in that plain white dress, but she's staring at Brother Doorock, her hand still holding Calvin's but limply, meaninglessly. *God has come between us,* Calvin thinks, and the thought, strangely, makes him feel like laughing.

"Exodus 21 tells us..." Brother Doorock says after a sweaty pause, "that whosoever striketh a man... so that he dies... shall himself be put to death."

A-men to that.

Calvin squirms. *Just a coincidence,* he thinks. With both of her thin hands, Money is mashing Calvin's hand against her breasts now as if she is praying. Her chest rises and falls, rises and falls.

Now Brother Doorock is looking at Calvin again, no question about it. "Whosoever striketh his father... or his mother... shall himself be put to death."

A-men!

Calvin's whole body is suddenly a tightly wound golf ball. Money has dropped his hand without looking at him.

"Whosoever *CURSES* his father... or his mother... shall himself... be put to death," Brother Doorock warns, still aiming his scornful eyes at Calvin.

Calvin tried to understand: the preacher knows. Does he know? Did Money tell him? That's fucking crazy! Money won't even look at him now. She's just sitting there like some innocent angel.

This is really pissing Calvin off, but he can't decide what to do about it. He moves his body forward and to the left just enough to lose all heated contact with Money. He feels the eyes of everyone in the church burning his skin.

"Love... is *Forgiveness*," Brother Doorock shouts, his eyes skyward now.

A-men!

"Love... is *Self-Sacrifice*."

Yes, lord.

Brother Doorock's voice plummets almost to a whisper. "And without... self-sacrifice... the famlee... will surely perish."

That's right!

Now Money stands; everyone but Calvin stands. The little girl taps his left shoulder, motions impatiently for him to stand, but he refuses.

"Love pulls us together," Brother Doorock chants.

A-men, the congregation replies.

"Love is *GRAVITY*."

A-men.

Calvin closes his eyes and grits his teeth. He's so confused. Money's heated, musky scent is strong in his nostrils. He still wants her, worse than ever.

Brother Doorock shouts, "There'll be a *NUCLEAR EXPLOSION* without love."

Yes, Jesus!

"The Lord is thy shepherd."

I shall not want.

"The Lord is thy shepherd!"

I Shall Not Want!

"The Lord is thy *SHEPHERD*!"

I... SHALL ... NOT... WANT!

Calvin opens his eyes; his throat is dry and sore. Was he chanting it too? He reaches for Money's hand, but she will not let him hold it. He feels like screaming. On the other side of him the little girl is swaying and moaning softly.

This is hell, Calvin thinks. *This is truly hell.*

"Brothers and Sisters," Brother Doorock says now, his wide brow raining sweat, his voice softer, quieter, back to earth. "Who among us today is ready to receive the Lord?"

Without a word or even a glance at Calvin, Money slides away, squeezing past the two fanning ladies out into the aisle, where she floats toward the front. Calvin stands in time to see her stop and bow toward the altar.

"All ye who would receive Jesus, come now to the doorstep of the Lord, take Him into your heart, join His famlee, let Him become your Nucleus," Brother Doorock says.

There is another tap on Calvin's left arm. The blue-clad little girl is looking up at him with what seems like deep comprehension and sympathy. "Go on," she urges, a faint smile playing underneath her solemn expression.

Calvin shakes his head firmly.

"I am a child of the Lord," the little girl says, the smile breaking over her face now like a thrilling sunrise, the face of God. *Who is this child?* Calvin wonders.

Calvin feels that familiar upwelling of emotion threatening to drown him again, and he looks away from her to the ceiling. *No,* he tells himself, shaking his head wildly. *Do NOT cry.*

Brother Doorock has stepped down from his pulpit and placed his big hand on Money's head, pushing her gently down to kneel. "Before Jesus, what is your name, sister?"

"Edmonia," she mumbles to the floor.

Brother Doorock raises his arms and shouts to the ceiling, "Sister Edmonia has come here today to join the Lord's famlee. Hallelujah, Jesus!"

Hallelujah, Jesus.

"Sister Edmonia, can you feel the Love of Jesus filling you this evening?"

"Yes, I can," Money says loudly, her head still bowed.

"Do you accept His love?"

"Yes, I do."

"Do you give your soul to His keeping?"

"Yes, I do."

"Will you be baptized in His Name?"

"Yes, I will."

Brother Doorock pulls her upright and leads her around behind the choir platform, through a door and out of sight. Everything for a weird few moments is still, as if hell has finally, as advertised, frozen over, then programs flutter again and the choir, on cue from the piano player, takes up "Amazing Grace." People sway slowly as they confess to being wretches who have been saved. Calvin lets the slow, mournful music wash over him, soothe him. He can certainly relate to feeling like a wretch, but he sure as hell isn't *saved.*

The little girl takes his left hand, curling her little fingers around his and resting them there, light and cool, easy, that eerie, beatific smile playing around her lips again, and the closest of the two unsmiling ladies, a tallish, thin woman with a white, lacey thing pinned over her hair, takes his right. Calvin allows himself to sway a little too, what the hell.

During the third verse, someone from the choir goes to the wall next to the crucifix and pulls back a curtain, revealing the big preacher and Money, waist deep in a huge water tank, both wearing heavy white frocks in place of their clothes. Brother Doorock raises his arms and moves his lips, but Calvin can't hear a thing over the singing. Money, eyes closed, moves her lips too, then the preacher puts one hand on her forehead, the other in the small of her back, Money pinches her nose, and he dunks her over backwards.

She comes up quick, hair plastered to her face, her body shedding streams of water like a duck does after a dive, her nipples showing through the frock. Calvin cringes with desire and acute shame, as if he's the one in that tank with her, naked, hard, wanting to disappear inside of her right in front of all these people. Money raises her chin, wipes the hair out of her face, searches out over the heads of the crowd until she finds Calvin, and when her eyes come to rest on him, her expression becomes a serene smile, just like the smile of the company Turtle, all knowing, peaceful, absent of any desire for him, and this begets another rise of anger in Calvin. She seduced *him* last summer, and then last night she said she *needed* him on the phone. He senses that somehow Karl must be involved in all of this. It's all so crazy.

The congregation starts through the first verse again and Money holds Calvin with that infuriating gaze until someone from the choir goes over and closes the curtain.

SHE IS THE LORD'S NOW

Calvin waits until the church is completely empty but Money never comes out of the back room. By the time he hurries out the main door, the Revival has lost its grip on him. All of Brother Doorock's dramatic admonitions about being put to death if you strike your mother or father ring as hollow as the inside of the church without all that fanning and shouting and swaying. Calvin's just not buying it. He didn't kill them anyway.

What hasn't lost its grip on him is Money. He's got to see her, talk to her, find out what is going on.

There is a barbecue supper taking place in the little yard behind the church. People are standing around talking, some of them holding plates, some still fanning themselves with the evening's program, their children weaving in and out of the grownups like bass dodging ancient tree trunks in the Old Reservoir. Calvin looks around for the little girl in blue, but doesn't spot her.

People reach out to shake his hand. "Welcome, Brother Calvin," they say. He forces weak smiles and grips the hands, all the while scanning the crowd for Money. Smoke rises from a pit of hot coals fitted over with two big metal grids laden with searing chicken parts. Calvin's stomach is empty; his mouth waters. Bowls and dishes of potato salad, baked beans, slaw, sliced tomatoes, corn on the cob, sliced raw onions and several pans of corn bread sit on two long, fly-infested tables, but he will not take these peoples' food. He has crashed their Revival and sung their songs with them, but he doesn't believe. What he wants is Money, not Jesus.

Brother Doorock strides up to him and offers a smooth, puffy hand. "Well, Brother Turtle," he says, "can we gitcha some barbecue?"

Calvin tries to hide the guilt and desire roiling inside him. "No thanks, Brother Doorock, but thank you for letting me attend your church today."

"You're most welcome, son."

Calvin fights the urge to say *I'm not your son*. Instead, he says, "Do you happen to know where, uh, Edmonia went?"

The benign look on the reverend's face dissolves. "Well, now, Brother Turtle, she didn't say, she didn't say."

He tries to sound casual. "Did she leave?"

"She walked out that back door yonder, but she didn't say where she was headed to." Brother Doorock nods warmly at a passing group of grey-haired ladies, then turns a cold, judgmental eye back to Calvin. "You might better just let her go, Brother Turtle, you might better just let her go." His tone is a mix of the sweet love of Jesus and the Almighty threat of condemnation. "You see," he continues, "sometimes when a body accepts the Lord, yes, praise Jesus, when a body accepts the Lord the way Sister Edmonia has done tonight, that body needs to be by herself, all right? You can understand that, now can't you?"

Calvin glances down the darkening, tree-lined street, trying to spot Money. "Yes," he says. "I can understand that."

Brother Doorock raises his arms and closes his eyes: "Let us thank the Lord for taking sister Edmonia into his arms this fine evenin', and let us git us some of that fine barbecue too, and be thankful, 'cause it's His food we're eatin'."

"Right," Calvin says, easing toward the road.

On the front seat of his car is a note scratched in pencil on the back of a Revival program:

> *You will not have me. I am the Lord's now.*
> *Do not try to find me. Go home.*

NORTH, TOWARD LOUISVILLE

The farther Calvin drives down the crooked, bumpy Bayou Meto road, the more angry he gets. *I am the Lord's now,* she said. The whole thing smells as bad as Gaheena's sulfurous air.

His headlights illuminate the trailer coming up on the left. No car, no truck in the driveway, no light on inside. He pulls in, kills the engine, rolls down the window, shuts off the headlights. Total darkness, no sound except a host of bullfrogs in full throat out in the bayou behind the trailer. He fetches a flashlight from the glove compartment and gets out of the car. The note on the handle of the trailer door is gone. He climbs the steps and knocks. No answer. Knocks again. No answer. He tries the door. Open. Finds a light switch, flicks it on.

The interior of the trailer is a red explosion, as if the world has suddenly been coated with blood. Everything – carpet, walls, curtains, even the couch – is red. The place smells weird too, a sweet oversmell like hippy incense topping a musky, exotic undersmell, Money's scent, no doubt about it.

"Money, are you here?" Calvin says.

Nothing.

"Karl?"

Nothing.

Calvin turns around in the doorway and listens. Nothing. Only uncommon darkness and the bellowing bullfrogs out in the bayou.

"Okay, shoot me, Karl," he yells. "See if you can hit me in the ear."

Nothing.

"Come on, shoot me, goddammit!"

Nothing.

"Money, are you out there?"

Nothing, just his car, the empty road, the bayou, and the bullfrogs. "Goddamn the both of you!" he shouts.

Calvin steps back into the trailer, collapses on the couch and let's out a sound like the scream of a shot rabbit, but he hates the miserable sound of himself so much that he gets up and goes into the kitchen (red linoleum, red Formica table, painted red cabinets) and turns on the faucet, expecting crimson blood to flow from the spout, but the water is greenish, tastes like a bayou, organic and warm, and smells like a bayou, too, musky and dangerous. Money.

Calvin washes his face and hands in the stuff, then washes again, but he can't get clean. He shuts off the water, dries himself with a crimson dishtowel, turns the light out and clicks the door shut behind him. From the trunk of his car he takes his shotgun, shucks a shell into the chamber, rests the gun beside him on the front seat, drives slowly back along the pitch-black Bayou Meto road to the highway where he turns right, north, toward Louisville.

SUNDAY, SEPTEMBER 3RD, 1972

Calvin wakes late in the morning, still tired. He scans his bedroom: drapes pulled against the daylight, door to the bathroom wide open, clothes piled in the floor, nothing unusual. He remembers every detail of the revival in Arkansas, but he doesn't remember the drive down there or the drive back, as if, now this is really crazy, the whole thing was a dream.

"That was no dream," he assures himself. His whole room smells like bayou, and on top of that he feels like he's been chewed up and spit out like a piece of bad meat. Brother Doorock was *real*. And Money, the smell and the heat of her so close to him in that church? Infuriatingly real. The little girl in blue? Heartbreakingly real. Money's notes? Real as rain. Money's trailer with the red interior? Real as fire.

He flicks on the TV: a Sunday morning news show. The topic? Watergate, what else? Calvin turns the TV off. He is hungry. Very hungry. On the way downstairs to scramble some eggs, he remembers that he never touched a morsel of that barbecue at the Revival, and this thought takes him back to Money. Did she really take that Baptism seriously? And where in the hell did she go afterwards? The whole trip really does seem like an insane nightmare, but it was all too real. Calvin decides that he must stop thinking about Money or *he* will go insane.

In the shower he remembers that today is the dove hunt out at the Kentlinger farm. He wants to go. It's just a dove hunt. Wouldn't mean he's joining the Hunt Club. Those assholes will think that's what it means, but too bad. Sooner or later the shit will hit the fan, but not today. Today he will play their game. Today he feels like killing.

A Gentle Morsel

The mourning dove is a gentle, cooing morsel, its tiny breast delicious wrapped in bacon and served with wild rice, but this soft, greyish-brown, delicately-spotted bird is tough to hit on the wing. With unearthly speed he will dart and flip and change directions on you, so it's not unusual to shoot and shoot without touching a feather. Some say it's the sportiest hunting there is.

Doves are plentiful in the fertile corn country of Kentucky. They feed twice a day, once in the early morning and again in late afternoon, but in the interim they wrap their little reddish feet around the branches of shady trees and mourn this sad sad world, *down up, down down down.* The season opens at noon on the first day of September and by mid-afternoon, when the birds are hungry again and beginning to feed, the fireworks have begun.

The high social event of the year for the Louisville Hunt Club is the annual Labor Day Weekend dove hunt, held on the Kentlinger farm out in Oldham County on the first Sunday of September. Each spring Mr. Kentlinger's tenant farmer plants a large field of corn, then towards the end of August he "harvests," leaving behind enough grain to feed Bangladesh. By Labor Day Weekend, every dove in Kentucky knows where *that* field is.

WELCOME TO THE HUNT CLUB

It's a hazy twenty-minute drive out Highway 42 to the secluded Kentlinger farm. The dove field is a few hundred yards from the main house, just below a freshly whitewashed barn. Adjacent to the barn is a slime-covered pond surrounded by high crickety weeds.

Four dust-coated cars are already pulled into those weeds when Calvin arrives. He parks next to the Georges' paneled station wagon, shuts off the engine and opens the door, letting in a blast of hot, sticky air. A dove darts overhead, desperate to get to the bountiful corn on the stubbled ground. A shotgun blast rips the air and the dove falls in a crumpled fluttery wad to the earth. Dr. George pops out from under a walnut tree to retrieve it.

The other men are posted at the best spots under trees or telephone poles. Standing together on the fence-row in a casual, chatty, shotgun-toting circle are three khaki-clad women, Sags Kentlinger, Dee Dee George, and, sure enough, Penny. Despite himself, Calvin is excited to see her. As he stuffs his vest with shotgun shells, it occurs to him that he and Penny are the Hunt Club's last hope for a future.

Calvin takes a stand along the weedy fence near the cars and Penny waves; he waves back. Now a dove sails over the field toward Calvin. It has been a while since he's fired a shotgun but he knows what to do. In a flow of motion familiar as any primal reflex, he sweeps the round sight on the tip of his gun barrel to a place just in front of the closing dove and pulls the trigger. The bird explodes. Its limp, feathery body thumps the ground like a fist.

"Nice shot," Penny hollers.

Calvin's heart thumps his chest the way the bird thumped the ground. Sweat trickles from his armpits as he takes a few steps out into the corn stubble. The dove is a mangle of shredded purple flesh and shuddering wings, the head jammed into the dirt beneath a cornstalk, blood dripping from the curved beak. As Calvin watches, the deep brown of the eye becomes the dull, dirty grey of clay, and the shuddering subsides.

"Too close," he mutters. He picks up the ragged carcass and tosses it into the high weeds behind the fence.

Now Penny eases up the fencerow toward him, looking so good in that hunting outfit, toting that shotgun.

"Since when are *you* a hunter?" Calvin says.

"Since now," she says, leaning up to kiss him on the cheek. "I've missed you, Calvin."

Calvin inhales the hot scent of her Shalimar. "Missed you, too." He feels the eyes of the Hunt Club upon them.

Penny catches his eye. "Calvin?" Her eyes are soft, pleading.

"Yes?"

"I still love you."

"I love you, too."

She frowns and looks away. "God, I wish I could believe that."

Calvin pulls her close and kisses her dry lips. "You can." He opens his eyes and glances over her head at a squadron of doves, fifteen of them, maybe twenty, dipping and diving and weaving, heading right toward Penny and Calvin.

"*Mark!*" he says, stepping away from her and dropping to one knee, releasing his safety. Penny swivels and crouches beside him. He hears her safety click off. "Which one should I shoot?" she says.

"Just pick one."

When the doves are in range, Calvin stands up and shoots three times. Nothing falls. "Shit!" he says, the pungent smell of gunpowder in his nose, the tang of it on his tongue.

"Too high?" Penny asks.

"Why didn't you shoot?"

She shrugs. "I didn't know which one to shoot *at.*"

"Maybe you should go on back down there."

"You don't want me around?"

Calvin strokes her smooth cheek. "No, that's not it, honey. Two of us standing here together is spooking them. I just don't think you'll get enough good shooting."

Penny laughs sadly. "Yeah, right."

As she starts back down the fencerow, four or five doves soar over Calvin's head and he raises up awkwardly and shoots three more times. Nothing falls. Penny looks back and grins: "Serves you right."

Directly across the wide field from Calvin, up against a fence-post at the edge of some woods, stands Kitsie Stanfull, alert, leaning slightly forward, watching the sky, more serious about hunting than the other wives. Calvin waves. Mrs. Stanfull raises her hand in an exaggerated salute, then she suddenly bends into a deep crouch. "*Mark!*" she hollers.

Calvin sees the dove cup its wings, float over her, then the urgent rise of her gun and the fire-flash, the jolting *BLAM*, the abrupt fall of the bird, a grey smear on the parched earth.

"Nice shot," he hollers.

"Thank you," she calls back. When Mrs. Stanfull picks up the bird, its wings flap a couple of times against her hand, so, with a quick, decisive motion of her free hand she yanks the bird's head off. The flapping intensifies for a few moments, then ceases altogether.

Dr. George waves to Calvin from under a giant walnut tree in the middle of the field. "Hey, Calvin," he shouts, then he suddenly raises his gun, shoots at a pair of doves trying to land in that tree. One falls dead, but the other wobbles off to a crash landing in the distant woods, too far away to retrieve.

Down the field under another tree, No-Knees Headmore clumsily wheels around to search the sky. Mr. Stanfull stands along the back fencerow, and at the far corner Barn Kentlinger's bulk dwarfs a telephone pole.

"Hey, Calvin," Mr. Kentlinger bellows, "welcome to the Hunt Club!"

A shot is fired and Mrs. Kentlinger pops out of the little circle of women to retrieve the fallen dove, but the dove isn't dead yet. It flaps through the grassy cornstubble, keeping just ahead of the tentative reach of Mrs. Kentlinger. Finally she stops chasing it and levels her gun: the bird is no more than ten feet away.

"Don't shoot!" Mr. Kentlinger yells.

"How about a little help, then?" Mrs. Kentlinger yells back, swinging her gun more or less in her husband's direction. She stares at him for a long moment, then at the escaping dove, and Calvin isn't sure which one she is planning to shoot. She waits. Mr. Kentlinger does not leave his post to help her. Finally, she turns and heads back to the circle of women, the wounded bird left to die in the stubble.

Late afternoon brings flight after flight of hungry doves, more than Calvin has ever seen. They dodge, dive and sail: everyone shoots and shoots. Calvin loses track of how many downed birds he has or in which direction they lie. His hands are coated with blood and feathers, his overheated gun barrel splattered with the brains of cripples whose heads he's had to bash. The world reeks of spent gunpowder and hot entrails. Calvin's overflowing game bag hangs leaden and heavy at his side like some grotesque organ. He tastes salt and blood and bile.

Back at the cars, their clothes splotchy with dirt and sweat and dried blood, flies buzzing above the stiffening doves piled in a bloody deranged heap at their feet, locusts keening their late afternoon serenade, the members of the Louisville Hunt Club start drinking. Penny wants to sit with Calvin on the hood of his car. Moving to make room for her, he spills cold beer down the front of his shirt. "Feels nice," he says, grinning at her. Dr. George pulls out a pack of Kools and lights one. Little swirls of cigarette smoke rise and vanish above his head.

"Did we get over the limit?" Sags Kentlinger asks in her girlish, high voice. Calvin thinks she sounds and looks like Marilyn Monroe today. She is sitting near Penny and Calvin on the tailgate of the Georges' station wagon, a sweating can of beer between her legs, a good bit of cleavage showing between the open topflaps of her shirt.

Mr. Stanfull snorts out a little laugh and shakes his head at her question. "Are you serious?" He lies on the vast hood of his white El Dorado, ankles crossed.

"We should've quit sooner," Mrs. Kentlinger says.

"No way," her husband grunts.

"Best goddamned hunt *I've* ever been on," Mr. Headmore says.

"Pretty good," Mr. Stanfull agrees. He slides down off the hood of his Cadillac and stands for moment with his head bowed, as if he is going to lead them all in prayer. "I miss Sonny," he says, looking up at Calvin.

Calvin feels a shadowy contraction of his heart.

Mr. Stanfull reaches in a cooler and pulls out a dripping can. "This hunt was for Sonny," he says, opening the trunk of the El Dorado. He takes out his shotgun, shucks in a shell and shouts, "To you, Sonny!" then he throws the can into the air, raises his gun, and blasts the spinning can full of holes. Foamy beer rains down as the spinning can hits with a thwop on the surface of the pond, into which it gradually sinks, leaving a small dark hole in the slime.

When everyone has swilled to the memory of Calvin's father, Mr. Kentlinger stands up and, breathing heavily, says, "Here, gimme that gun." He takes Mr. Stanfull's shotgun and shucks in another shell. "Watch this, Calvin." He reaches in his pants pocket and pulls out a large shiny coin. "Silver dollar," he says. "Virgin mint." He tosses the silver dollar out over the pond but not high enough. By the time he gets the gun up and pulls the trigger, the dollar has already sunk into the slime. His low shot hits the barn roof, pellets rat-tat-tatting across the rusty metal.

"Helluva shot!" Mr. Headmore says, laughing.

"Give me that gun, you idiot," Mr. Stanfull barks.

"Fuck you," Mr. Kentlinger says, dropping Mr. Stanfull's gun onto the pile of dead doves.

"Now don't start, you all," Mrs. Stanfull warns.

No one says anything for a time. Calvin sucks down the last of one beer, fetches another, holds the cold can to the back of Penny's neck. She arches into it, inhaling deeply, then drops a hand on Calvin's thigh and whispers, "God, that feels good."

Now two Negro women come bumping down past the barn in a battered old pickup truck. They stop some distance away and don't get out until Mr. Kentlinger motions to them. "Here come my gals," he says as they approach.

The women are both heavy-boned and full-breasted. One of them has a small, quiet face with recessed, averted eyes, but the other has a full, wide-open, bright face. She looks at the group and says, "How're yall?" The small-faced one holds a cardboard box.

Mr. Kentlinger says, "Calvin, Penny, I'd like you to meet Peaches and Loretta." He puts his big arm around the shoulders of the quiet one. "This is Loretta."

Penny says, "Hi, Loretta."

Mr. Kentlinger puts his free hand behind the other woman, just above her ass. "And this is Peaches."

"Nice to meet ya," she says, moving away from the hand.

Loretta pulls some plastic bags out of her cardboard box as she and Peaches kneel and begin sacking up the heaps of doves. Flies buzz off in all directions.

"Calvin, those are two of the finest cooks in the world," Mr. Kentlinger says, as if Peaches and Loretta are animal specimens at the State Fair.

"Naw we ain't," Peaches argues.

"Yes you are, too," Mr. Kentlinger insists, circling his lips with his huge tongue. "Wait'll you taste those barbecued doves, Calvin. God damn!"

"It'll take you all night to clean those," Calvin says.

Peaches looks wearily up at him, "Uh huh."

"Just do enough for our supper," Mr. Kentlinger says, "then take the rest home to your Daddy, all right girls?"

"Yessir," Peaches says as she drops the last of the doves in a plastic bag, then she and Loretta lug two of the loaded sacks to their pickup. Calvin drops down off the hood of his car and carries the remaining bag to the truck.

"At least there's one gentleman in this crowd," Mrs. George says when he returns. Calvin catches her eye and smiles. Mrs. George is so nice. She could be his mother-in-law some day if he could just get his mind off of Money. *Never mind*, he tells himself. *Stop thinking about Money!*

Now a whiskey bottle goes around. The sun has disappeared behind a layer of afternoon grey, but the heat is still oppressive. The keening of the locusts has diminished, and crickets in the high grass around the pond begin to chirp. A dove on the powerline out over the field sings *down-up, dowwwn, dowwwn, dowwwn.*

"Sure is hot," Mr. Headmore announces.

Mrs. Stanfull hops down from her perch on Mr. Headmore's tailgate and sets her beer carefully on the ground. "God it's hot," she says, standing upright as she pulls her hunting shirt out by the tails and unbuttons every button until the wet khaki hangs open, revealing the part of her bra where the cups join.

"Ho, Ho, Ho," Dr. George says.

Calvin tries not to look at Mrs. Stanfull's flattish chest.

"It's so *hot*," she insists, glancing at her husband, then she pulls the shirt away, over her arms, dropping it to the ground, and sits back on the tailgate next to Mr. Headmore where she begins to unlace her

161

dusty and blood-specked leather hunting shoes, then Mrs. Kentlinger and Mrs. George begin undoing the buttons on their own sweaty hunting shirts.

"Sure is hot," Mr. Kentlinger says, his voice full of boozy excitement.

"And getting hotter," Dr. George adds. His hand makes its way behind Mrs. George to rest easily against her butt.

Calvin feels the world changing, just when he thought he understood. In his ear there is a warm, low hum. It's Penny. She rubs her hand up his leg to his knee, then down his thigh. "I'm so drunk," she whispers.

Mrs. George, shirt off now, revealing large wrinkled breasts that droop a bit in their plain white bra, suddenly stops the flow of things. "Wait everyone. We forgot something."

"What's that, baby?" Dr. George says absently, his hand now firmly on her backside, his eyes glued to the overflowing bra on her front side.

Mrs. George raises her silvery beer can: "To Anna."

Calvin feels another dark contraction of his heart as everyone toasts his mother. He is staring at the dusty, bloody, feathery ground when Mrs. Stanfull's hunting pants fall to the grass in a heap.

"Oh, baby!" Mr. Kentlinger says.

Now Mrs. Stanfull, tanned and trim as any age-spotted fifty-year-old woman could be, turns and tip-toes in her underwear through the high grass and wades into the bubbly green slime of the pond. "It's so warm!" she says. Calvin gets a strong whiff of musky, organic gunk. "Come on in, you chickenshits!" Mrs. Stanfull yells, then she dives into the slime.

"Let's go get her," Mr. Stanfull says, sliding down the hood of that big Cadillac and unbuckling his pants.

"I wanna make love," Penny whispers in Calvin's ear. Her hands are all over him now, but no one pays any attention. The husbands and wives of the Louisville Hunt Club are ripping off their clothes and heading for the slime. Over Penny's shoulder Calvin watches Mrs. George shove her pants to her ankles and bend over to remove her shoes, shooting him a stretch-marked, lace-pantied moon in the process. There is something vaguely wrong about all this, but Calvin can't think about that. Penny wants to make love. Who could resist that? They can slip away and go to her apartment. No one will notice or care.

Now Penny fiddles with the buttons of her own shirt.

"What are you *doing*?" Calvin says.

"I'm going in," she says, looking at him as if he is the biggest idiot in the world. "Come on. It's so hot!" Her hands dive to Calvin's crotch and skillfully take the zipper down, then she rips her own shirt off, a wild gleam in her eyes.

Mr. Kentlinger bellows, "All right, Penny!"

This is fine, Calvin tells himself. *It's so hot.* He shucks down to his underwear and follows the Louisville Hunt Club into the slime.

Monday, September 4ᵀᴴ, 1972

Calvin wakes with the foulest hangover of his life. His teeth hurt, his jaw muscles are knotted and cramped, and his poisoned blood presses at the thin, hyper-sensitive membrane of his skin. There is dense hammering at the frontal lobes of his brain, and his limbs feel cold and remote. A coarse splatter of wet vomit covers half the bed. He can't even remember how he got home. It's still dark outside.

Still in his filthy hunting clothes, Calvin slouches into the kitchen and fixes a Coke and three eggs, then another Coke with a shot of whiskey. In the den, he gets out a deck of Turtle Cards and starts a hand of Klondike. There are three cards in the free piles when he runs to the bathroom and throws the whole mess up.

In the shower he begins to feel a little better, but when he is dry he thinks he can still smell that vomit on himself, so he gets back in the shower and uses more soap this time. Under the hot spray he closes his eyes and tries to understand something: it has occurred to him that he's felt dirty, not on the outside but on the inside, for a long time now, maybe his whole life. Filthy dirty. Yes, there has been something befouling his life every day every hour every minute every second no doubt about it, but what, exactly, is this thing and how can he get rid of it? It's like trying to conquer a foe you can't even see. Like playing Klondike.

After shower number two, Calvin stuffs his blood-stained hunting clothes along with the fouled sheets in the washing machine, turns the dial to the hottest setting and dumps in a cup of soap. Then the phone rings.

"Good morning, glory," Penny says so sweetly.

"What did we do last night? I am so hungover I can't see straight. I don't remember what happened after we went swimming."

"You took me home and we made love, don't you remember that?

"Yes, we made love."

"It was wonderful."

"Yeah, it sure was."

"You don't remember, do you?"

"Yes, I do, honey. It was truly wonderful for me too."

"You don't even remember making love. That's great, Calvin. Really great."

The image in Calvin's mind is that pile of doves, bloody feathers, mangled bodies, crushed heads, vacant eyes, flies buzzing. "Jesus," he says, his voice low and slow, "I feel like hell."

"Try tomato juice and a raw egg. Want me to come over and fix it for you?"

Calvin feels like vomiting again. "No thanks. Anyway, I thought you were done with me. Going to U of L, getting on with your life, all that."

Penny sighs. "I can't stop loving you, sweetheart. I've tried, God knows I've tried, but I can't do it."

"I don't even know *how* to love anybody."

Penny lets out an insane little laugh. "Hey, I could write a song: I CAN'T STOP LOVING YOU..."

"Are you still drunk?"

"Or *you* could write one: I CAN'T *START* LOVING YOU..."

"Please don't make fun of me."

"How about, SET ME FREE, WHY DON'TCHA BABE, GET OUTTA MY LIFE, WHY DON'TCHA BABE, *WOO-OO WOO WOO*..."

"Stop it."

"YOU DON'T REALLY LOVE ME, YOU JUST KEEP ME HANGIN' ON, *WOO-OO WOO WOO*."

When Penny finally quits the crazed singing, there is nothing between them but the faint hiss of the phone line. Finally, Calvin says, "Penny, I do love you, I swear to god I do, and I think I wanna marry you some day. I want so bad to have a family, you have no idea. Christ, I would *love* to be in your family, it's just...I can't do it yet. I don't know what it is. I feel like I've got to do something first, take care of something and I don't even know what the hell it is. I think I'm going crazy. I need time. *Please.*"

"Don't keep me hangin' on, okay, babe? Don't call me again unless you mean business."

"You called me."

"Oh, you're so fucking smart, aren't you? Nobody gets on top of Calvin Turtle, do they?"

"Were you on top last night?"

Penny slams the phone dead.

LORDAMIGHTY, BOY.
YOU THAT IGNORANT?

Johnnie **comes** through the back door into the kitchen at the usual hour.

"What are *you* doing here?" Calvin says.

"Well, why wouldn't I be here? I ain't dead."

"Today's Labor Day."

"I don't take off for Labor Day." She gently shuts the basement door in his face.

Johnnie always changes into her uniform, a faded blue smock-dress with white trim, in the basement, then emerges singing that song, "Sweet Surrender," and begins to clean. Calvin knows so little about her. When she comes out of the basement, he says, "Have you got a family?" He has known her all his life and never asked.

"I've got one," she says, eyeing him suspiciously.

"Shouldn't you be home with them on Labor Day?"

"Who's gonna clean this house? Looks like a tornado hit."

"I want to meet your family."

A shadow of something like menace passes over her face. "Naw you don't."

"Yes I do, too. You can clean tomorrow."

"There's no bus till this evenin', now git outta here and let me start on them dishes." She tries to push him out of the kitchen.

"I'll take you home. Today's a holiday."

"Ain't no holiday for me."

"I want you to take the day off, Johnnie. Please."

She stops stacking dishes and puts her hands on her hips. "Do I git paid?"

"Full pay. Where do you live?"

She keeps a narrowed eye on him and says nothing.

"So where do you live? Downtown somewhere, right?"

"Thirtieth Street."

"Is that in the West End?"

Johnnie shakes her head. "Lordamighty, boy. You that ignorant?"

ARE YOU PREPARED?

My **Old** Kentucky Home is not in Louisville's West End. Down there the darkies are not always gay and the birds don't sing sweetly all the day, but the sun shines bright, too bright. It's the first thing you notice as you leave the East End behind. By the time you hit 15th Street, the light is so bright you can't miss the tenement buildings that stand like minimum security prisons in the middle of empty patchworks of concrete playgrounds and dying grass. There must be a thousand people living in those buildings, you figure, but there's not a human being in sight.

By 20th Street you've secretly eased an elbow up to the slick little lock-knob on your car door and pushed it down. You're not afraid, you tell yourself, just careful. The road narrows and people stare at you from porches and sidewalks; the houses are small and close together. Some of the little yards sprout trash and junk, others sprout flowers and trees and bicycles. Like a hardening artery, the road is clogged on both sides with parked cars, most-ly big cars, not little foreign jobs. Some kids are playing jumprope; they part just wide enough to let you through. You smile and give them a little wave. Surprised and sus-picious, they wave back tentatively.

On a corner there's a package store, bars on every window, the sidewalk glittering with broken glass. A young shirtless man waxes his car out front. His angry stereo rattles your head. His angry stare makes you swallow.

A little further down there's a church, dull orange brick with a sign:

Greenwood Baptist
Reverend William Cowherd, Pastor
ARE YOU PREPARED TO MEET GOD?

Around 25th Street there's a Laundromat with a faded sign, *W A S H 25¢*, and a brawny woman wearing lime-green shorts and pink curlers is standing in the doorway smoking. A few kids play in the weedy vacant lot next door.

A low building, *BILLIARDS*, dominates the next corner. Several old men sit in the scant shade of the awning and watch you pass. You hear a siren. Somebody's always getting killed down here. The ambulance catches up and passes you. *LOUISVILLE GENERAL HOSPITAL*, it says on the door. Can this be the same city you live in?

Finally you hit 30th. Your eyes hurt. You're edgy and ready to get the hell out of here. The next ambulance could be coming for you. You calculate the quickest route east. You need the wide shady lawns of the East End. You need a drink.

I KNOW WHO YOU ARE,
MOTHERFUCKER

"**C**assius Clay lived around here someplace, didn't he?" Calvin asks as they turn onto 30th.

"Muhammad Ali," Johnnie says.

"Yeah, Muhammad Ali." Calvin feels funny saying it. "Do you know him?"

"I spanked his dirty little behind."

Johnnie's house is a narrow, one-story affair with fresh white paint, well-cropped grass in the little fenced yard, and on the front porch one of those green metal rocker-couches.

"Thank you, Calvin," Johnnie says, reaching for the door handle. "I'll see you tomorrow."

"Can I meet your family?"

"Maybe another time," she says, not looking at him. Johnnie gets out of the car, shuts the door, heads up the sidewalk, but then she stops and turns, hands on hips, and frowns. She comes back to the car and pokes her greying head back in the window. "You really wanna meet my family?"

Calvin can hear a dog barking somewhere to the rear of her house, a big one with a voice like a 12-gauge shotgun. "Sure," he says, and gets out of the car.

Two children pop out of the screen door, letting it slam, and run down to hug Johnnie's skirt and stare up at Calvin. "These are my grandbabies," Johnnie says. "This is Lucilla." The little girl, maybe seven years old with corn-row hair and yellow bows, sways shyly against her grandmother's thigh. "And this is S.B." The pudgy little boy, maybe five, steps forward and holds out his hand. Calvin offers his hand for a shake, but instead S.B. slaps his palm.

"Bro," S.B. says.

"Hey, S.B.," Calvin says, "how ya doing?"

"Cool."

The dimly lit house smells of cooking and clean laundry. Lucilla and S.B. run ahead through the living room and down a hallway. In the living room the television is on, some game show, but no one is watching. Beside the television stands an ancient oscillating fan, idle now in the cool of the morning. A faded portrait of Jesus, long blondish hair, neatly trimmed beard, hangs on the wall over the couch, and small tables at either end of the couch display family pictures in free-standing frames, several of which depict a handsome young man in military uniform.

Calvin says, "Is that your son?"

Johnnie nods. "That's Lucius Junior. He was killed in Vietnam."

"Oh, no." Calvin feels a sudden blast of shame. All he has ever really understood about Johnnie is the color of her skin. That brownness has existed in his mind like a protective membrane between them, but now the membrane is ruptured.

"How long ago?" he says weakly. The Vietnam War has always seemed like make-believe to him.

Johnnie has an amused look on her face. "Four years ago."

"I'm so sorry. Did Mom and Dad know about this?"

Johnnie's amusement vanishes. "No."

"Why not? You're part of our family, and we care about you. You should've told us."

Johnnie says nothing, but her expression is penetrating. Calvin lowers his eyes to the scuffed wooden floor.

"Here now," Johnnie chirps, holding out a beckoning hand. "No more of this. I want you to meet my girl."

On a small day-bed in a little cove under some stairs lies a body, an old man in fetal position, his back to the world. Calvin looks closer to see if he is breathing; yes, under the tattered housecoat Calvin detects the slight rise and fall of an emaciated chest. The skin of his neck is as dark and rough as the bark of a wet tree. A few curly white hairs grow at the edges of the bald head. Ahead of Calvin, in the bright kitchen, Johnnie is speaking to someone.

Now S.B. comes skittering back from the kitchen to fetch Calvin. He points at the man on the day-bed. "That's my great granddaddy. He ain't dead." S.B. takes Calvin's hand and leads him into the sunny kitchen. The walls are deep blue, with trim the color of clouds. A young woman, the mirror image of Johnnie, only newer and smoother and tank-topped, sits at the metallic kitchen table, a hefty book opened before her. She rises halfway and holds out a warm, fragile, open hand. "I'm Babe," she says, meeting Calvin's eyes.

"Nice to meet you, Babe," he warbles.

S.B. wedges himself between Babe and the table. "Mama's in college," he brags, slapping a hand on the book, flipping some pages over, "at the University of Louisville!"

"Boy, you leave that book alone," Babe says, jerking S.B.'s chubby little hand away. Graphs and tables fill the pages of the textbook in front of Babe.

"I dropped out of college," Calvin announces.

Babe glances at her mother and says nothing. Johnnie goes over to the sink and runs water into a pan. S.B. is still between his Mama and that textbook, gazing at its mysterious pages. Lucilla, hovering in the narrow space between the stove and wall, stares at Calvin.

"What are you studying?" Calvin asks Babe.

"Business."

"That's what *I* do. Business."

"Mama's gonna be rich," S.B. says, slamming his hand back down on the textbook.

Babe yanks him away from the table. "Go outside and play!" S.B. struggles to get free of her grip. "Lucilla, take him outside."

"Aw, Mama," Lucilla says.

"I ain't gonna tell you again."

The kids push out the back screen door just as a heavily-muscled man wearing a sleeveless T-shirt and a couple of days' stubble comes in from the hallway. He flashes a tight-lipped scowl at Calvin, then bends down and kisses Babe noisily on the lips. "Mornin', sugar," he says, then he gets himself a bottle of juice from the ice box, takes a long pull on it, puts it back in the ice box and sits down across from Babe at the table.

"This is Donte," Johnnie says, coming up behind him and laying a hand on his big shoulder. "My son in law."

Calvin holds out his hand. "I'm Calvin Turtle. Nice to meet you."

Donte does not take Calvin's hand. "I know who you are, motherfucker."

"*Honey*," Babe pleads.

Calvin's heart is blamming. "I don't know what you mean."

Donte backs up his chair and stands. "What I *mean*, white boy, is I work for you in the shipping department, or at least I did until you laid me off. Now, you get the fuck outta this house." Shrinking into a kind of crouch, Donte starts toward Calvin as if he might lift him up and throw him thirty feet, maybe forty, right out the door.

"*Donte!*" Johnnie screams, her eyes full of wrath.

Donte freezes, presses his lips hard together, glares at Johnnie for a moment, then he backs up, yanks the chair under himself and sits down.

"I better be going," Calvin says, but he doesn't move. *Shipping?* he thinks. *Does he work on the dock? Boxing room? Truck driver?*

Before Calvin can move, a small man in a tuxedo glides into the kitchen on a cloud of fruity cologne.

"Mornin' Daddy," Babe says quickly.

Johnnie starts to say something but the man lands a cufflinked hand on the back of her neck, pulls her to him and kisses her on the mouth. "Thought you wus at work," he says.

With her head Johnnie motions for him to look over his shoulder, and when he turns and sees Calvin for the first time, his relaxed demeanor evaporates.

Johnnie says, "Lucius Clay, this is Calvin Turtle."

Lucius steps forward, offers Calvin a limp handshake, and nods. "Howdydo, sir. I knew your Daddy from the Pendennis Club." He gestures at his tuxedo. "That's where I work. Been a waiter thirty-five years."

"Don't be Tommin' him," Donte snarls.

Johnnie steps in front of Lucius and takes Calvin by the arm. "You best be goin'." She turns and glares at Donte: "And you keep your mouth shut, young man, you hear me?"

"Don't be tellin' me to shut up, old woman."

Babe smacks her textbook closed. "I've had enough of this shit." She stands up and tries to leave, but Donte grabs her arm. "Let *go* of me!" she yells, jerking her arm free, then she slams out the back door.

When she gets Calvin to the front door, Johnnie whispers, "I didn't think he'd be outta bed."

Calvin glances back toward the kitchen and shakes his head. "I shouldn't have come down here."

She takes both of his arms. "No, it's awright. You're my boy, remember that, and I'm not gonna let anybody do bad to you. Now I'll see you in the mornin."

She eases him out the door and closes it gently behind him. The harsh sunlight burns his eyes. Somewhere in the alley that 12-gauge dog barks.

My Hero

On the way home from the West End, Calvin stops in at Our Lady of Peace. Aunt Virgie is lying in bed, eyes closed, her skin a deathly yellow. She seems older and thinner this morning. When he knocks, she opens her eyes and blinks.

"Sorry. Didn't mean to wake you up," Calvin whispers.

Virgie peels off the covers, swings her thin, scaly legs around to the side of the bed, and a little color returns to her face. "That's all right, sonny boy, now let's play cards. I'm gonna whip your skinny little butt today."

Calvin sets up the card table and Virgie deals out a hand of gin. As he discards the three of spades, he says, "Tell me something about Mom and Dad, would you? Anything."

Virgie rests her cards on the table and looks at Calvin sadly. Her empty hands dart under the table to straighten her billowy nightgown, flit back above the table. "I remember their wedding," she says, her voice gentle as a child's.

"Tell me about it."

Virgie's bony hands come to rest on her cards. "I was a bridesmaid. My dress was pink satin, with bare shoulders and a wide sash, and my bouquet was all red roses. Ohhh, I was beautiful that day, sonny boy. Heads turned, I'll tell you, heads turned. But your mother, oh, my! Anna was positively heavenly in that wedding gown,

the most beautiful thing I've ever seen. That long train, that lacy veil..."
Virgie looks out the window and Calvin remembers the picture of his
mother in that milky wedding gown on Grandma's backroom wall.

Virgie sighs and turns back to him. "When your father lifted
up the veil and kissed her, I just cried and cried. Oh, Calvin, I do hope
you will marry that George girl some day soon."

Calvin's gut clenches. "Was there music?"

Virgie pauses. "Oh, yes, you mean at your mother's wedding.
Well, there was an organist, and the music was just..." Virgie's hands
descend to her lap again, and she closes her eyes and shakes her head
slowly.

"What's the matter?"

Her eyes pop open with anger. "I just remembered that infernal singing. When the wedding was over, we all went to the River
Valley Club, and of course your father and his friends got drunk. They
sang filthy songs and sailed silver platters into the river. Charlie took
me home."

"Mr. Stanfull?"

"Oh, that man! With God as my witness, what a horrible beast
he is."

"What happened?"

Virgie begins to cry, not the long mourning-dove wails of
Calvin's mother, but an inward, high-compression, silent crying. It's
the first time he has ever seen his aunt cry, and that familiar feeling of
dread rises inside him. He gets up and shuts the door to her room, sits
beside her on the bed, their legs almost touching. When he reaches
out an arm to hug her, she cringes and shrinks away.

"What's the matter? What happened?"

Virgie remains hunched over, hiding her face with her hands.

Calvin waits until she stops crying. "May I ask you a question?"

"No."

Calvin gets up off the bed and returns to his seat behind the
little makeshift card table. "How did you wind up in this hospital?"

Virgie straightens, removes her hands from her face, but does
not look at him. "None of your business."

"I don't understand why you're here. Mom would never tell
me. Does it have something to do with Mr. Stanfull?"

She wipes her nose and pushes the cards to Calvin's side. "Deal
another hand, sonny boy."

"Want me to kill him for you?" Calvin says, grinning.

Virgie smiles, showing a sliver of old yellow teeth as she clasps her hands together, rolls her eyes and chirps, "My *hero!*"

Kill You in Two Minutes

Calvin spends the last hours of Labor Day playing Klondike, Donte's words banging around in his head: *I know who you are, motherfucker.*

In his restless sleep he has the sharks and minnows dream again, except this time the gorgeous lifeguard pulls him from the pool and stretches him out on a soft mound of grass in number one fairway. She pounds his chest and he coughs up water and duck moss.

"Don't die," she says, stroking his face. "You're all I have."

The shark's bite-holes burn like fire on his backside, and he begins to shiver. She takes off her bikini and lies on top of him. Giant cones of color fill the sky over their heads, *BLAM, BLAM, BLAM*, the Fourth of July fireworks. He strokes the soft contours of her bottom. She moans under his hand, *down-up, dowwwn, dowwwn, dowwwn*, and lowers a breast to his lips. The finger-sausage nipple drips cloudish white liquid into his mouth.

"Kill you in two minutes," a deep voice says.

THE PARADOX OF KLONDIKE

People play cards for three basic reasons: Solace, Fortune or Dominion. Dominion is just an illusion, of course. You're going to lose in the end, God will make sure of that, but don't cheat just to take that smirk off His face. Honor counts. For example, if you miss a play and turn over another card from the deck, don't go back and make the play as if you knew about it all along. Live with your shortcomings. Embrace defeat.

Sooner or later there will be a game of Klondike where you won't get even a single card in the free piles. You wait and hope, flipping card after card from the deck thinking surely at least one ace will show up, but then you run out of cards. Calvin calls this the Apocalypse.

Of course, it's hard to say when the Apocalypse might happen. Some people play game after game and always seem to luck out with at least one free card, while for others it happens as often as once a night. But about one thing there is no doubt: it happens to everyone eventually.

Calvin's philosophy? When the Apocalypse happens, you can't just lie down and die. You're still breathing, aren't you? To shuffle is to hope.

Here's the paradox of Klondike: you are in control; you are not in control. You can win. You can never win. It's all about the Indomitable Human Spirit. Says so right there in the Rule Book.

It's late in the day and Calvin's got his office door shut so he can play a little Klondike and think. Business is way off and nothing he's tried has worked. The factory is a dismal place, everybody scared or angry or both, and in the main office people seem to drudge about the workday, no spirit, no humor. Even Violet has stopped making suggestive remarks.

As he builds strings of cards and watches the wastepile for possible plays, Calvin wishes he could talk with his father about it all, then he realizes this is the first time he has thought anything good about his father since the accident. No, he doesn't want that father back, the one who hit his mother and berated Calvin and whipped him and made everything a big joke, Mr. Big Shot Sonny Turtle. That father is dead, good riddance. But how about the father who knew how to run the playing card business and who hugged Calvin when he was sick and taught him to hunt and stuck up for him that day in Arkansas when Karl had the snake? That father is dead too.

A little rivulet of sadness leaks into Calvin's heart. He sighs. *You killed him*, he tells himself, then he recoils from the guilt of it. "NO. Not guilty!" he says out loud, banging his fist on the desk, but it doesn't work. Calvin still feels it. His father and mother are gone, and he pushed them into the wall.

Today, right now, with everything turning to shit,

Calvin needs a father in the worst way. Dr. George would do, and Calvin picks up the phone to call him but, in the end, doesn't. He hasn't called Penny either. He can't. It feels like if he does, he will never be a man. Well, maybe that's a tad melodramatic, as Penny would say, but it does feel like his life is somehow in danger if he marries her right now, before.... There is something he has to do first, on his own, by himself, something big, but he won't know what it is until he actually does it. The cards aren't telling him a thing. God is so frustrating!

This, at least, he now believes: He does love Penny George and Penny loves him. She is smart and beautiful. She will make a good wife, and her parents will make a good family. He needs to hurry up and figure things out so he doesn't lose her.

One big thing he decides to do right now: help Johnnie's family. Ever since his trip to the West End, Calvin has felt terrible that he didn't even know Johnnie lost a son in Vietnam. Donte's words, *I know who you are, motherfucker,* keep flashing in Calvin's mind.

Well, maybe Donte doesn't know everything he thinks he knows. Calvin gets out the phone book and looks up the University of Louisville. He calls the Bursar's Office, and after talking to three different women, he finally gets the Bursar himself, a man named Paul Norman. Mr. Norman knows who Calvin is, says he knew Calvin's dad, thought a lot of him and so forth, and says how sorry he is about the accident. Calvin explains to Mr. Norman that he wants to help a student financially, but that the student is not to know who paid the bill. He tells Mr. Norman that the student's name is Babe, but he can't remember her husband's last name.

"You're kidding," the Bursar says. "There are 21,000 students at this university, Mr. Turtle, and you want me to find the one named Babe."

"Sorry. How stupid of me. Can you hold on just a second?"

"Of course."

Calvin puts Mr. Norman on hold and asks Betty to find the name of the employee named Donte who got laid off last month. She already knows who he's talking about and with a worried look, tells him the full name, "Donte Miller." Calvin gets back on the line with Mr. Norman and before the end of the week, Babe Miller's tuition and fees are paid through to graduation.

MORE LAYOFFS

By October, the national energy crisis has deepened, inflation is raging, and all you can hear about is Watergate, Watergate, Watergate. Nixon is screwing with the very foundations of free society.

Bad news for the nation is usually good news for the playing card business – people play cards for Solace and to give themselves the illusion that they can influence things – but so far the buying spree hasn't begun. Calvin and Fornton Bruhall have tried everything from discount gimmicks to zippy new ads, but people just aren't buying cards right now. The factory mood is grim. Orville speaks to Calvin only when he has to, and Nelle Brown won't speak to him at all.

One morning Forny comes into Calvin's office and says, "We can't pay our bills."

Calvin calls Mr. Stanfull for permission to borrow some money.

"Lay off another ten percent," Mr. Stanfull says.

"That will destroy this company."

"Don't exaggerate, Calvin. The one major expense you can reduce is payroll. A ten-percent reduction now will put you in the black, then when sales pick up, you can hire some of them back and be more efficient than ever. That's the beauty of it."

"It's not beautiful if you're the one out of work."

"God, you sound like my son."

There is a pause, during which Calvin imagines

that Mr. Stanfull longs for his estranged firstborn, but when Mr. Stanfull speaks again, his tone is assured and lawyerly. "Life is tough, Calvin. Business fluctuates. People get laid off. It's that simple. We can't get distracted by individual hardship stories and lose sight of the big picture. If the whole company goes under, everyone loses."

Everyone except you, Calvin thinks. "We could take out a short-term loan until sales pick up, just until Christmas. Things will pick up by then. The economy's in our favor."

"You could lose your stock, too, if you default on a loan. Look, I'm still Trustee of your father's estate and I can't let the company go under. I owe it to your father."

"Don't give me that."

"I don't want to fight with you this morning, Calvin. Just do what I say, okay?"

"No, it's not okay. Why don't you let me run things? I've *been* running things."

"Yes, you *have* been running things since your father died, and the company is in bad shape. Do as I say, Calvin, or I'll have to go to court."

"I'm applying for a loan," Calvin says, and hangs up.

Within two hours Mr. Stanfull strides into Calvin's office with a court injunction barring Calvin from making any financial moves on behalf of the corporation until his twenty-first birthday. He flutters the document under Calvin's nose.

"You don't give a damn about these people," Calvin tells him.

"Don't be a hypocrite, Calvin. You're just like my son and all the other self-righteous, judgmental young pricks of your generation. You hate your fathers, but you're the same as us. Some day you'll understand that."

THURSDAY, OCTOBER 19ᵀᴴ, 1972

Just before the second round of layoffs is to take effect, it happens again, this time on a batch of regular Turtle Cards. Violet calls Calvin with the news: "We got a big problem, hon."

A dealer from Minneapolis has called the switchboard and complained that the Turtle's tiny smiling eyes are a different color on every ace in a recent shipment. Calvin asks Violet to take the dealer's number, runs to the warehouse, rips open several cases of Turtle Cards and sure enough, they all have marked aces. No question about an accident this time. Someone has deliberately altered the inking on the printer roller.

Calvin is suddenly and painfully alive to the end of every nerve in his body. This, finally, is it. He feels like he has been waiting like a lonesome bridegroom for this moment since the death of his parents, maybe even since Jewel's death, maybe even since he was born. This crisis at Turtle Cards begins the biggest card game of his life. He must shoot the moon. Everything, the family business, his future with Penny, his very life, hangs in the balance. Though he is too old to believe this anymore and he knows it's crazy, he senses that somehow this crisis is his chance to get Jewel back too.

He must be sharp. He must be bold. He must not miss a thing.

Calvin sprints to shipping and tells them to hold all orders until further notice, then goes back to his office and calls the dealer in Minneapolis, asks him to destroy every deck of Turtle Cards he has in stock and urges him not to tell anyone what happened. Calvin promises him enough replacement Turtle Cards to cover what he destroys plus an extra six-month's supply.

"What the hell's going on?" the dealer says.

Calvin tells him it's only a minor problem with the inking machine, that it happened on just a few decks of cards before they caught it, and wasn't it funny that it was the aces, ha, ha.

"Guess you fucked up, didn't you, buddy?" the dealer says. "You send me that six month's supply, plus a set of your best bridge cards for my wife, and we'll see what we can do."

"Who discovered the flaw?" Calvin asks him. The dealer gives Calvin the number of a pool hall in rural Minnesota.

Calvin calls the pool hall, explains to the owner who he is and asks to speak to the person who discovered the marked aces. After a long silence, someone picks up the phone and says in a low voice, "Yeah."

"Who am I talking to?" Calvin asks.

"Joe."

"Are you the one who found the flaw in the Turtle Playing Cards?"

"Bout got me killed. The boys said I done it."

Calvin hears some yelling in the background. "Well, I'm glad nobody got killed."

"Mister, you're not nearly glad as I am."

More yelling in the background. "How can I make it up to you, Joe?"

Joe hesitates. "Who is this, anyhow?"

"I'm Calvin Turtle, owner of the Turtle Playing Card Company down here in Louisville."

"Iszat so? Well, whaddayou want, mister playing card company? I got a poker game goin."

"I'd like to send you some new playing cards, Joe, with no imperfections, for free. How's a hundred and forty-four brand new decks of cards sound?"

"A hunderd and forty...What is this? I already took them bad cards back to the store and got me a different kind. I don't care what cards I play with, long as they're not marked. Now listen, mister, I gotta go. You keep your hunderd and forty decks a cards, thank you, but no thank you."

"Could I ask you one favor, Joe?"

"Whatzat?"

"Try Turtle Cards again sometime, would you?"

Joe laughs. "Hell, they're marked!"

Calvin sets the receiver back in its cradle but does not let go. He studies his left hand gripping the receiver. The skin is clean and taught and reddish, veins bulging and pulsing underneath, muscles clenched. He is alive and strong and it's time to take charge.

"What's happened?" Betty asks as Calvin comes out of his office.

Calvin motions toward the factory and speaks quietly. "Sabotage."

Betty's thin eyebrows jump up and her glossy lips form an O, then she puts a forefinger to her lips and nods. She follows Calvin back into his office and shuts the door behind them. Calvin feels a sudden desire to tell her everything, all about Penny and the Hunt Club and Johnnie's dead son and what Donte said to him and even about Karl and Money.

"Betty," he begins, but as she gazes at him with watery concern, loving motherly urges written all over her powdered, droopy face, the feeling passes. This is a business crisis, after all, and he can't be telling Betty about all his sordid troubles, even if she has known him since he was a baby. He invites her to sit, then settles behind his Dad's desk and tells her about the sabotage.

"Some guy in Minnesota reported it; I don't know how many decks got out the door. We can't tell anybody about this, especially not Charlie Stanfull."

"Of course not," Betty says, her face reddening against her sprayed blue-white hair. "I know what to do. This happened to your father, you know."

"I didn't know that. When?"

"You were just a boy, and sales were down like they are now, and your father had announced layoffs, just like now. He never told a soul about the bad cards besides me and Orville, not even your mother, I don't think." She glances furtively at Calvin as if to gauge his reaction, and he wonders if there was something between his Dad and Betty. She might've been pretty good looking 20 years ago, but she must've been soft and passive even then. The whole idea of his father and Betty having a secret love affair makes him feel weary. *Too many secrets*, he tells himself. *The whole goddamned world is a lie.*

Betty continues, "We got all the bad cards out of the warehouse that night and destroyed them. Orville found the bad plate and destroyed it too. He said it must've been an accident."

"That's what he told me last month when we had that bad batch of Casino cards."

She squinches her lips and nods. "I know."

"When it happened before, did my father go ahead with the layoffs?"

Betty seems annoyed at the question. "Well, yes he did. We were losing money!"

"How many people called about bad decks of cards back then?"

"Well, it was only two, I believe, a dealer in Alabama, then this lady from a nursing home right here in Louisville. She was very grateful to us for helping her cheat." Betty laughs.

"Was that it?"

"Yes, near as I can recall. We traced the shipments and got them all back."

"Okay, here's what you can do for me."

Betty raises a hand to her cheek. "Oh my. You sound just like your Dad. Taking charge."

Calvin takes a deep breath. "First, ask Orville and Nelle Brown to come to my office, then swear Violet to secrecy. If she gets another call about a bad deck, have her transfer it directly to me or to you, nobody else, okay?"

"I sure will, hon, and Violet can keep a secret." Betty's eyebrows raise again in a sly smile. "She's kept a few around here."

"What do you mean by that?"

Betty turns her back and opens the door. "Just girl secrets, that's all."

New Deal

Calvin plays a little Klondike at his desk. The more he thinks about all that has happened, the more obvious it becomes that Orville has to be behind the sabotage. No way something like this could happen without Orville knowing about it, and the same thing happened to Calvin's father. But Orville has worked for Turtle Manufacturing for more than twenty-five years. He has a family somewhere in Indiana, and friends in the plant. *Orville, you're fired*, Calvin imagines himself saying, sending hot waves of fear and guilt through his body. And how the hell are they going to make playing cards without him? Orville knows more about the process than anyone else.

Betty buzzes and tells him that Orville and Nelle are waiting outside. Calvin braces himself, feet on the floor, hands flat on the arms of his chair, as she escorts them into the office and shuts the door. Neither Orville nor Nelle will sit down. Betty stands behind them, blocking the door.

"What's up?" Orville says, his face colorless.

Nelle stands back of Orville a step, sullen and edgy.

Calvin feels his heart pick up speed. "You're fired, Orville," he says, leaning slightly forward in his chair. "Give your keys to security and get your stuff out of here immediately. We'll mail you your last check."

Orville screws his face into a bloodless, half-smile. "What'd I do?"

Behind him, Betty shakes her head. Nelle lowers

her eyes to the carpet.

"You tried to sabotage this company," Calvin says. In his lap now, his own hands are shaking.

"I what?"

"You let marked Turtle Cards go out of here, Orville. Are you going to deny that?"

Orville shifts his feet and glances at Nelle. "I don't know nothing about no marked cards."

"You did it with the Casino decks last August, and you did it years ago when my father had to lay off employees, didn't you?"

Orville's expression is angry now, his lips pressed hard together. "I never did no such a thing."

"My father let you get away with it, but I won't. Betty, please ask Ed Hurley to get in here immediately."

"You little son of a bitch," Orville growls, taking a step toward Calvin.

Calvin jumps up to receive the attack, but Orville hesitates, casts a look backwards at Betty as she disappears out the door, then looks back at Calvin, his fists balled up at his sides. "I been workin' here since before you was born," he yells, his hollow eyes starting to brim over with years of resentment.

For a few seconds, nothing happens. Beneath his menacing glower, Orville seems to be calculating his next move, but then Ed Hurley, head of security at Turtle, strides into the office, one hand near the gun at his side. Ed is usually a sociable fellow, but big and brawny and bearded enough to scare the hell out of you when he needs to. Calvin's father called him Burley Hurley.

"Hi, Ed," Calvin says, profoundly relieved to see that badge and that gun. "Orville has been fired. Please make sure he turns in his keys, then make sure he leaves the building."

Ed Burley is the best kind of security guard, good-natured but dead serious about law and order. Even though he is friends with Orville, Calvin knows he will respect the power structure and do his job. Ed shoots a look at Nelle, then one at Orville, then nods at Calvin. "Yessir," he says.

Orville shrinks away from Calvin a step.

"Let's go, Orville," Ed says, touching Orville's elbow.

"What about the others?" Orville says, waving at Nelle. "I ain't the only one."

"Now don't go lyin' about me," Nelle threatens, her eyes alert and fiery now.

Orville glares at her a moment, then turns to Calvin. "You ain't like your Daddy. I don't care to work here any more." He storms out of the room, Hurley Burley and Betty right behind him.

Now Nelle collapses in a chair and blows out a long gust of air. "Am I next?"

Calvin sits down too, his heart still hammering. "What did you have to do with the sabotage, Nelle?"

"Nothin'. I knew 'bout it is all. One of the inspectors come to me when the run went through and said Orville talked 'em into it. I *told* him not to send them cards out. You don't cut off your own head for spite, but I don't blame him for bein' mad, neither. We ain't been treated right around here."

"I want to do better."

Nelle snorts and shakes her head. "I heard that before. You ain't never gonna do right for us."

"How about an immediate raise?"

Nelle sits up and inspects him with cold suspicion. "You put that in writing?"

"In blood if you want me to."

She lets out a snide little laugh. "Be all right with me."

Calvin holds out a wrist and smiles. "Cut me."

Nelle does not laugh. "What about the layoffs?"

Calvin withdraws his hand and leans back in his leather chair. "I'll cancel the latest layoffs, and maybe after Christmas we can hire back some people who've already been laid off."

Nelle is still suspicious. "I thought you didn't have no money for no raises."

"We don't, but if I cut my pay entirely, and if I can get a little short-term loan, I think we can come up with maybe two percent. That's got to be enough for now. Of course, if we don't have strong Christmas sales, we'll *all* be looking for work."

Nelle studies him for a moment, those untrusting eyes burning into him. "You're gonna cut your own pay?"

"I won't take any salary at all until things get better. And we won't hire anyone to take Orville's place."

"You put that in writing too?"

"I'll put it all in writing if you'll go out right now and tell everybody that the second round of layoffs is canceled and that they're all going to get a two-percent raise immediately." Calvin is thinking that

Nelle might make a pretty good replacement for Orville.

She stands up and, still wearing a suspicious frown, sticks out a dry, calloused hand. "Deal."

Calvin extends his own sweaty hand. "Deal."

Nelle's grip is strong.

WE GOT ANY DUCKS YET?

The squarish Kentucky National Bank Building sits downtown along the edge of the Ohio like some fancy food crate washed up after a flood. Calvin feels dense and cold as a raw potato as he enters the elevator. Mr. Kentlinger's office is on the top floor.

After a short spell on a plush couch in the frigid waiting room, an indifferent young secretary ushers Calvin into a huge office. Mr. Kentlinger's grip is flabby and hot. He motions for Calvin to sit, then crash lands in his own swivel chair. "Just a little harmless fun," he says.

"Pardon me?" Calvin says.

"A little harmless water play." Mr. Kentlinger's breath is rapid, as if he's just jogged up the stairs, little BB's of sweat popping out on the pink folds of skin above the tight white collar of his shirt.

"Oh, you mean the Labor Day dove hunt." Calvin pictures Mrs. Kentlinger in her wet underwear and a wave of something like shame washes through him. She looked pretty damned good, actually. He can't imagine the two of them making love. Outside Mr. Kentlinger's window Calvin can see the intricate pattern of triangles in the George Rogers Clark Bridge over the Ohio, pigeons looping around and around the rusting steel.

"Right," Mr. Kentlinger says, then he clears his throat. "Now, did you know..." He pauses, a professor about to hold forth on the deepest philosophical question, gazing wistfully at the ceiling as if he can see all of human history there. "Did you know, that in the time of the Greeks, everybody went naked, and everybody fucked everybody else?"

"Everybody fucks everybody now, too," Calvin says, grinning.

Mr. Kentlinger laughs, then shifts forward in his chair. "That's right," he says, studying Calvin with surprise. "That's pretty funny, young man. Now what can I do for you? Haven't seen you in a while, good to see you, hail to the Hunt Club and all that. How ya been? How's business?"

One of Calvin's lower back muscles begins to spasm. "Not so hot."

Mr. Kentlinger takes a filterless cigarette from a silver case and lights it, draws a thoughtful puff, blows the smoke out without inhaling, then puts his free hand under one of his chins. "Sorry to hear that."

Calvin bends forward to ease the quivering in his back. "Didn't Mr. Stanfull tell you about it?"

Mr. Kentlinger's tone is cold. "Haven't talked to him."

Good! Calvin thinks. "We need a short-term loan to tide us over through Christmas, otherwise we'll have to lay off a bunch of people. I'm afraid if we do that, there will be trouble. A strike, maybe."

Mr. Kentlinger takes a quick pull on his cigarette and narrows his eyes. "Fire the bastards. Can't let labor control you." He leans back and gazes at the ceiling again. "Let me tell you about Karl Marx, that communist son of a bitch. Had everybody believing in equal distribution of wealth, for Christ's sake."

"I don't mean to be rude, Mr. Kentlinger, but I've got to get back to the office. Can you loan us the money?"

Mr. Kentlinger sucks in and exhales a deep gale of smoke and closes his eyes, as if he is about to receive a blow job. "How much do you need?"

"Fifty thousand, 90-day renewable. Mr. Stanfull and I talked it over." The back spasms intensify. He can barely stay upright in this chair. "We should be able to pay it off before Christmas. I'm sure business will pick up soon."

Mr. Kentlinger clears his throat and opens his eyes. "Sure it will, sure it will, be better by Thanksgiving, no doubt. God I'm looking forward to duck season, aren't you? Have you heard anything from Karl? We got any ducks yet?"

The mention of Arkansas freezes Calvin's heart. The Hunt

Club is not going to duck hunt this year, but now is definitely not the time to talk about that. "I've really got to go," he says.

Mr. Kentlinger tilts forward in his massive chair, stabs out his cigarette in a clean glass ash tray and puts both hands together in a ball that he rests in front of him on the desk, his expression stern and paternal. "Young man, you're the first person in a long time to tell me to hurry the fuck up and give him a loan."

"I'm sorry. I didn't mean to say that."

Mr. Kentlinger exhales loudly and allows his body to settle back in the chair. "Okay, no big deal, buddy, and listen, no big deal about Labor Day either, okay? Hell, we're the Louisville Hunt Club, right?"

"Right on," Calvin says, raising his fist a few inches.

Mr. Kentlinger smiles and picks up the phone. "How much did you say you need?"

"Fifty thousand. 90-day renewable. We'll pay it back before Christmas."

"And you talked it over with Charlie?"

Calvin's back muscles are wild. "He said to go see you and take out a loan."

Mr. Kentlinger dials and tells someone to write up a fifty-thousand-dollar note with Calvin's stock as collateral. Thirty minutes later the money for raises is in the Turtle Company account.

FRIDAY, OCTOBER 20TH, 1972

About a third of the bad decks of Turtle Cards have gone out the door. Yesterday afternoon Calvin and Betty hunted down the remaining unshipped cards, maybe a hundred cases, and dumped them in the incinerator at the corner of the warehouse while Forny contacted every dealer that received some of the bad batch and recalled all the tainted cards with apologies, double compensation, etc. Nelle has passed the word about Orville, the rescinded layoffs and the raises, and Calvin has asked Ed Hurley to hire and post a guard for every floor in case Orville or anybody else tries to do more damage.

Mr. Stanfull calls in the middle of the morning. "I heard you fired Orville."

"Yes, I did. He sabotaged a whole run of cards."

"And you took out a loan without my authorization."

"Yes."

"You have violated a court injunction, young man, and you lied to Barn Kentlinger. He is *furious*."

"I won't let you destroy my company."

"Oh, cut the crap, Calvin. I'll go to court this afternoon and the judge will order the bank to rescind the loan."

"I've already sent out word to every employee that the layoffs are canceled and that they're all getting a two-percent raise. If you take it back now, they will shut down this factory. Is that what you want? You think my father would go for that?"

"You're breaking the law."

"This is my company and I don't care what the law says."

"You don't understand business the way your father did."

"I understand that layoffs will do more harm than good to this company, not to mention the people that work here. I'll get my own lawyer, and we'll see what the judge thinks about how the Trustee is handling things."

Mr. Stanfull makes his voice cool and reasonable. "All right. I *will* seek legal recourse if I have to, but you won't make me do that, will you? Let's have a Board meeting. We've got to make plans for Arkansas anyway."

"You're not going to Arkansas."

"Beg your pardon?"

"You're not hunting on the Old Wilson Place this year. None of you."

"Calvin Turtle, what the hell is *wrong* with you?"

"It's my land, and you're not hunting."

"The fuck we're not!"

Monday, October 23RD, 1972

Calvin receives a registered letter at the office:

LEGAL NOTICE

Petitioner: *Mr. Charles Milton Stanfull III*
30th Floor, Citizens Tower
Louisville, Kentucky 40204

Respondent: *Mr. Calvin McGraw Turtle*
Turtle Manufacturing Co.
100 Washington Street
Louisville, Kentucky 40204

Pursuant to Kentucky Revised Statute 387.550, you are hereby given notice of a hearing on a petition by Mr. Charles M. Stanfull III for his appointment as permanent Guardian of Mr. Calvin M. Turtle, said hearing to be held in District Court, Jefferson County, Kentucky, on Monday, November 20th, 1972, at 10:00 a.m. Your presence at said hearing is required by law.

Petitioner seeks guardianship on grounds that Respondent is disabled. (KRS 387.530)

Pursuant to Kentucky Revised Statute 387.560, should you not be able to afford an attorney, you have a right to court-appointed counsel.

Calvin calls Mr. Stanfull. "So now you're trying to permanently screw me?"

Mr. Stanfull's voice is smooth and caring now, like that old barber pole, Reverend Bushrod. "I knew you'd be upset, Calvin, but I'm not trying to do anything except what's in your best interest."

"Your concern is touching, but what you really want is to take control of my father's estate, right?"

"That's not true. I care about you, that's all. Your father's not around now and, well, I think you need someone to look after things, at least until you get well."

"I'm not sick."

"You're distraught over the death of your parents, and you're making the wrong moves at Turtle Manufacturing against the wishes of your father's Trustee and the company's Board of Directors. In my opinion, you are jeopardizing the future of the company. It's my duty to look after that company, and I don't believe you're well enough to handle it."

"What a crock of shit."

"All the members of the Board agree with me on this, Calvin."

"Dr. George agrees with you?"

"Jim has given his assent to the petition."

"You're all assholes."

"We're doing what your father would want us to do."

"I don't need a guardian, and especially not you."

"The judge will decide that."

PHIL GOUGAN, ESQUIRE

Phil **Gougan is** around forty, maybe forty-five, with a cratered face, teeth yellow as a legal pad, and a mouth always cranked open to accommodate a cigarette. His law office is way out in the West End near Iroquois Park. He defends drug dealers and whores, drunk drivers and petty thieves. He has no respect for big-time lawyers like Charlie Stanfull, and he doesn't like Calvin at all.

"*Calvin Turtle?*" he says, when Calvin first calls him. "Am I supposed to laugh?"

"Yes, I'm Calvin Turtle, and I'd like to hire you to defend me in a... I don't know what the legal term is, but Charlie Stanfull is trying to become my legal guardian. Do you know him?"

"How'd you get my name?"

"Out of the phone book. Do you know Mr. Stan-full?"

"I know of him."

"Will you take my case?"

"Kid, you got more money than King Midas. Whaddayou want with me? Just bribe the judge."

"Are you saying you won't represent me?"

"It'll cost you."

"How much?"

"Ten thousand. Up front."

"Fine. When can I see you?"

"Mi casa es su casa."

Calvin drives out there the next morning.

"Go see a shrink," Phil says when Calvin shows him the court summons. His office is on the first floor of a nice old house under some stately trees just at the edge of Iroquois Park. The inner walls are lined with paintings of sleek race horses with jockeys in brightly colorful silks.

"Why?" Calvin asks, staring at one of those perfect horses.

"Find one who will say you're not crazy, and get him to write a letter. Stanfull has to show that you're disabled, which means crazy, so get a letter that says you're not."

"I'm not crazy, Mr. Gougan."

"If you say so, pal."

MONDAY, NOVEMBER 6TH, 1972

Calvin has made an appointment with Dr. Nancy Strim, one of the resident psychiatrists at Our Lady of Peace and Aunt Virgie's long-time doctor. Dr. Strim's office is immaculate and furnished like a living room with large, comfortable chairs, a coffee table and a beautiful yellow-brown Persian rug. In a dark blue skirt, ruffled white blouse and matching dark blue suit jacket, Dr. Strim is an impeccably dressed lady, her thin grey hair pinned in a tight bun behind her head.

"Take your time," she tells him, her voice quiet, steady, easy, her eyes warm.

Calvin is trying to explain his failure in college, why he has no friends, what he feels about Penny, why he has defied Mr. Stanfull and the Hunt Club. He has told Dr. Strim a little about Karl Buntingstrife and the Old Wilson Place down in Arkansas, but he hasn't told her about Money.

He says, "The best way to explain it maybe...." A long-suppressed image is trying to swim its way into his head. A Christmas tree. Dark dead tree lights. That bitter smell. Calvin does not, will not, must not, he *absolutely must not* allow this image to surface, so he looks up at Dr. Strim, who is studying him, but not in a threatening way. "It's all like a game of solitaire," he says, looking away from her sympathetic countenance to the window and the leafless trees outside. There is something inadequate about this analogy.

"Why don't you sleep on it and come back tomorrow?" Dr. Strim suggests.

Tuesday, November 7ᵀᴴ, 1972

"**W**hat is your least favorite outcome in solitaire?" Dr Strim asks.

"What do you mean?" Calvin has tried to explain to her that life, for him, is like Klondike, that the situation at Turtle Cards, his relationship with Penny, the stuff with the Hunt Club and Arkansas and Karl Buntingstrife, all of it feels like he is battling with God Himself, the Wizard of Klondike. He has surprised himself with how open he's been with this woman, more open than he has ever been with anyone. She doesn't seem to need anything from him, and this reassures him, but in a vague way it also pisses him off. She just sits there in that chair across the coffee table from him, calmly receiving everything he says but not talking much.

"Do you think I'm crazy?" he asks.

She smiles and cups a hand under her chin. "Soooo...." she says very slowly, gently, the pitch of her voice rising just a tad at the end. "Tell me your least favorite outcome in Klondike, your least favorite number in the free piles."

"Three," he says, and wonders why he didn't say zero. Who likes zero, anyway? He's getting even more irritated with her goddamned questions.

WEDNESDAY, NOVEMBER 8ᵀᴴ, 1972

"**W**hen did you** start playing Klondike?"

"I don't know, when I was a kid."

"Does that question bother you?"

"No."

"May I ask you another question, then? A very painful question?"

"Shoot."

"Are you sure? I sense that you are getting tired of my nosey questions."

"Ask away."

"What are your feelings about your sister?"

"What do you know about her?"

"I've known your family a long time, Calvin. I know what happened."

"She's gone. That's it."

"I'm so sorry."

"My parents killed her."

"How do you mean that?"

"All the fighting and drinking, that's what killed her. She's gone. That's it. World without end, amen."

"World without end... hmmm. Your family attended the Episcopal Church, yes?"

"Episcopal without end, amen."

"And your sister's name is Jewel, right?"

"Was."

"I don't believe she's gone, Calvin."

"You mean she's in heaven, right? Well, I don't

believe in heaven."

"Do you believe in hell?'

"Yes, I do. Life is hell."

"You started playing solitaire after she died."

"Yes."

"To win her back?"

"...Yes."

"Have you ever beaten Klondike?"

"I beat it twice in one night when I was a kid."

"How old were you?"

"Ten, I think. I was playing in my Grandparents' back room and ran into the living room to tell everybody and slipped on a rug and broke my grandmother's precious china hands."

"My God! The best and the worst of nights, all at the same time."

"My father whipped me with a belt for it."

"Oh my God, Calvin. I am so sorry. What did your mother do?"

"I have to go."

Thursday, November 9TH, 1972

Calvin has not said a word today, nor has Dr. Strim. When he came in, she did not touch him on the shoulder and guide him to his chair the way she usually does. Now she just sits there, waiting indifferently for him to begin talking. This is really pissing him off.

Yesterday he said too much, way too much. His disclosures still hang in the room like heavy stormclouds. Dr. Strim said he didn't have to come back today, but for some reason he wanted to.

He hears a siren outside. Police, probably, or maybe an ambulance bringing someone to Our Lady of Peace. Do they bring people to a place like this in an ambulance? Not likely. People arrive here slowly, by daily, monthly, yearly accretion, and they leave here even more slowly, if ever. Calvin wonders if he belongs in Our Lady of Peace too.

At the end of today's interminable session of silence, Dr. Strim shifts in her chair, lets out a sigh and says, "Three."

"Three?"

"Yes."

"In solitaire, you mean?"

"No, I mean the three of you, Calvin. Your mother and your father, with you in the middle."

FRIDAY, NOVEMBER 10TH, 1972

They are strolling down the sloping lawn at Our Lady of Peace; Calvin is more than a head taller than Dr. Strim. The sky is powdery blue today and the air is warm for November and moist, springlike even, yet there are no leaves, no green grass, no birds.

"So, what you're saying is, the two of them still exist inside me like demons or something, and that I'm still fighting with them, even though they are dead?"

"Precisely. The two of them had you locked in a kind of hell on earth, and even though they are dead now, the hell lives on inside of you. Your current struggles reflect that."

"I don't buy it. They're dead!" Calvin stares at the brown grass moving under his shoes. He is thinking about another threesome: Karl, Money, and him.

"It will take time to see this, Calvin. Years, perhaps. For now, just remember, you did not do anything wrong. You were the child, they were the parents. World without end, amen."

"I'm not a child."

"Of course not."

"And I didn't kill them."

"No, of course not, not really. They had been slowly killing themselves for years. But you certainly had a right to want them dead."

"I feel a big explosion coming."

"Meaning...?

"I don't know. Nothing. Right now I have to get back and run the card business and figure out how to save the company and fight the Louisville Hunt Club and deal with things down in Arkansas and be with Penny."

"That's a tall order, Calvin. I believe I can help you if you will let me."

They walk a while in silence. As they near the entrance to the drab building, Dr. Strim asks, "Is there anything else you want to tell me?"

"No."

"Would you like to come back for another session next week?"

"No. I don't ever want to talk about this stuff again."

"I understand, Calvin. I really do."

"So, do you think I'm crazy?"

Dr. Strim stops, touches his arm, and smiles. "What does crazy mean?" She gestures at the brick hospital looming over them. "Why is this place here, and why is your aunt a resident? I don't have all the answers, Calvin." She shrugs. "Wish I did."

"Does that mean you can't write a letter to the court that says I'm not crazy?"

"On the contrary. I'll say you're as sane as anyone I know."

CHRISTMAS IN AMERICA

It begins as soon as people get the egg washed off their doors and toss the Halloween pumpkin in the trash. As the grocery bins fill with Thanksgiving turkeys, city workers start hanging boughs of holly and Angels of Peace. Snowflakes and candy canes appear in store windows, and the Ray Conniff Singers wish you a Merry Christmas from hidden loudspeakers. Vacant lots fill up with living-room-sized conifers, and families of ruddy-cheeked children and grouchy parents wander in and out of the tight rows of greenery under the watchful eye of some seedy guy in a plaid overshirt with a money pouch on his belt.

First in the working-class neighborhoods, then in the wealthier ones, strings of colored lights appear on the bushes and trees and eaves. On a few roofs, Santa rides off in his sleigh behind wiry, lighted reindeer, and in a few yards Baby Jesus snoozes in his little manger surrounded by his magnificent Mother and Father plus a contingent of long-robed dignitaries.

Jesus has saved the day at Turtle Manufacturing, you might say. People are finally buying playing cards for Christmas. Production lines are nearing full capacity and Calvin wants to rehire some laid-off workers, but Phil Gougan has told Calvin to hold off. "Look like a sensible, conservative businessman," Phil said. "And get yourself a confident business suit for the hearing. Let's really impress the judge."

SATURDAY, NOVEMBER 18TH, 1972

At Rhodes men's store Calvin buys a sleek double-breasted number plus some tasseled loafers, then on his way out of the mall he runs into Penny. She is wearing a bright blue jumper over a white blouse, and in her hair rests a little spray of red holiday flowers. *Red, white and blue*, he thinks. *America the beautiful.*

They buy ice cream cones – butter brickle for Calvin, strawberry swirl for Penny – and sit on a bench to watch the throngs of package-toting shoppers. Over the mall's sound system, Ray Conniff and his gang are prancing through their lively Christmas repertoire, and down toward the middle of the mall, Santa is hefting terrified kids onto his pillowy lap for a quick photo and a halting run-through of their little hearts' desires. It isn't long before Penny and Calvin are talking about their hearts' desires too.

Penny points to his purchases. "What's in the bags?" Her tongue shoots out and captures a little mound of strawberry swirl on its crimson tip.

"I bought a new suit and some shoes for the big legal fireworks on Monday." He searches Penny's face for signs that she knows what Mr. Stanfull and her father are up to. When she averts her eyes and shoots out that tongue for some more strawberry swirl, he knows.

"Do you think I'm a pathetic mental case?" he asks her.

Penny lowers her ice cream cone, licks her lips clean and studies Calvin as if she is seeing him for the first time. "Honestly, I don't know *who* you are anymore, Calvin. My Dad said you told them they can't hunt in Arkansas. What is that all about? He said you got a loan from Mr. Kentlinger by *lying* to him."

"Guilty as charged."

She takes another lick of ice cream and shakes her head. "Unbelievable."

He stands up and grabs his packages. "Merry Christmas, Penny."

She clamps a hand on his arm. "Wait." She pulls him back down to the bench and takes his free hand. "I'm sorry I'm being such a snit. I just don't know what to do here. Give me a clue, will you?"

"Well, whose side are you on, that's what it comes down to. I've got a fight on my hands, to the death. Are you with me or against me?"

Penny blinks and her face wrinkles. "You're being melodramatic. I don't really like the way my father and Mr. Stanfull are treating you, but it's *not* a matter of life and death. I guess I'm sort of on your side, but I just don't understand you anymore."

"It feels like life and death to me."

"Will you please tell me what is going on with you? Please, sir?"

Calvin takes a bite of butter brickle and swishes the delicious creamy mass around in his mouth. "Always call me *sir*," he mumbles through the ice cream.

"Gross, Calvin. Swallow!"

Calvin swallows the ice cream, sets his cone on the bench and gives Penny's slender hand a squeeze. "I've been thinking about you. I can't even begin to tell you what I've been through since Mom and Dad died, but maybe after about a thousand years I will be able to figure it all out, and then I'll tell you everything."

Penny lowers her eyes to her lap. When she looks back up at him, a tiny tear is inching its way down the valley at the edge of her nose. "Is that a proposal?"

In the air above them, the Ray Conniff singers are roasting chestnuts on an open fire. Calvin holds onto her hand. "Not exactly. I need to be alone for a while longer. I have to do a few things. This court fight, then some other things down in Arkansas." *Money*, he thinks. *What am I going to do about Money?*

Penny sniffs and tries to retract her hand, but he holds on. "Penny?"

"What?"

"Please look at me."

She does, but the look is full of mistrust.

He rubs her hand. "Please forgive me for being so weird and running away from you so many times. There's just some things I need to do first, and I'm not even sure what they are. I can't begin to explain it right now, okay?" He pulls her close and slides a hand inside the back of that blue jumper. "You're the American Dream," he whispers. "You're *my* American Dream. You're what I really want in this world." Keeping his grip on her hand, he pulls back, gets on his knees, fires a soulful look into her eyes and starts to sing: "Oh beautiful, for spacious skies, for amber waves of grain..."

Penny casts an embarrassed look at the passing crowd and pulls at his hand. "All right, Calvin, get up."

Calvin stops singing but stays put. "Hey," he says, rubbing her cold hand with his thumbs. "How about if we meet at St. Mark's for the midnight service on Christmas Eve?"

"Calvin, if this is one of your melodramatic stunts..."

"No, baby, no." He rises and pulls her up, closing his arms around her, his belly against her belly. "I love you," he says into her sweet-smelling hair.

Penny pushes back and gives him a deep, strawberry kiss. "I do so love you too."

"See you on Christmas Eve, then?"

Penny holds his face, glances again at the passing crowd, leans into him and whispers, "You're making me so hot."

MONDAY, NOVEMBER 20TH, 1972

The hearing is in the courtroom of Judge John Herrington, Louisville's first black district judge. Before they go in, Phil instructs Calvin on what to do: *Nothing*.

"Aren't you going to coach me on what to say?"

"No."

"Well, then what am I paying you for?"

"To do the talking."

"Verbal whores."

"Beg your pardon?"

Calvin grins. "That's all you lawyers are. Verbal whores."

Phil laughs as he pushes through the big swinging door.

There are twenty-five people seated in the stately old courtroom, maybe thirty, all of them looking haggard or bored or scared except the lawyers, who are fresh and alert, hair in place, dark suits a-gleaming. Phil and Calvin sit on the benches to the left. Mr. Stanfull is already sitting across the aisle, not looking their way.

The clerk finally hollers out their case – hear ye, hear ye, case number such-and-such, guardianship petition by Mr. Charles M. Stanfull – and the three of them, Phil, Mr. Stanfull and Calvin, step forward.

Judge Herrington, a jowly, benign-looking man, takes a few moments to look over the petition and supporting documents, which include financial statements from Turtle Manufacturing.

Mr. Stanfull's petition is a work of art. He portrays Calvin as a spoiled, irresponsible mental case without using any of those words. His tone is warm and loving. Calvin is like a son to him, he says. He is heartsick over Calvin's "total collapse," and he feels obligated, certainly not burdened, to take care of him. As Trustee of the Turtle estate as well as Calvin's guardian, Mr. Stanfull will manage Calvin's "substantial and complex" affairs solely with Calvin's interest and the interest of the employees at Turtle Manufacturing in mind. Of course, he will never take a red cent for himself. He will even welcome Calvin into the bosom of his own happy family if the Court thinks it appropriate.

Finally the judge removes his glasses and speaks. "Good morning, Mr. Stanfull."

"Morning, Judge."

"Mr. Gougan."

"Judge."

The judge turns to Calvin. "Mr. Calvin Turtle, I presume?"

Calvin's gut constricts. "Yes, your honor."

Judge Herrington's eyes are weary, but not unkind. "How are you this morning?"

"Fine, sir."

"Good, that's good, glad to hear it. May I call you Calvin?"

"Sure."

"All right, good, that's fine. Now, uh, Calvin, do you fully understand what we're here for today?"

"Yes, sir, I do."

"Well, could you explain it to me?"

"Why do I have to do that?"

Phil grabs Calvin's elbow and whispers in his ear: "Do what he asks or you're fucked."

"Counsel, have you instructed Mr. Turtle on this procedure?"

"Sure have, your honor." Phil releases Calvin's elbow.

"Well, Mr. Turtle, are we to have the pleasure of your cooperation this morning?"

"Yes, your honor. I'll do whatever you want."

"It's not what *I* want, young man, it's the law. We have to follow certain procedures in the Commonwealth of Kentucky. Now you can understand that, can't you?"

"Yes, sir."

"Well, fine, good, now let's start again. Can you explain to me what you think is going on here this morning?"

"Well, Mr. Stanfull has filed a petition to be my guardian because I supposedly can't take care of my own affairs, but what I really think is happening is that Mr. Stanfull is trying to take control of my land down in Arkansas before I turn twenty-one."

"I'm not interested in what you think about Mr. Stanfull's motives."

Mr. Stanfull adjusts the jacket of his suit. "Your honor, I think the mental condition of this boy is apparent. I respectfully ask that you grant this petition and appoint me guardian."

Phil jumps in. "With all due respect to Mr. Stanfull, your honor, nothing's happened here to indicate anything more than nervousness and a little anger on the young man's part. I think he's entitled to that. This is a groundless, vicious and self-serving petition, with all due respect, your honor."

Mr. Stanfull glares at Phil, then turns a sweet face back to the judge. "Your honor, it's clear that this young man had a complete breakdown after his parents' death. At work there immediately was a problem. Flawed playing cards were shipped to a long-time customer, jeopardizing the economic well-being of the entire company. Since the death of his parents, Calvin has taken frequent time off for trips to Arkansas or to play golf or go dove hunting, while things at the family business have been getting worse and worse. Recently there has been an even more serious breakdown in employee morale at Turtle Manufacturing. The company is in dire financial condition and young Mr. Turtle here has resisted attempts on my part, as trustee and legal executor of his father's estate, to right the company ship. The Board of Directors has met and unanimously supports my efforts to correct the situation, but Mr. Turtle has, totally unauthorized, fired people and promised raises, borrowed money, and, in my opinion, put the very existence of Turtle Manufacturing seriously at risk. I submit to you that this young man is traumatized by the death of his parents and is incapable of functioning at a responsible, adult level. He needs supervision, probably for the foreseeable future, and I, as his father's best friend and trustee, am the logical one to do it."

Judge Herrington replaces his glasses, glances down at a piece of paper, then over his glasses at Mr. Stanfull. "A psychiatrist, one Dr. Nancy Strim, has submitted this evaluative report that says he's mentally and emotionally competent, Mr. Stanfull."

"Not a binding determination, your honor."

"Point taken."

"Your honor," Phil says, "you have a signed statement from a highly reputable psychiatrist to the effect that Mr. Turtle is fine, and you can see on the company financial statements that the business is now recovering. They are approaching full production at the plant, and they will be able to pay back the loan on time. This young man knows the playing card business better than Mr. Stanfull, and he has righted the company ship without more layoffs. He doesn't deserve this treatment, your honor. Mr. Stanfull here seems to think he knows more than the psychiatrist."

The judge reads back over some of the documents before him. "Mr. Turtle," he finally says, eyeing Calvin over the top of his glasses.

"Yes, your honor?"

"Is it your wish that Mr. Charles Stanfull become your legal guardian?"

"No, sir."

"Well, what do you plan to do when you turn twenty-one? Can you tell me that?"

"I plan to run the family business and manage my father's estate as he would have wanted me to do it."

"Yes, but the family business is in pretty rough shape right now. How do I know you're going to be able to handle it?"

"Your honor, I am not having a breakdown. I'm fine. My parents were both killed in a car accident and I have been upset, naturally, but I haven't been playing a lot of golf or taking a lot of trips. That's a lie." Calvin glances over at Mr. Stanfull, who stares straight ahead. "Since they died I've played golf one time and I've taken one very short trip to Arkansas where I met with the man who takes care of my land down there." A shiver races down Calvin's spine with the lie. "I went dove hunting once, on a Sunday over the Labor Day weekend, *with* Mr. Stanfull as a matter of fact. I have been going to work every day at Turtle Cards, and I've been doing the right things. Business has been down but it's nobody's fault. We are now making more high-quality playing cards with fewer employees than ever, and we are currently turning a small profit. Sales will only get better with Christmas on the way. Mr. Stanfull doesn't understand the playing card business, and he doesn't understand the employee situation at Turtle Manufacturing either. If I had done what he told me to do, my family's company would be ruined by now."

The judge rubs his whiskery chin like Grandpa Calvin used

to do, and Calvin thinks the judge might just utter Grandpa Calvin's favorite word, *Oomska*, but instead, he says this: "I remember that accident. Out on Highway 42, wasn't it?"

"Yes, sir."

"Terrible thing." The judge pauses, as if he is trying to picture the accident, then he says, "Your 21st birthday is coming up next summer, is that not correct?"

"Yes, sir. The 28th of June."

"All right, fine, that's what – six, seven months from now? Tell you what I'd like to do, if it's all right with you and your attorney. I'd like to save the Commonwealth of Kentucky the expense and bother of a jury trial to determine whether you are mentally disabled or not. Does that sound all right to you?"

Calvin looks at Phil, who nods. Calvin says, "Yes, sir."

"All right, then, fine. Jury trial to determine disability is waived. What I'd like to do, then, is postpone my decision on this petition until you've had time to prove you can handle your own affairs. Say... six months from now?"

"Your honor!" Mr. Stanfull interrupts, "I respectfully submit that there is enough evidence now to indicate disability. A waiting period serves no purpose. It's in the boy's best interest to grant this petition today."

"Garbage, your honor," Phil says.

"Mr. Gougan ought to look in the mirror, your honor," Mr. Stanfull snaps.

"Gentlemen, gentlemen, let's keep it civil this morning, shall we? Mister Turtle, as I was saying, I'll give you six months to prove you can handle your own affairs, but until your twenty-first birthday you must do what your father's trustee, Mr. Stanfull, says. Agreed?"

Calvin feels too heavy to move. "Yes, sir."

"Agreed, Mr. Stanfull?"

Mr. Stanfull mutters, "Agreed, your honor."

"All right with you, Mr. Gougan?"

"Yep."

"Good, fine. Petition is denied pending a second hearing to be set for six months hence. Jury trial as to disability is waived, therefore guardianship will either be granted or denied at the second hearing." The judge bangs his gavel. "Good day, gentlemen."

Mr. Stanfull packs up his papers, comes over to Calvin, offers a handshake.

Calvin refuses.

"Do whatever you see fit at the plant, and I'll see you in Arkansas," Mr. Stanfull says, then he swivels and walks away.

Phil Gougan is already leaving the courtroom. Calvin chases him through a cloud of cigarette smoke into the marble hallway. "Hey, Phil, will you represent me when this comes up next year?"

Phil squints and speaks around the cigarette in his mouth, the long ash releasing little gray flakes like dirty snow: "That won't be necessary, kiddo. He'll drop the petition."

"Why do you say that?"

"Because that's the way the world works, son." Phil steps into the revolving door and pushes.

OVER HIS DEAD BODY

That afternoon Calvin calls the Café down in Gaheena. Karl calls back an hour later.

"I told the Louisville Hunt Club they can't hunt in the Old Reservoir this year," Calvin says, his heart racing. He is thinking about Money on the front porch of the Shack. He still wants her, goddamn it. You have to take the Queen if you're going to shoot the moon.

"Awright, that's good, then," Karl says.

"I'm going to hunt, though."

"Naw you ain't."

"Karl, it's my land now, and I can do whatever I want. I'm coming down after Thanksgiving and I want to kill a few ducks. One hunter won't hurt a thing."

"You'll have to kill me first."

Calvin swallows and his voice wobbles a tad: "What if I fly down early and we talk about it?"

"Nothin' to talk about."

Calvin clears his throat, pauses, composes himself. "Karl, please listen to me. The Old Wilson Place will be legally mine soon, and there's nothing you can do about it. If I say I hunt, I hunt."

"Whose is it now?"

"What?"

"You said it wasn't legally yours yet. Whose is it now?"

"Mine. I'm the sole heir to my father's estate, but until I turn twenty-one, which is next June, Mr. Stanfull is trustee. It doesn't mean anything."

"Means you don't own it yet."

"No, I'm the owner, Karl, not you, and not Mr. Stanfull."

"You're a smart little shit, ain't ye?"

"I'm coming down the day after Thanksgiving and we can talk about it, okay?"

"You can come, cain't nobody stop you, but you're not duck huntin' in the Old Reservoir. You'll have to stop me first, and you ain't near man enough to do that."

Thanksgiving is the first big holiday for Calvin without his mother and father. The house feels too big and too sad. Johnnie has cooked him a small turkey. "Just warm it on 350 for thirty minutes," she says.

"Is your family getting together?"

She is suspicious. "Uh huh."

"Don't worry, I'm not going to show up at your house for dinner."

They both laugh.

"How's Donte?" Calvin asks.

"He's about to drive me crazy, is how he is. If he don't find a job, he's gonna drive us all crazy."

"Maybe I can hire him back at Turtle Cards."

Johnnie shakes her head in warning. "Don't let Donte get to you."

"I'm not!"

She comes over and puts her hands on his shoulders the way she did at the funeral and examines his face. "I know it was you paid my daughter's bill at college, but don't you worry. I'm not gonna tell your secret."

Calvin feels his face flush. "What are you talking about?"

Johnnie smiles, her cracked old teeth beaming at him. "My daughter is going to get a college degree!"

They hug. Her droopy old woolen coat smells like flowers.

Johnnie starts out the door, then stops and looks over her shoulder. "Thirty minutes on 350."

Calvin waves her out the door.

THANKSGIVING DAY, 1972

Calvin leaves the turkey in the icebox and drives over to Our Lady of Peace. Aunt Virgie is in the recreation room having a holiday meal with the whole long-termer gang. She looks gaunt and tired, almost ghostly, but she perks up when she sees Calvin.

"Hey, sonny boy!" she says, her mouth full of food. The long-termers are a family today, the room as intoxicatingly noisy as any dining room in America. Calvin spots Dr. Strim at another table, waves to her, then ducks down into a chair next to Aunt Virgie.

"Happy Thanksgiving," he says to her.

"Eat!" she says. Someone passes Calvin a plate.

They have a hell of a good time at this table today, imitating that old Phisohex bottle Mrs. Bonson, spitting up food, that sort of thing. After dessert, Calvin follows Virgie back to her room and they get out the cards.

"Gin," Calvin says, early in the first hand.

"You lucky dog." Virgie throws down her hand. "You must be the luckiest man in the world."

"You're right about one thing: I *am* a man."

"Ha! What'd you do, slay a dragon?"

"I told them all to go to hell."

Virgie's smile drains away as she fiddles with the cards. "Told who?"

"The Hunt Club."

Her hands come up off the table as if she wants to embrace him, then they suddenly halt and fall back to a rest on top of her cards. "Don't cross the Hunt Club, sonny boy."

"I didn't cross 'em. I just told them they can't hunt down in Arkansas anymore."

Virgie's thin, speckled hands press and rub each other. "Oh, my precious boy, my precious little boy." Virgie gathers the cards into a neat pile and points a crooked finger at Calvin. "Don't be a hero. Let those men have their way. They *will* have their way."

Friday, November 24TH, 1972

Calvin meets Sleepy Jim at Bowman Field. As the Cessna lurches into a cloudless Louisville sky, he closes his eyes and pictures Karl standing in the doorway of the Shack with that big black pistol: Mister Karl Buntingstrife, King of Gaheena. Beside him, folded into that chair, is Money, sweet Money. Where has she gone?

Jim falls asleep soon after they level off, placing them in the hands of the automatic pilot again. Calvin plays hand after hand of Klondike. When they come over the confluence of the Ohio and the Mississippi at Cairo, he searches the wispy sky for ducks. Sometimes there's a flight or two right up there with you heading for Arkansas, unaware that they are about to be shot.

An hour past Cairo, Jim wakes up and calls the airport. "This is Seven Six Padre, Stutgart, hello Stutgart."

In the hazy distance the grain towers at Stutgart look like a child's carefully stacked blocks.

"Gotcha, s'em six pod-ray." It's Eli.

Calvin's heart blams against his ribs.

"Seven Six Padre, permission to land."

"Come on, then, we ready for ya."

Like a giant steel mallard, they bank and soar down to the flat and dangerous land.

STORM COMIN'

Eli, expelling foggy blasts of breath, meets them on the runway, the wind whipping his breath against his greying temples. "Welcome to Arkansas, Land of Opportunity!" he hollers

Calvin jumps from the wing to the pavement. "You always say that, Eli."

"What you want me ta say?" There is a peculiar light in those old eyes today.

"How about, 'Welcome to Arkansas and BEWARE OF SNAKES'?"

"You *better* beware," Eli grumbles, his eyes averted now.

"Beg your pardon?"

Eli looks heavenward. "Storm comin."

"What are you talking about?"

Eli hefts Calvin's bags. "They's a storm comin' tonight's all I know. I'm sposed to tell y'all bout it, dat's the law, and I done that, so lemme put these heah bags in one of dem Foad's yonder." Eli hurries off toward the rental cars.

Jim is climbing back in the cockpit.

"What's he talking about?" Calvin asks.

"Federal regulations. Has to give me a weather report before he can clear me for takeoff. Guess I better get back in the air if there's a storm coming." He leans out and reaches for the small door of the Cessna. "See you Sunday?"

"Ten four. Thanks for the ride, and have a nice sleep."

Jim laughs, shuts the door, locks it.

Calvin swings his shotgun over his shoulder and marches toward Gaheena.

A HOT & DANGEROUS LONGING

Calvin checks into his father's customary room in the Hunt Club's customary wing at the far end of the Mallard Motel, then walks over to the Buck and Doe Restaurant for lunch. They serve him a man-sized cheeseburger, but he's too nervous to eat. His back aches and his heart seems to fill his whole chest.

On the way to Gaheena, Calvin detours down Bayou Meto Road. Money's trailer is not there. He drives a mile or two past the spot to make sure he hasn't missed it, comes back to where he is sure the trailer should be. Not there. Nothing but an empty patch of weeds and then the bayou, no overturned boat, no car, no sign there was ever a trailer there. Goddamn her!

The Café is too warm, too smoky, full of men in thermal hunting clothes who go quiet as Calvin walks in. Karl is sitting at his customary table in the middle of the room, the customary court of admirers around him. He stands up and crushes Calvin's hand.

"C'mon," he grunts, yanking his coat off the back of his chair.

They ride in Karl's pickup to the corner of the Old Wilson Place and park on the shoulder of the W.P.A. road next to that old bullet-riddled sign:

POSTED
THIS IS MY LAND
I DON'T WANT YOU ON IT
D.P. Wilson

Karl opens the glove compartment, takes out that big black pistol and lays it on the seat between them. He rolls down his window, scans the sky, listens for poachers. Calvin is trying not to tremble. Several shotgun blasts go off to the north.

"Sounds like that's on our place," Calvin says, feeling strange about calling it *our* place.

"Naw. Wind's comin' thisaway. Them shots is way over in Harden's beans, probably Old Man Harden himself, him and that nigger of his."

"Anybody try to slip in on us this year?"

"Two old boys from Little Rock tried last Sunday. Thought I'd be at church, I reckon." Karl grins. "I follered 'em into the woods and cut 'em off, and when they seen this pistol," Karl pats the forty-four magnum between them, "I reckon they thought better of it."

"They did the right thing," Calvin says, glancing at that big gun. "But what if one of these times some guy decides he's gonna shoot it out with you? Aren't you afraid of that?"

Karl's grin changes to a smirk. "He better git me on the first shot's all I gotta say."

They sit there a while longer, the sky clouding over, the afternoon light going soft. Calvin knows Karl is hoping he will just cave in and not try to hunt on the Old Wilson Place tomorrow. Sitting so close to that pistol, Calvin is *tempted* to cave in.

Karl finally leans forward and starts the truck. "Come on," he says, "I gotta run my traps."

They drive up to the gravel turnoff. "Git the gate," Karl orders, handing Calvin the key.

Calvin steps out, carefully searching the roadside grass for snakes, even though it's November, and opens the gate. When he gets back in the truck, he hands the key back to Karl.

"Keep it," Karl says.

"Are you sure?"

Karl smirks. "You the new owner, ain't ye?"

There is no sign of Money or her trailer at the Shack. Karl goes inside for a moment, and in the sudden quiet Calvin hears all those ducks peeping and quacking out in the Old Reservoir, millions of them, a sound that would boil any hunter's blood. When Karl comes out of the Shack, Calvin expects Money to be right behind him.

"She's gone," Karl declares, striding past in hip boots, that pistol in a holster on one hip, a hatchet flapping in its leather sheath on the other.

"Where?"

Karl ignores the question. Calvin feels a hot and dangerous longing for Money running like venom in his veins as he follows Karl to the Green Timber.

SO WHO'S THE BOSS?

Green Timber is what you call a duck hunting hole if the woods are under water only during duck season. Mallards commute from the Old Reservoir to feed on the soggy acorns a foot or two beneath the water's surface. Find an opening in the trees, put some decoys out, blow on your call, and the mallards fly right down on top of you. It's murderous good hunting.

Karl moves swiftly atop the levee, stopping only to search where he's set his traps. Calvin hurries along behind in his L.L. Bean snake-proof super-hikers and bulky hunting jacket. None of Karl's leg traps has been sprung. At one point Calvin notices that out over the water the trees are filling with blackbirds.

The blackbird, of course, travels not in flocks but in nations, and when a nation of blackbirds fills the woods, the incessant cheeping and shitting can drive you insane. Karl seems indifferent to the growing blackbird din. They flap and cheep and shit monsoons upon the water. Calvin is puffing, sweating, stumbling.

Suddenly Karl stops and draws that big black pistol. Calvin freezes a few feet behind Karl and closes his eyes. *This is it*, he thinks. *That bastard lured me into these woods and now he's going to kill me.* Calvin waits for the hot hunk of lead to slam into his ear, but when he blinks opens his eyes, Karl is taking one-handed aim at a blackbird in a low leafless bush out over the water. He fires and the bird explodes in a Fourth-of-July shower of blood and feathers, the echoing *BOWWWW* of the magnum pistol lifting the entire nation of blackbirds into the air with a sound like the sudden ignition of a long pool of gasoline, and then, as if the world has ended, there is silence, no more cheeping and shitting, no sound at all.

Karl says, "Showed you who's boss, didn't I, Mr. Blackbird?"

Calvin starts laughing, a deep crazy uncontrollable laughing that bends him over at the waist. Karl gawks at him for a moment, as if Calvin is some strange animal that Karl has never seen before. A few feathers float on the water near the shredded wad of skin, bone, and beak.

"You're skeered of me, ain't ye?" Karl says as he spins around and heads down the levee. After a minute or two, Calvin stops laughing and runs after him.

At the western edge of the Green Timber they find a raccoon, ragged but still alive, cowering in one of Karl's leg traps. Karl unsheathes his hatchet, eases down the levee and pulls on the trap chain, causing a ferocious lunging snarl from the masked beast, whereupon Karl strikes a powerful chop to its head, spattering his own whiskery cheek with blood. No more snarls.

Karl hauls the bloody raccoon out of the water and unhooks one back leg from the trap while the other leg pushes frantically at the air.

"He's not dead," Calvin says.

"He's dead awright. He just don't know it."

Karl tosses the dying raccoon on top of the levee at Calvin's feet, resets the leg trap, then bends down to wash his hatchet and his hands. The animal twitches and kicks and sucks rhythmically through its crushed, bloody teeth. The sky is fully grey now. Rain seems imminent.

"How long you been hunting out here?" Calvin asks Karl.

Karl climbs back up the levee, drops the hatchet to the ground and squats next to it. "Twenty-three years."

"Longer than I been alive."

Karl gazes out over the Green Timber. "When you first come down, I toted you out in the Old Reservoir on one arm."

"I don't remember that."

"Your daddy said to just leave you in the boat, but I didn't mind totin' you. I'da done anything for your daddy. Wasn't for him, I'da never had nothin.'"

"What about *your* daddy? Didn't you ever hunt with him?"

Karl snorts. "Sure, when he wasn't knockin' the shit outta me."

"Sorry."

Karl picks up a small stick and pokes the dirt. "Sorry fer what? Cause a daddy whips his boy? That ain't nothin' to be sorry about. He was my *daddy*." Karl looks out into the Green Timber, still poking the dirt. After a long time he stops poking and aims those dark eyes at Calvin: "You still wantin' to hunt?"

Calvin imagines there might be little crosshairs in those dark eyes, so that Karl sees things as if through the scope of a rifle, pin-point clear, every twitch.

"Yes," Calvin says. It is his right. It is his land now.

Karl stabs the dirt again. Next to him the raccoon emits a soft, gurgling noise, the final death rattle. Carefully, making sure the thing is not going to snarl out and bite him, Calvin takes the coon by the warm, wet, hairy tail and pulls it aside so he can squat next to Karl. They look out over the water and say nothing for a while.

Calvin spots a pair of mallards swimming toward them through the Green Timber, two little wakes spreading out in the shallow water. The hen stops, ducks her head under the water, then the drake follows her lead, and the two search the leafy bottom for acorns while their upturned butts do a little dance. Calvin points and whispers to Karl, "Look."

Karl follows Calvin's point and spots the mallards. "Uh huh," he says, and Calvin feels the possibility of a shaky peace with Karl. They are just two human beings, after all, insignificant before the awesome beauty and mystery of Nature. Perhaps a shaky peace is the best that can come between two men in this life.

The tufted, upturned duck butts tilt and spin, tilt and spin. Karl pokes around with his stick. "The Hunt Club comin' down?"

"I told them not to, but I think they might try to hunt in the morning anyway, I don't know. We'll have to make sure they don't get in."

"Nobody hunts but you?"

"Nobody hunts but me. Just once. After tomorrow, no more hunting this year."

The two mallards have surfaced now and spotted Calvin and Karl. They swim a couple of quick pirouettes to find the best escape route, then take off with great flapping urgency, climbing through the scraggy maze of leafless branches to join their brethren in the evening exodus to the grain-laden fields surrounding Gaheena.

Specks of rain begin to fall. Karl throws the stick in the water and stands up. "You don't own this Place," he declares, a nasty, bloodless look on his face.

So much for peace, Calvin thinks. Tensed, ready for an attack, he says, "Well, who does?"

"I farm these fields and flood these woods and maintain these levees, and I set there in that truck all day guardin' this Place. Cain't nobody own a Place that don't work it and live on it. Y'all come down here a coupla times a year. That ain't ownin."

"So *you* own it?"

Karl's jaw is set. "Man does the work, owns the results."

"My father paid a lot of money for this Place, Karl, and he left it to me, and now I own it."

Karl's lip raises in a sneer. "You ain't like your daddy. You got a smart mouth."

Calvin shifts his weight, ready to run. "My father was afraid of you, but I'm not."

A shadow of surprise passes over Karl's weathered face. "You don't own this Place and neither did your daddy. Difference is, your daddy knew it." Karl takes a step and Calvin flinches, nearly falling down the levee into the water. Karl hisses a little laugh as he grabs the dead raccoon by the tail and heads back down the levee toward the Shack.

Rain comes harder now. Thousands of ducks flap and whistle and quack in the darkening sky. When Karl is out of sight, Calvin begins to shiver.

It is dark by the time he gets back to the Shack. Karl is waiting in the idling truck. The raccoon is a matted black heap in the truck bed. Calvin, wet and matted himself, gets in. Karl puts the truck in gear and guns the engine.

On the way out to the gate, Karl suddenly slams on the brakes, skidding the truck in the wet gravel. Calvin sees it too, flashing across the road in the rainy blackness, a grey blur with an erect white tail, bounding toward the Green Timber. Karl gooses the engine, races up to where it crossed and skids the truck to a stop again.

"Doe," Karl says.

"Yeah," Calvin agrees.

"One in behind, too. Buck. A big'un."

"Where?"

Karl is a shadowy form in the faint glow of his dashboard. "He took off the other way."

"What makes you think it was a buck? I didn't see anything."

Karl's voice is full of contempt. "I *know* it was a buck, son. That's how a buck will do, follow behind a doe, let her go first so she gets shot and not him."

Calvin's insides flood with anger. "Call me *son* again and you're fired." The dimly lit truck cab feels like the inside of a skybomb ready to explode. Calvin doesn't know where Karl's pistol is, but he doesn't care. He will die before he lets another man call him son, so he sits like a statue in the gauzy darkness, the engine idling, rain plopping like spent bullets on the roof. He can feel Karl's murderous gaze on him.

Finally, with a little snort, Karl puts the truck in gear and drives on to the gate. Calvin gets out, unlocks the gate, lets Karl through, locks it back, and Karl takes him to his rented Ford at the café, all without a word between them.

THEY'RE ALL HERE

A **drowning rain** blurs the windshield. Calvin creeps along, focused on staying out of the snake-infested ditches along the highway. The Mallard Motel is a dim, yellowish island in the downpour. No lights are on in any of the traditional Hunt Club rooms. Maybe they haven't come.

Calvin takes a shower, drinks a little whiskey, tries to calm himself. He puts on some dry clothes and runs through the rain to the Buck and Doe for dinner. Traditionally, on the night before the opening-day duck hunt, the Hunt Club has a big feast at the Buck and Doe. The owners, Holace and Shirley Battle, always treat them well, despite the racket and the mess. Holace partitions off a back room and appoints two waitresses to spend their whole evening catering to the Hunt Club. These men tip wildly, and the Battles wildly pad the bill.

"They're in the back," Shirley says as Calvin walks in. Over the quiet murmur of people in the front part of the restaurant, Calvin can hear the unmistakable roar of Barn Kentlinger's laugh.

"Shit," he says.

"I'm sorry?" Shirley's eyebrows are raised.

Calvin apologizes and walks back to the partition. Through the crack he can see Mr. Stanfull, Mr. Kentlinger, Dr. George, and No-Knees Headmore, the whole damned bunch. Open whiskey bottles stand like orphans amidst the devastation on the table. A smiling young waitress dressed in a white blouse and Razorback-red skirt squirms between Mr. Stanfull and Mr. Kentlinger.

"Come here, baby," Mr. Kentlinger bellows, "let me *fix* it." He reaches up and rubs at a splotch of shrimp sauce on her breast. The waitress tries to laugh as she fends off Mr. Kentlinger's big hands.

On his way out of the Buck and Doe, Calvin orders a sandwich and asks Shirley if she can have someone bring it to his room. "In this rain?" she says.

Calvin pulls out a twenty and hands it to her.

"Okay, hon," she says, smiling sweetly.

Calvin heads straight to Mr. Stanfull's customary room and tries the door. Unlocked. He flips on the light and the familiar mix of smells hits him, good Kentucky bourbon, acrid tobacco smoke, the rankness of boiled shrimp smothered with hot horseradish sauce, the pungent gun-oil-and-blood aroma of old hunting clothes. Mr. Stanfull's shotgun lies in pieces atop a towel on the bed. He's been cleaning it.

Back in his room Calvin paces, drinks a little whiskey, eats the sandwich and sails playing cards into the hotel wastebasket. Goddamn, what a night. Karl is ready to kill him and the Hunt Club is ready to hunt as if nothing has changed. Calvin takes a pull of whiskey and angrily picks up half a deck of Turtle Cards and hurls them at the block wall of the motel room. Cards flutter to the floor like so many shot birds as someone knocks on the door. It's Dr. George, drink in hand, eyes bloodshot, hair soaking wet.

"Shirley told us you were here," he says

Calvin cannot look him in the eyes. "I'm here."

Dr. George sips from his drink and stares at Calvin.

Calvin finally looks up at him. "Having fun?"

Dr. George blinks a couple of times and clears his throat. "I've been appointed to say that you're the only son of the Hunt Club who is worth a damn." He glances down the breezeway toward Mr. Stanfull's room, then takes another sip of his drink.

Calvin steps back and starts to shut the door.

Dr. George holds up a hand to stop the door. "Wait, Calvin. We wanna have you over for a friendly game of poker." He follows Calvin into the room.

"You're kidding."

"No, come on over and have a drink, play some poker."

"Hope you guys don't think you're gonna hunt in the morning."

243

Dr. George sets his drink on the TV. "Oh, come on, Calvin, it's so goddamned silly for all of us to be down in Arkansas like this and not go hunting." He raises and lowers his hands, letting them slap against his khakis. "Oh, fuck it. I don't even care." He pauses to light a cigarette, clinks closed his lighter. "We won't go hunting if you don't want us to."

"What does Mr. Stanfull say?"

Dr. George blows a thin stream of smoke at Calvin. "Charlie wants to talk to you. He's sorry about all that guardian stuff, and so are we. Really. What we did stinks, and we all feel terrible about it. Now come on, play some poker, whaddya say?" He grins. "We might even let you win."

FATHERS AND SONS

They are sweet to him, sweet as Thanksgiving pie. "Calvin, let me fix you a drink, old buddy," Mr. Headmore says. He struggles up from the bed, limps over to the makeshift bar, fixes a strong bourbon and water and hands it to Calvin the way a butler might.

"How was your flight down?" Dr. George asks. He fingers a deck of Turtle Cards, shuffles them, makes a fan, pulls out a card, the Queen of Spades, then stuffs it back into the deck and shuffles again. When he turns the deck upside down, the Queen of Spades is on the bottom of the deck.

"How do you do that?" Mr. Headmore says, his mouth open and eyebrows raised. Calvin knows that Mr. Headmore has seen Dr. George do this trick a thousand times.

"Here, have some," Mr. Kentlinger says, sweat trickling down his puffy face as he passes a giant glass bowl of peeled pink shrimp. "How's business?"

"Better," Calvin says.

"Attaboy," Mr. Kentlinger replies.

"Penny sends her love," Dr. George announces. He takes the shrimp bowl from Calvin and sets it back on the makeshift bar. "Did you meet with Karl today?"

"Yes." Calvin bites into a large, succulent shrimp smothered in spicy cocktail sauce.

"Good," Dr. George says, sneaking a glance at Mr. Stanfull, who reclines on his bed in a plush blue bathrobe and brown slippers, his freshly oiled shotgun now back together and resting quietly at his side like a good wife.

"Hey, Calvin," Mr. Stanfull says, his expression pained, his mouth full of shrimp. "Let's be friends. Sorry about that petition. Hell, I was angry. You know how I get when I'm angry. Your father could tell you. I lost my head. Wasn't thinking. You're a good man, good as your father."

"Thanks," Calvin says, thinking *What a pile of horseshit.*

The shrimp bowl comes around again and Mr. Headmore limps over to the bar and makes another round of drinks, serving Calvin first, of course. Someone turns on the TV, a football game, and when Calvin has had all the shrimp and whiskey and pampering he can stand, they set up the card table and give him the most comfortable seat. Dr. George deals out the first hand of seven-card stud as Mr. Kentlinger says, "Just a friendly game, fellas. Dollar limit?"

"If it's just a friendly game, we don't need a limit," Mr. Stanfull says.

"Fine with me," Calvin says.

"Doggonit," Mr. Headmore says, when he first looks at his cards. "What a lousy hand." He shakes his balding head at the cruel fate of it, then folds.

"Me too," Dr. George says, slapping his cards on top of Mr. Headmore's. He takes a sip from his drink and moans: "I never get any good cards."

Mr. Kentlinger folds too. That leaves Charlie and Calvin, the classic showdown. Calvin knows who will win.

Dr. George deals the last card down: Calvin has a pair of tens showing; Mr. Stanfull has four cards to a straight showing. He presses a shrimp between his lips and says, "Whatcha got under there?"

"Two more tens," Calvin lies.

"I think he's got it," Mr. Headmore says, tipping his chair back. "You better fold, Charlie."

"Bet he does too," says Dr. George.

Calvin tosses a wad of dollar bills into the pot, looks up boldly at Mr. Stanfull.

"Call," Mr. Stanfull says sullenly, and Calvin knows something is wrong.

"You call?" he says.

"I call." Mr. Stanfull shoves in a wad of money to match Calvin's. "Show us what you got, hot shot."

"Well, I've only got the tens."

Mr. Stanfull flips up the fifth card to his straight. "You lose," he says, then he reaches for the money and stuffs it in the pocket of his bathrobe.

"What the hell are you doing, Charlie?" Dr. George says. "That wasn't the plan."

Mr. Stanfull gets up from his chair and plops back down on the bed, robe open nearly to his crotch, drink in hand. "We're going duck hunting tomorrow, boys. Let's get some sleep."

Calvin stands. "You're not hunting on my Place in the morning, none of you."

Mr. Stanfull jumps out of the bed and cocks his arm as if he is about to throw his drink at Calvin, his reddened, hairy belly poking out of the bathrobe. "I'm not kissing your ass any more, you spoiled little shit. I say we are going duck hunting in the morning, and that's that." He turns to Dr. George, whose face is flushed and grim. "And don't argue with me either, asshole. I'm tired of arguing with all of you. The little son of a bitch never would have changed his mind. Well, fuck him. We are going duck hunting in the morning." He falls back on the bed, then instantly jumps up, sloshing his drink. "You oughtta be ashamed," he says, stabbing a finger at Calvin. "If I were your father, I'd whip your little ass."

"You don't know *how* to be a father," Calvin says. "That's why you lost your son."

"You little *fucker!*" Mr. Stanfull shouts. He spins around and his drink falls to the floor as he grabs his shotgun from the bed, turns back to Calvin, his face red and twisted, eyes bulging. Dr. George wrestles with him and the gun goes off, a quick flash, a murderous *BLAM*, blowing a small hole in the ceiling. As white flecks of plaster float down like snow, Calvin yanks the door open, runs through the wet darkness to his room, gets his shotgun and some other gear, throws it all in the car and drives off into the night.

GOD'S DARK,
UNKNOWABLE PLACE

The rain has stopped, but now there is fog thick as skybomb smoke. Calvin drives about ten miles per hour, terrified he's going to ram someone and have to watch them burn to death. It takes a lifetime to get to Gaheena.

A vaporous halo shrouds the spotlight on the front of The Washeteria, and the Café is an island of hoary light. Not a soul, not even the sheriff, prowls the highway.

Calvin creeps through town and on out to the W.P.A. road, where he turns off the highway and inches through the heavy grey fog until he finds the gate to the Old Wilson Place. He leaves it open and takes the padlock with him in case he needs to make a quick getaway.

The Shack is dark. Karl's truck is not there. Calvin knocks. Nothing. He opens the door, hollers "Karl." Nothing. He shines his flashlight all around. The Shack is empty, no Karl, no Money, only the bed, the couch, the sink, the cluttered shelves and the metal table where he and Money played strip poker. The air is cold and odorless. Karl's pistol and shotgun are missing from the gun rack.

On the front porch, next to that rocking chair where he first saw Money, Calvin sets his shotgun, two boxes of shells, his hunting gear and the whiskey bottle. It is his intention to stay awake until dawn, in case someone comes after him. Inside he finds some matches in the table drawer, right next to the playing cards, and gets a couple of stove burners going. The flames spurt and wane, pop and flicker. Shadow-shapes dance like weird, angular ghosts across the cluttered walls. Calvin pulls up a chair to sit and wait for warmth, but he can't stay still, so he stands up and begins to circle the room, around and around like a pigeon, burner light crawling all over him. He pounces on Karl's unmade bed, the springs groaning under him the way they groaned under Karl and Money that night, then he jumps up and flaps his arms like a duck and flies around the room for a while, then he gets too dizzy and sits back down at the table, panting. After a few blank minutes, he takes the playing cards from the drawer and begins to deal out a hand of Klondike, but the acrid smell of that burner flame reminds him of something so horrible he can't even think, so he bunches the cards and slips them back in the drawer. It's about seven hours until daylight, maybe eight.

Calvin leaves the burners going to warm up the Shack and steps outside on the porch, where he laces on his snake-proof super-hikers, zips on some hunting pants and a waterproof hunting jacket, jams his reversible all-purpose camo-cap on his head, takes a pull on the whiskey bottle, and with the little flashlight beam stabbing the way through the cold, damp fog, eases through the darkness toward the boat dock at the edge of the Old Reservoir. There are no snakes this time of year – they're all deep in their dens for the winter – but Calvin watches the path anyway.

Leaden vapors hang over the surface of the Old Reservoir like the breath of some giant creature. *This is mine now*, he thinks. There is no sound, not a peep nor a quack from a duck; they are all out in the fields, gorging. Calvin pictures Money and himself on the dock last summer. He wants her still.

Calvin steps into one of the aluminum johnboats and cranks the motor, the fog muffling its rhythmic putter. He throws off the line, puts the motor in reverse, backs away from the dock, puts it in forward and heads down the narrow bar ditch that circles the Old Reservoir. With his weak little flashlight he can see only a few feet in front of the boat.

When he gets around to the east side of the Old Reservoir, maybe 500 yards from the dock, he leaves the bar ditch and steers the small boat through tangled branches, raising the motor every minute or so to loosen the duck moss clinging to the prop. Progress is very slow. If he doesn't crash head-on into some underwater stump, he takes the wrong way around a rotting log and ends up stuck on top of its barely submerged continuation, then he has to idle the motor, raise and lock it out of the water, move up to the front of the boat, push back off the log with a paddle, lower the motor, then try another route, all of this with only the lame little flashlight to show the way.

When he finally gets to what he judges is about the middle of the Old Reservoir, he kills the motor, flicks off the flashlight and floats in a cocoon of cold foggy blackness. He is warm – good thing he put on all that gear – and he is not afraid of this empty blackness. The world still spins, but he cannot see. There is nothing to hear. This is God's dark, unknowable Place.

After a time, Calvin reaches over the side of the boat and dips his hand into the frigid water, grabs a heavy wad of duck moss and hauls it dripping into the bottom of the boat. He pulls off a single strand of it and holds it up in the beam of his flashlight. Little green shoots sprout like tiny fingers all along a single, central spine, reminding him of the tinselly stuff you wrap around a Christmas tree.

"So this is what all the fuss is about," he says.

Calvin stuffs the strand in his mouth and chews it a while. It has a sharp, rubbery taste, vaguely reminiscent of the Gourmet Green Salad on the evening menu at the Country Club. He swallows some and pretends he is a duck, clapping his beak together a couple of times, shaking the water off his back, raising his head to look around, stretching his wings.

Calvin eats a little more duck moss, then drains the water from a big hunk of it and, using it as a pillow, lies back and watches the fog slowly twisting and billowing through the beam of the flashlight. After a while he shuts off the flashlight and closes his eyes. The boat drifts noiselessly until it nuzzles up against a big log and all movement stops. Calvin falls asleep and dreams that he is on the practice tee at the Club, waiting for the Parachute to emerge from the smoke of that one and only skybomb.

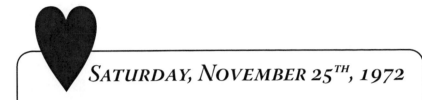

SATURDAY, NOVEMBER 25TH, 1972

A wet coldness stirs Calvin out of sleep. He has fallen down onto the soggy pile of duck moss in the bottom of the boat and water has seeped through all his layers, including his supposedly waterproof hunting jacket. He struggles upright, flailing around to get back on the seat, then he sees it, a faint flickering glow of orange through the fog. The Shack is on fire. He left those damned stove burners lit.

Calvin cranks the motor and heads toward the dock, but hurrying a boat over all the hidden stumps and tangled limbs in the Old Reservoir is futile, especially in this fog. By the time he makes it to the dock, the Shack is a huge wall of flames. He runs clumsily down the path into the intense heat. His gun, his waders and his whiskey are on the porch, but there is no chance to get them now. Sparks disappear into the fog, which seems to swallow and compress everything into a tight nuclear inferno. *Like my family,* Calvin thinks. *Gone up in flames.*

Somewhere in the inferno shotgun shells begin to explode like firecrackers and Calvin ducks behind a thick tree. When the shells stop exploding, Calvin peeks around and sees that the two left-side tires on his car, which he pulled right in front of the Shack, are on fire. They soon blow out with a couple of muffled *fummphffs* and the car lists to that side. Now he is stranded, no car, no whiskey, no playing cards, and worst of all, no gun. All he has left is that impotent little flashlight and the soggy clothes on his back.

Calvin sags against the tree and watches the Shack burn. His stomach aches and he has begun to shiver. As the flames wane, the heat and light grow less; fog begins to reclaim the night. Finally the charred skeleton of the Shack caves in with a sad racket of tin and timbers, and snakes, yes *snakes*, shoot out from under the fiery rubble, seems like dozens of darkly writhing snakes racing desperately away from the inferno in all directions, including right at Calvin. They were denned up under the Shack, apparently, all snug for the winter, then all hell broke loose above them and they had to evacuate.

When a long one slithers by Calvin, he shudders. Cottonmouth. No mistaking that evil diamond-shaped blackness it has for a head. *Kill you in two minutes.* Seems like every cottonmouth in Arkansas was holed up under that Shack, and Calvin is certain one of them will crawl right up one of his L.L. Bean snake-proof super-hikers and bite him in the neck, then he'll fall screaming to the ground and quiver away the last two minutes of his life.

Calvin remains frozen to the tree until the Shack is nothing but embers. His flashlight has died, simply given up its puny existence, and with killer snakes all around him, no light, no car, no gun, Calvin can only hug that tree and wait for dawn. It seems like twenty years before the fog begins to whiten and Calvin hears a vehicle.

"Oh shit," he says.

A pair of headlights stabs out of the fog and eases up to the Shack. It's Karl's pickup. He shuts off the truck and steps out slowly, circling the smoking rubble, taking his time to look it all over, now disappearing for a moment in the fog, then drifting back into view like some eerie specter. He walks over to inspect Calvin's scorched car, bends down to look at the popped tires, opens the passenger door, searches all around inside, looks under the car, walks back around the Shack another time or two, then gets back into his pickup and sits, smoke from his cigarette curling out the open window of the truck to join with the fog. Calvin can't see Karl's face clearly, but he has the impression that the man is grinning.

Calvin waits. Fog clings to the barren fingers of the treetops like great wads of damp cotton. As the daylight grows, a slight breeze begins to push the cottony fog across the forest floor in a patient, twisting dance. Karl gets back out of his pickup and starts down the path to the Old Reservoir.

"Watch out!" Calvin says, and Karl jumps back, his hand slapping at the pistol on his hip.

"What the *fuck* are you doin'? I almost shot you."

Calvin lets out a long breath. "Glad you didn't."

Karl looks Calvin over from head to feet. "I thought you burned up in that fire."

Calvin shakes his head and hears his own teeth clicking against each other. "I'm not dead, just cold."

Karl turns to glance at the Shack. "What happened?"

"The Shack burned down."

There is that smirk again. "No shit."

Calvin is suddenly fighting back tears and trying to keep his voice even. "Well... I took a boat out on the Old Reservoir...and while I was gone, the Shack caught on fire. I left a couple of burners on."

"You left burners on in *my* house."

"Sorry."

"What were you doing in the Reservoir?"

"Nothing. Just..."

"Why'd you leave the burners on?"

"For heat."

Karl snorts and turns back toward his truck.

"Watch out for cottonmouths," Calvin says, hoping one will lunge out and bite the son of a bitch on the leg. Karl hesitates, glances for an instant at the ground, then looks over his shoulder at Calvin as if Calvin is speaking in riddles.

"A whole bunch of them came out from under the Shack when it collapsed. I haven't moved."

Karl's thick eyebrows are curled in genuine surprise as he looks toward the smoldering rubble. "Well, I'll be damned. Musta been a den under there." Now he turns back to Calvin and there is new light in his eyes, almost friendly. "Guess I been sleeping with the snakes."

Calvin tries to laugh. "Yeah."

"Hey, cut loose of that tree and show me. I wanna see if I can find where them snakes was at. You're not skeered of a little ol' snake, are you?"

Calvin can't stay next to this tree like some big baby, not now. It's plenty light enough to see there aren't any cottonmouths in the vicinity, so he takes a couple of tentative steps and, like a newborn animal, reels and wobbles around, nearly falls, regains his balance and feels the incredible tightness and soreness he's been storing up in every muscle. He stretches and limbers up, struggles with cold hands to unzip his wet hunting pants, pees, then strides over to his charred car like he ain't skeered of no snake and together he and Karl survey the damage.

"Melted them tires," Karl says.

"Probably my gun, too." Calvin sees no sign of it in the rubble.

"Your gun was in there?"

"On the porch. My shells too. When they all went off, I thought I would be killed."

"A shell don't shoot lessen it's in a gun," Karl says, as if Calvin is the stupidest human being he's ever known. "In a fire it'll just pop, like a firecracker." Karl walks off into the woods, finds a long stick, comes back and pokes all around in the hot rubble. Calvin expects a big cottonmouth to lunge out at him any second.

"Yonder it is," Karl says.

"What?"

"Your gun. Nothin' but melted steel. You'll have to git you another one."

It occurs to Calvin that Karl has lost his home. "We'll build another Shack, too."

Karl studies Calvin, then studies the rubble. He seems fascinated with the whole smoking pile, certainly not as angry as you might expect. Calvin hears ducks overhead, flight after flight of them, pouring back into the Old Reservoir after a night's feed. Karl hears them too.

"You wanna hunt?" Karl says, looking up at the grey fog obscuring all those ducks.

"You're kidding."

"Naw, I ain't kidding."

"What changed your mind?"

Karl pooches his mouth up in a conciliatory smile. "It's your Place now, ain't it?"

Calvin feels excitement close around his heart like a pair of warm hands. This is the best duck hunting hole in the universe and, yes, it's his. "But I don't have any waders, or a shotgun."

Karl's tone is all buddy-buddy now. "I got an extry pair of waders, and you can use my gun. I don't need to shoot." Karl leans into his truck bed and pitches out the extra pair of waders and Calvin wonders about the Hunt Club. It's well after daylight now. They would be here by now if they were going to try to hunt.

Calvin's clothes are still wet and cold against his back, but he doesn't care. He is going duck hunting, a one-man opening-day hunt. While he hops around trying to pull on Karl's waders, Karl unstraps his pistol, lays holster and gun on the seat of his pickup, fishes another pair of waders from the floorboard of the truck and starts pulling them on. Calvin takes Karl's shotgun, a .12-gauge pump, plus a box of Karl's shells, and waddles up the path, watching every step of the way for cottonmouths. The fog-shrouded staubs sticking up out of the Old Reservoir look like the skeletons of ancient hunters this morning, all but their central structures long since fallen into the Soup.

Karl, waders on, duck call dangling from his neck, comes up the levee behind Calvin and steps into the boat that Calvin used a few hours before, the soggy pile of duck moss Calvin ate from and slept on still in the bottom. Karl tosses the moss into the water without comment. "Let's go," he orders, so Calvin climbs in and sits down on the front seat.

Karl fires up the motor and steers them through the fog to the east side of the Old Reservoir, the boat cutting a rippled V in the smooth, opaque surface. Flights of ducks whistle without warning into the visible part of the world, then, spooked by the sight and sound of the boat, flare higher and higher until they disappear like winged apparitions into the misty void. Though Calvin knows there are thousands of ducks out here, their bellies full of rice, he can hear no quacking or peeping. Fog drapes everything like an eerie shroud.

Now Karl turns the boat out of the bar ditch and heads west into the middle of the Old Reservoir. At one point they ride up on a sunken log and have to violently rock the boat to get off. Calvin turns around and says all buddy-buddy to Karl: "Hard work!"

Karl nods and looks away.

"Why do we have to go all the way to the middle? Can't we just stop here? There's plenty of ducks."

"Naw, we need to be in the middle." Karl yanks the motor out of the water and guns it to get rid of a hunk of duck moss.

Finally they are more or less in the middle of the Reservoir and Karl kills the motor. "Awright," he says, as the boat rides its own wave for a moment, then settles.

Calvin loads his pockets with shells and hoists a booted foot over the side of the boat. The water compresses the dull green rubber tight and cold around his calf. The pressure of all that water squeezing his waders always makes Calvin a little uneasy. So many unseen forces in this world can flatten you. He swings his other leg over and the duck moss swallows him to the waist. He lifts Karl's gun out of the boat and takes that first slow, careful step, his legs heavy as gold. You don't want to move too quickly in the Old Reservoir. The minute you try to hurry, you trip over some submerged log or tree limb and you've got instant disaster, frigid fingers of watery evil reaching down into your waders.

Calvin eases toward a tall, rotting tree trunk, the remnants of some long-dead oak, once the king of the forest perhaps, but now only a scraggy, rotting, branchless trunk, pitted and jagged and sad. He loads three shells into the pump shotgun and turns to look at Karl, who still sits in the boat, staring at Calvin the way he did yesterday when he shot that blackbird, as if Calvin is some weird creature he's never seen before.

"You coming?" Calvin says, studying the fog overhead for dark, speeding forms.

"Lemme get this boat outta sight." Karl cranks up the motor. Even in the fog, a boat will spook a duck, so you take it off a ways from where you plan to shoot. Karl putters into the fog until Calvin can no longer see him. The motor screams once when Karl raises it to get the duck moss off the prop, then Karl lets the motor fall back in the water, muffling the scream. When he is fifty yards away, maybe fifty-five, Karl kills the motor and there is silence.

Now the ducks come, and Calvin decides not to wait for Karl. There isn't much need for a caller anyway, not with only one hunter, and not with so much fog a duck couldn't find the source of the calls anyway. Calvin watches a few sail overhead, not able to tell what kind they are – mallards, pintails, gadwalls, they all look the same in a fog like that – so finally he just picks one out, releases the safety on Karl's gun, raises it and pulls the trigger, *BLAM*, obliterating the eerie, fog-bound quiet. The duck slaps the water only a few feet away.

It's a hen mallard. She swims in desperate circles, her wings splayed out like pontoons, her beak in the water as if she is looking for some of that duck moss to eat. Feathers drop like little parachutes to the water around her. When she lifts her head, a string of dark red beads trickles down the mottled brown softness just below her eye, then the head drops, and the eye goes under. Again she tries to raise her head all the way out of the water, again the dark beads form below the eye, and again the head drops into the water. She tries to raise her head several more times, each nod weaker, the head not coming up as high, the splotchy orange beak not quite making it out of the water now. She is still swimming in circles, but wider and much slower circles now. Then the nodding stops, the circling ceases, the wings flutter one last furious time, and the body shudders. She is still now, mangled wings askew, her beak kissing the duck moss forever.

That familiar flood rises inside Calvin now and he feels like he is suddenly drowning. He closes his eyes and concentrates on his lungs. *Suck. Suck.* He tries to yell, but nothing comes out. *Suck, Calvin, suck.* The foggy air is like smoke, too heavy to breathe. With his free hand he reaches to the water and cups some to his face. The coldness is a slap, causes him to yell out, and following that yell comes cool, damp air into his lungs. His body relaxes, sucking, expelling, breathe in, blow out. *What is the matter with me?* he wonders. Calvin dries his face on the sleeve of his hunting jacket, restores the safety to the *on* position, and shoves another shell into the magazine of Karl's gun. The fog is moving more noticeably now, giving definition to a gentle wind. More streaking forms come into view, then disappear into the shroud. Calvin listens for Karl: nothing. He should be wading back into view by now.

"Hey, Karl," Calvin hollers, the fog deadening his voice.

Nothing.

"Karl," he hollers more loudly.

Nothing. No movement but the soft fog crawling over the Soup.

"Karl!" Calvin shouts, loud as he can. "Answer me!"

Nothing.

Calvin reviews the situation. Maybe Karl has fallen in, gotten tangled up in the duck moss and drowned. *No chance*, he muses, smiling at himself. Karl has waded this tangled Reservoir a million times. Maybe he's lost, wandering around in the fog, but no, that's stupid too, he would've heard Calvin shooting and hollering.

Maybe Karl's been bitten by a cottonmouth. *Oh shit.* Calvin has forgotten about the cottonmouths. It's hard to believe that a snake could be out here in this cold water, but all that heat and fire has stirred them up, confused them. Calvin holds his gun ready. Every little watery sound is a swimming cottonmouth now. *Kill you in two minutes.* The wind has pushed the lifeless hen mallard nearer to him. He will not look at her. He will not think about her.

"Karl!" Calvin shouts "Where the hell are you?"

Nothing. Panic seeps into Calvin's heart like frigid water

through a hole in a boot. He takes a step in the direction Karl went and stumbles on a submerged log. Water laps over the top of his waders before he can get upright again, its icy fingers reaching down to grab his balls. "Karl!" he screams. "Where are you?"

Nothing.

Ducks flap and sail overhead. One lands just a few yards from Calvin, a spoonbill drake. *Working class duck*, Calvin thinks, remembering the perennial Hunt Club joke. Spoonbills are fish eaters, plentiful and stupid. No good to eat. Not even worth killing.

The dead hen is just at Calvin's side now, though he does not see her. The wind spins her until the feathered tip of a wing lightly touches his waders, as if she is reaching for him, trying to tell him something, but he is not listening. Calvin is studying the fog, trying to decide what to do.

"Karl!" he shouts.

Nothing.

Calvin takes another step toward where Karl should be. The spoonbill jumps and flaps rapidly back up into the fog. "You don't know how lucky you are," Calvin tells the escaping bird. His foot clunks against a sunken log. He has to leg-lift about a thousand pounds of duck moss to step over it, and as he does so, a little more water pours over the top of his waders.

"Karl!" he bellows.

Nothing.

Calvin eases ahead, gun ready to blast any charging cotton-mouths, the fog coiling more rapidly around him now. He tries to move in a straight line toward where he believes the boat to be, but straight lines are impossible in the Old Reservoir. You have to walk around all those fallen treetops and log-jams, and when you've finally leg-lifted yourself to the other side, the future looks just like the past. You're not even sure you've moved at all.

When he's gone what he thinks to be about fifty yards, he stops and searches all around. No boat, no Karl.

"Karl!" he shouts into the mist.

Nothing.

Calvin moves a little to his left, then a little to his right, straining to see *anything*, maybe even the cottonmouth that has done Karl in, but there is no boat, no Karl, no snake. He is shivering constantly now; cold water has nearly filled his waders. He spins around and realizes he has no idea which way he came. The fog has reduced everything to its essential form: every tall rotting trunk looks just like the one he was originally standing by; every log-jam looks just like the last one he leg-lifted around. Calvin is dead lost.

"Karl!" he shouts.

There is a sudden splash behind him and he whirls around, sure that he will find Karl, but he sees nothing. He searches the murky surface of the water as far into the fog as he can see. No Karl. No boat. Then he sees it, just beyond his clear vision, something vague and dark, small, right on the surface, cutting a small V in the water, headed his way. *Cottonmouth.* His heart slams as he raises the gun, releases the safety, and takes aim. He will have to make a good clean shot. If he misses, the damned thing might go crazy and streak right toward him.

It's moving closer, almost in gun range now, and as the distance diminishes, the evidence grows. Yes, the head is above the water, just like a cottonmouth. Yes, it's swimming slowly, erratically. Calvin massages the cold steel trigger of Karl's shotgun.

A little green head emerges from behind a stump. It's a *teal.* Just a goddamned little teal, swimming innocently along. "Fuck!" Calvin says, lowering the gun. The teal spots him now, swims in a quick circle, then flutters the hell out of there.

Several minutes pass before Calvin calms down enough to push the safety on and move. He heaves his legs through the duck moss, and, like the teal, circles around and around, looking for the best escape route. His heart is slamming against his shivering chest. "Karl!" he shouts.

Nothing.

Calvin has two choices. He can just give up like a helpless child and let himself sink into the duck moss and drown, or he can keep trying to find Karl and the boat in this impossible foggy Soup. *I can do this*, he tells himself. *I'm no child.* He strikes out boldly for maybe two steps then goes down all the way over his head into the cold, dark nothingness. *This is death, then*, he thinks. Calvin is drowning for real. The cold, sad water pulls him down down down and he hears Johnnie's voice: *Swee-eet surrender.*

But there is something else down here, just a feeling, not like death but a buoyant feeling, the hand of God, maybe. He doesn't understand where this comes from, but he doesn't need to understand. It touches him in the way the hen mallard touched him: beneath his awareness. He hears his own voice: *Sparklers and Diggers, Pumpers and Puppytoes, Into the Free Pile, Here I Goes,* and decides to live.

Calvin flails and stumbles and thrashes as he tries to get his head above the frigid water again. His waders weigh a ton and it seems like he will never get to the surface, but finally, using Karl's gun like a crutch, Calvin pushes off the bottom and forces his head to the surface, where he sucks in the heavenly air. As he struggles back to his feet, strands of duck moss clinging like entrails to his gun and his soaked hunting coat, he shuts his eyes, shakes his head violently and screams at the top of his lungs. This goes on for a while.

When his screaming subsides, Calvin scans the shifting fog. He feels empty now, profoundly empty, as if for the first time in his life he has no substance, no history, and in this state of clarified emptiness his mind sharpens. It dawns on him that maybe Karl has *left* him out there to die. He wipes the snot from his nose and pours water from the barrel of Karl's gun.

Maybe Karl just walked the boat right on out of the Old Reservoir. He would have known the way, even in this fog; Karl lives here, after all. Maybe the son of a bitch knew that Calvin would fall in and drown, or that he'd just wander around in the fog, cold and lost and confused, until he gave up and died.

"You motherfucker!" Calvin screams into the fog. The skin of his hands is blue and he is totally exhausted, but for a second wind there's nothing like having someone try to kill you. He studies the fog-shrouded Reservoir in every direction until he remembers something: when weather moves in, it always moves in from the west. This fog is moving consistently in one direction, which has to be east, and since Karl took him to the east end, the way back to the boat dock must be against the wind, so Calvin turns and heads westward, dripping gun poised. He makes a lot of racket, of course, thrashing over logs and flailing past stumps. Soon he has to stop and rest, but at the moment he quits thrashing there is another noise for the briefest moment, off to the side and behind him, like an echo, then it stops. He turns to look, but can only see shrouded trunks and stumps. *Can fog cause an echo?* he wonders. Calvin decides that he must be losing his mind.

He thrashes forward into the wind until he has to rest again, and again he hears the echo. He sees nothing but stumps and logs in the billowy fog, but he knows it's Karl, strong and cunning and lethal, the King of Gaheena.

"Karl, I know you're there," he says quietly.

Nothing.

Calvin is shivering. "Karl?"

Nothing. Calvin considers the possibilities: He could go after Karl, try to confront him. Calvin knows that Karl doesn't have his pistol because he saw him lay it down on the seat of his truck. Of course, Calvin could just keep on thrashing his way west until he finds the dock and then he can just get the hell out of the Old Wilson Place. If it *is* Karl behind him, Calvin knows there is no chance of losing him, but as long as Calvin has the only gun, Karl will have to stay beyond the foggy veil.

"Karl, are you there?"

Nothing. No movement, only fog and staubs and stumps. Ducks whistle through the fog overhead as Calvin eases forward one little baby step, his leg struggling against a huge tangle of duck moss, the gun at his shoulder, safety off. He stops.

Nothing. No echo this time. Maybe the whole thing is just his imagination. Calvin takes another baby step and one of the rotten old tree trunks downwind of him comes to life, dances a little sideways jig, then is still. Calvin swivels around and points the shotgun at it. The old tree trunk moves again, keeps moving this time, and like the mythical figure Calvin always believed was attached to the Fourth of July Parachute, Karl Buntingstrife emerges from the smoky billows. He is coming straight toward Calvin now, head up, eyes locked on Calvin, his powerful body cutting a shimmery V in the water.

Calvin keeps the shotgun pointed at Karl. "I thought you were a cottonmouth," he says through his chattering teeth, and tries a friendly little laugh.

Karl says nothing, just keeps coming, his face a terrifying mask. He stops ten yards away, maybe fifteen, and raises that big black magnum pistol. Fire spits from the barrel, staining the eerie fog. Calvin feels the sharp strike of a snake at his temple, hears the murderous burst of a skybomb in his ear, falls back against a submerged log, same as he fell against the roof of his flipping Mustang that fiery Fourth-of-July night.

BORN AGAIN

Dr. **George** is yanking Calvin into a boat, same as he yanked Calvin into the world twenty years ago. The doctor lays him out in the bottom like a caught fish, then steps around and pulls Calvin's waders off, draining the water from them. Dr. George covers Calvin with his hunting coat and probes at the wound on his temple. Karl's bullet gouged a small trench in Calvin's skull, nothing too serious. Dr. George gives him a swig of whiskey from a small silver flask. The sky is ice-blue now, heavy with interlaced strings of ducks, a great din of quacking and peeping rising from the Old Reservoir. Freezing wind bites at Calvin's face.

"You're all right," Dr. George says with gentleness.

Calvin's head pounds and stings, and he is shivering hard. "Where's Karl?"

"You tell *me*."

"He tried to kill me." Calvin raises up on his elbows and peers over the side of the boat, expecting to find Karl, eyes fiery, cottony mouth open, those mighty hands gripped around that big pistol, the round cavernous metal mouth of the thing aimed right at his head, but there are only trunks and staubs and stumps jutting out of the glistening water like the ruins of some war. The dull green boat that Karl and Calvin took out this morning rocks impotently in the wind not fifty yards away.

WHAT THE HELL HAPPENED
OUT THERE?

Karl's pickup is gone, but Calvin expects him to jump out of the woods any second and blast them to Kingdom Come. Dr. George puts Calvin in the back seat of his rented station wagon, fires its big engine and turns on the heat. The doctor wraps a whiskey-soaked Mallard Motel hand-towel around Calvin's head, then gets in the front seat, passes Calvin the whiskey and a half-full can of cocktail peanuts. When Calvin has warmed up enough, he sits up. This makes him feel a little woozy.

Dr. George starts asking questions. "What the hell happened out there, Calvin?" The doctor's face is pale and tired, his expression wary.

Calvin tells him about leaving the Mallard Motel and driving to the Old Wilson Place in the fog, about turning on the stove in the Shack, going for a boat ride, then the Shack burning down and the cottonmouths, then Karl showing up and taking him out into the Old Reservoir to hunt this morning. "We went out there to duck hunt, but when I got out of the boat, Karl took off and left me in the fog. I couldn't find him or the boat. I called and called, but he wouldn't answer. Then I tried to make it back to the levee, and he followed me and shot me."

"Jesus Christ!" Dr. George says, stroking his unshaven cheek. He reaches into his shirt pocket and pinches out a cigarette.

"I don't know how he missed. It *was* foggy, but he was

pretty damned close." The whiskey burns Calvin's stomach and his headwound throbs. He watches out the window in case Karl is sneaking up on them.

"Why would he shoot you, Calvin?" Dr. George lights his cigarette and pockets his shiny lighter with a clink.

Calvin thinks about Money, the two of them on the dock last summer. "Because I wouldn't do his bidding? I don't know." He scans the duck-infested sky and wonders where Karl was all night. *With Money,* he concludes. How could she do this to him? He remembers that poker game in the motel, Mr. Stanfull in that blue robe, the shotgun blast. His anger rises. They were *all* in on it. "Maybe you all put him up to it," he tells Dr. George.

Dr. George gazes out toward the Old Reservoir and sighs. "We've been hunting down here a long time, Calvin, but we would never, *ever,* do anything to hurt you. I really mean that. What do you mean you wouldn't do Karl's bidding?"

"Yesterday Karl and I had a little discussion out in the Green Timber. I told him I was going to hunt this morning and there was nothing he could do about it. I think you *all* wanted me dead."

Dr. George strokes his cheek. "Oh, come on, Calvin, that's a little melodramatic, isn't it? We were pretty mad at you, but come on." The car is filling up with quiet swirls and clouds of smoke.

"Mr. Stanfull would do it."

"Charlie Stanfull is a decent man. He would *never* try to kill you."

"He tried to kill me in the motel room last night."

Dr. George turns the heater down a notch. "No, Calvin, that's not what happened."

Calvin senses that the Hunt Club has discussed it, and that they will stick together. He chews and swallows a handful of cocktail peanuts. "Did you find the gun?"

Dr. George looks at Calvin. "What gun?"

"The one I was hunting with. It was Karl's. He loaned me the waders too."

"No, I didn't see a gun. Where's yours?"

"Melted in the fire."

Dr. George glances out at the ruins of the Shack and Calvin's disabled car. "So where is he now?"

"I have no idea."

"Are you quite sure you remember everything? Did you and

Karl get in a fight?"

Calvin is starting to feel a little nauseous. "I *told* you what happened. How do you think I got this bullet wound in my head?"

Dr. George rubs his forehead wearily. "Don't get upset, Calvin. I believe you."

"No you don't."

"I know Karl Buntingstrife. He's a hothead and a bully and I think he's capable of doing what you say he did, but I'm worried about the sheriff. Karl Buntingstrife is a big man around here, and they all know about your little discussion with Karl yesterday, you can bet on that. Karl might be talking to the sheriff right now. What if he says you tried to kill *him*?"

"He's going to have to explain this bullet wound in my head."

Dr. George shifts positions in the front seat and gazes out the window at the smoldering rubble of the Shack. He takes another hit of whiskey and another puff on his cigarette. His profile, sleek nose, gentle chin, reminds Calvin of Penny. God, he wishes she were here. Dr. George shifts again and turns to look at Calvin straight on, obviously worried about something, his voice low and gentle. "I heard two shots, Calvin."

Calvin's stomach flips. "How could that be?"

"Two right together, ba-boom, like a heartbeat." Dr. George is watching Calvin carefully.

"I had my gun up."

The doctor's thin eyebrows squinch together. "Calvin?"

"Safety off."

"You shot him."

"No, I *didn't*." Calvin points to the wound on his head. "He shot *me*. He was coming toward me like a goddamned monster. I tried to talk to him, then I saw the flash of his gun and that's all I remember. Maybe my gun went off too, but I sure as hell didn't shoot first."

Dr. George taps himself on the head. "Sorry, Calvin. I sound like a goddamned lawyer."

Calvin doesn't answer. His headwound pounds. The heat and smoke and so many questions are making him dizzy.

Dr. George sucks on his cigarette, blows out a blast of smoke and says, "When I got here this morning the gate was open and unlocked, so I figured you'd be back here hunting, but when I saw the Shack and your car toasted to a crisp, I was worried no joke. Then I heard the shots. I went out on the levee, but you couldn't see a damn thing in the fog. I yelled and yelled but I didn't hear a damn thing either, so I decided to take a boat out there."

"Maybe I shot him and he sank," Calvin says, cranking down the station wagon window.

"Well, if you shot him, then where the hell is his truck?"

Calvin rubs his eyes. "I don't know."

"My smoke bothering you?"

"Yes, a little."

Dr. George flicks his cigarette past Calvin out the open window, then says, "I looked all around out there." He smiles. "Maybe Karl went for help."

"Yeah, right!" The fresh air is not helping. Calvin's head spins and his stomach hurts. He cups his face in his palms and thinks of that hen mallard, still out there in the Old Reservoir, dead, stiff, wasted. Maybe Karl is lying out there too. Calvin hopes so, the motherfucker. "I'm sure as hell not going back out there to look for him."

"Me either."

"How'd you find me?"

"Well, it took quite a while. I'm not very good with boats and motors, and I kept getting stuck, but eventually the fog lifted enough that I could see your boat, so I went over there and farted around until I found you draped over that log. You were damned lucky!" Dr. George shakes his head. "If you hadn't fallen back on that log, forget it. You would have drowned."

"Lucky," Calvin says, then he throws up all those peanuts on the station wagon floor.

Dr. George gets out, comes around to the passenger door, yanks it open and fusses around with hotel towels and hunting socks, trying to clean up the puke. Calvin tries to help.

"No, no, I've got it," Dr. George says cheerfully. "I do vomit for a living."

When the car is clean, Dr. George slides back in the driver's side and starts to light another cigarette, then stops and looks at Calvin. "Okay, if I smoke this? Are you feeling better?"

"Yes."

The Doctor's eyes are kind. "You sure? You look like hell."

Calvin laughs and says, "I feel fine."

Dr. George lights the cigarette, takes another slosh of whiskey and says, "I know you probably think I came out here to hunt, but that is not the case. We decided last night after you left that we have no right to hunt on this Place if you don't want us to."

"Who decided?"

"Barn, No-Knees, and me."

"What about Mr. Stanfull?"

Dr. George pulls a lung-full from his cigarette and crushes it in the ashtray. His next words come out with the smoke: "After you left, we had a little pow-wow. I suggested that maybe this whole Arkansas thing has gotten out of hand, and that we should never have filed that petition and then come down here to hunt. Barn and No Knees agreed with me. We tried to tell Charlie that it was better to let you do as you wish, but he wanted to go ahead and hunt this morning. As a matter of fact, he insisted on it. He was pretty drunk, as you know. He said we owed it to your father, and when I suggested that maybe we owed *you* something, he started quoting the Bible. *Honor thy father*, and all that."

Calvin takes another handful of peanuts. "That's laying it on pretty thick."

"Yes, very thick. No-Knees told him to forget about hunting and go find a whore."

"What did he say?"

"He left."

"Where'd he go?"

"Don't know. He put on his clothes, took a bottle, called us chickenshits, and left."

"I'll bet he went to find Karl."

"You don't know that."

"Where else could he have gone?"

"Maybe he did go hunting a whore, or maybe he just needed to let it all sink in. You don't know how much this thing means to Charlie. Hell, hunting down here means a lot to all of us, but not as much as it does to Charlie Stanfull. He really does love you, Calvin, I know he does, but nothing's more important to him than this Place. I don't know why. It's just a goddamn swamp full of ducks." Dr. George lights another cigarette.

"When did he come back?"

"Don't know. I went to bed."

"Did he take his gun?"

Dr. George casts a firm look at Calvin. "No. We wouldn't let him."

"Why didn't he try to hunt this morning?"

"When I woke up this morning, Charlie was in his room playing solitaire. When I asked him why he didn't go hunting, he wouldn't answer."

"I'll bet a million dollars he went to find Karl."

"I doubt it."

Calvin looks at the smoldering ruins of the Shack. He swallows hard and moves his gaze upwards. The sky is empty of ducks now. God, what a beautiful blue. He lowers his eyes to the doctor and says, "I think Karl and Mr. Stanfull cooked up a scheme to get rid of me."

"That's pretty far-fetched, Calvin." Dr. George is thoughtful for a moment. "Whatever you think about Charlie Stanfull, we treated you shabbily, and I'm sorry. We owe it to your father not to treat you that way, and I came out here to find you and apologize." He grins. "Besides, I was too hungover to hunt this morning."

"Where is everybody now?"

Dr. George blows out a long, smoky breath. "Back at the motel, packing. We're flying back to Louisville this afternoon."

HE IS NOT CRAZY

The Café isn't crowded, just a few old timers in the red-vinyl booths drinking their coffee and gawking at Dr. George and Calvin. While the waitress rounds up a bandage and some salve to put on Calvin's headwound, Dr. George calls the sheriff. Calvin imagines word spreading through Gaheena like high-voltage current.

Darrell Woodburn, Sheriff of Gaheena, is about forty, tall, stocky, with short, pale hair and narrow, almost Asian eyes. Decked out in crisp brown uniform – gleaming badge, wide black belt stuffed with cuffs, nightstick and bullets, and a big gun holstered at his hip – the sheriff strides into the Café scowling like God Himself, weary of all the sinning but patient too, all-knowing. He reports that no one in town has seen Karl Buntingstrife this morning. "Y'all come on," he says. "We're goin' back out yonder."

The sheriff leads them back out to the Old Wilson Place in the town's patrol car, a white Chevrolet Impala with glow-in-the-dark decals and antennas quilling from every surface. A couple of local boys ride with him.

The Shack is still smoldering. The November sun, already high as it's going to get, does nothing to warm the day. The two local boys, lanky fellows about Calvin's age, maybe a little older, both wearing hunting boots, baseball caps and hunting jackets, inspect the ruins of the Shack. "I'll be shit," one of them says.

The sheriff makes a full circle around the Shack,

then around Calvin's rental car, adjusts his belt, and with a curled forefinger motions for Dr. George to come along with him. To Calvin he says, "You stay right where you're at. We're gonna go out yonder and look around."

The two local boys take waders out of the trunk of the patrol car and pull them on. Dr. George gives Calvin a wink and a thumbs-up, then leads the procession down the path to the boat dock.

When they are out of sight, Calvin inspects the hot-tin-and-charcoal ruins of the Shack. He spots his shotgun, a sagged has-been, and tries to imagine being inside a fire like that, so hot, no water, no life, just the stench of your own burning self and you want to scream but of course you can't. He hears a slight rustling in the woods and flinches. It's just a squirrel, but it could have been Karl. Calvin hopes he is dead and stiff and sunk so deep in the frigid water and tangled duck moss that they'll never find him, but if Karl is dead, then where's his truck? There is something just beyond his grasp here, some piece of this puzzle that feels like it ought to be obvious, but he can't quite get his hands on it.

The boat is stirring up ducks in the Old Reservoir. Calvin watches them rise and form lines like crazy stitching across the powdery sky, then the stitches break up and the ducks begin to spiral back down to the west end of the Old Reservoir, far away from the search party. Arkansas overflows with wild things – snakes, blackbirds, raccoons, deer, ducks, people. Calvin thinks of Money again. He wonders where she is, but his desire for her has diminished. So many wild things have happened. Everything is so *crazy*.

He reaches up and touches the bandage on his head. "No, you are not crazy," he tells himself. Those snakes were as real as the smoking embers of the Shack are now, and Karl *did* try to kill him. And last summer with Money was real, too, so real.

Over and over, Calvin hears the boat motor suddenly rev higher, a desperate moan, then return to a low whine. They're in the duck moss now, hefting the motor every few feet to clear the prop. Calvin stares at the sky, ducks everywhere. He hears a hen mallard calling to her mate, to her group, to the whole damn universe of ducks. For a time he is lost in that skyfull of ducks as if he has become one of them, up there in line, part of a V formation, finally getting the hell out of this godforsaken Place.

WHO CHASED WHOM?

Now the whine of the boat motor is getting closer to the dock; the sheriff and Dr. George are coming back. Calvin climbs in Dr. George's rented station wagon and shuts the door. He expects to see the two local boys coming down the path with Karl's stiff body jouncing between them like some great trophy buck, but when they emerge atop the levee and start down the path to the Shack, they have no body. Behind them come the sheriff, who is carrying Karl's waterlogged shotgun, and Dr. George, looking worried as hell.

The sheriff puts the shotgun in the trunk of his squad car, comes over to the station wagon, motions at Calvin, who rolls down the window.

"Get out of the car," the sheriff says.

He takes Calvin by the arm, leads him past Dr. George to the passenger side of the patrol car, opens the door, guides Calvin into the front seat. The car reeks of men's cologne. The sheriff gets in on the driver's side, taking care not to snag his gun or cuffs on the textured cloth seat, fires up the engine and turns on the heater. A blast of hot air pours out at Calvin's feet. The sheriff beckons with another motion of his hand, and Dr. George climbs in the back seat, behind a metal screen. The hotter it gets in that car, the stronger that gaggingly sweet cologne gets.

Now the sheriff picks up the radio mike hanging from the dash, calls the state police, reports a *missing white male, age 46, Karl Buntingstrife, K-a-r-l...B-u-n-t-i-n-g-s-t-r-i-f-e, six foot one, last seen Friday afternoon wearing blue jeans and a dark camo hunting jacket.* Then the sheriff turns to Calvin and says, "Tell me what happened."

Calvin tells the whole story from the drive to Gaheena last night in the fog, to the fire and the snakes, to the moment he saw that flash from Karl's gun.

"Did you shoot him?" the sheriff asks.

"No."

"Then how come there was a spent shell in the chamber of Karl's shotgun?"

"It must've gone off when he shot me. I don't remember."

The sheriff scratches the back of his hairless neck. Heat pours out of the dashboard. The noxious cologne fumes are making Calvin feel sick again.

"You afraid of snakes?" the sheriff says, a brief smile flickering over his ruddy face.

"Yes."

"I'm terrified of them," Dr. George adds from behind the screen.

Sheriff Woodburn looks out the windshield at the two soggy young men gawking at the ruins of the Shack. When he turns back to Calvin, his expression is full of suspicion. "Why were you out here in the middle of the night?"

Calvin glances at Dr. George behind the partition. "I came out to guard the Place."

"Against what?"

"Against anybody who tried to hunt this morning. I told people they couldn't hunt out here and..."

"Karl didn't want anybody hunting this year," the sheriff says.

"We didn't hunt," Dr. George says.

"I did," Calvin says. "Yesterday Karl told me he didn't want me to hunt, but this morning he loaned me his waders and his gun, and he boated me out there."

"Karl let you hunt?" the sheriff says.

"Yes."

"And he loaned you his gun?"

"Yes, I've already told you that."

"Where's *your* gun?"

"Melted in the fire."

"Lemme see that cut you got," the sheriff says.

Calvin pulls the bandage loose and the sheriff leans across to examine the wound. "Karl's a better shot than that," he says, falling back over to his side of the front seat.

"It was foggy," Calvin says.

"Karl chased him halfway across the Old Reservoir," Dr. George says.

The sheriff swivels around, leather squeaking, to look at Dr. George through the steel mesh. "We don't know for a fact who chased who."

"Whom," Dr. George says.

"What?"

"Sorry," Dr. George says. "It's a bad habit of mine. Correcting people's English. Please go ahead. Sorry I interrupted."

The sheriff pauses for an indignant moment, then says, "How do I know this boy didn't stage the whole thing? He coulda taken Karl's pistol and shot himself to get that scratch."

"That's ridiculous. You can test for gunpowder burns on his forehead, but you won't find any. I'm a doctor and I've seen suicides. There are no powder burns on this boy's face, and why would he burn down the Shack and park his car close enough to burn it too, and throw his gun into the fire, and then talk Karl out of his own gun and shoot him with it? Nobody in his right mind is going to believe he came out here with such a wild scheme. And where's Karl's body? For that matter, where's Karl's truck? I think this boy did exactly what he says he did."

"I'm not a boy," Calvin says quietly.

The sheriff is trying to hold his temper. "You're a doctor?"

Dr. George nods.

"And you heard two shots?"

Dr. George fires a worried glance at Calvin. "Yes."

"You were here when the shots went off?"

"Yes!"

"Was Karl's truck here when you arrived?"

The doctor pauses. "No, it was not."

The sheriff nods triumphantly. "Well, then, Doctor, tell me how Karl shot this boy and hightailed it out of here."

Dr. George goes pale, looks at Calvin again. "Maybe he had an accomplice who heard me coming and hid the truck."

Calvin pictures a headline in the Courier: *MURDER PLOT THICKENS: YOUNG TURTLE'S LIFE HANGS IN BALANCE.* His head spins with it all, and his guts are all churned up again. It's so damned hot in this car

"You know who this accomplice was?" the sheriff asks.

Dr. George's voice is subdued. "No. I'm just speculating."

"How do I know *you* didn't move that truck? Maybe all of you Louisville boys are in on this."

"Preposterous." Dr. George sounds tired now.

The sheriff swivels back around, picks up the radio mic, then twists back around to look at Dr. George. "I'm taking this boy in on suspicion of murder."

Dr. George comes to life. "You don't even have a body!"

"I'm not a boy," Calvin mutters, then he leans over and pukes on the floor of the squad car.

"Aw, shit!" the sheriff says, slamming the mic back on its hook. He opens his door, comes back to Dr. George's door, yanks it open, tells the doctor, "You get the fuck outta here."

LES PLAY CARDS

The Gaheena jail is a windowless concrete-block cellar beneath the pool hall. The sheriff leads Calvin into the smoky pool hall and introduces him to Ace Berliew, a fat, red-haired man in a dirty t-shirt, manager of the pool hall and keeper of the jail.

"Suspicion of murder," Sheriff Woodburn says.

"I heard," Ace says, taking a swipe at the Formica counter with a worn towel. "Shot Karl in cold blood, didn't you, boy?"

"No, I didn't," Calvin says, "and don't call me boy."

Ace guffaws, revealing racks of cavity-riddled teeth. The overly warm room has gone still, pool games suspended, players frozen, cues at-ease in their hands. Sheriff Woodburn leads Calvin past the young studs of Gaheena, Calvin staring at the filthy wooden planks underfoot, the young studs staring at him. At the back of the pool hall, behind a partition, a door leads down a narrow wooden staircase to the cellar, a cold damp room running the length of the shotgun-style building. Near the foot of the stairs is a sprawling heap of wooden restaurant tables, broken shelves and empty soft-drink cases. A floor-to-ceiling chain-link fence marks the beginning of the Gaheena jail.

The sheriff follows Calvin through the open door of the chain-link wall into a small space containing a little metal desk. Beyond the desk are two fenced inner cells, cages within a cage, one on either side of a central aisle.

The cage on the right has someone in it, a grey-haired old black man clenched in fetal position on a cot, his back to the door, a dirty army blanket pulled halfway over him. Calvin thinks of the old man lying under the stairs at Johnnie's house. "He ain't dead," little S.B. had said.

Sheriff Woodburn takes Calvin's belt, his wallet and his waterlogged watch, mashes his fingers on an inky pad, rolls each fingerprint onto an Arkansas State Police record sheet, points to a black telephone on the little desk and says, "Wanna call somebody? Collect?"

"I've got a credit card in my wallet."

"Figures." The sheriff tosses Calvin's wallet to him.

Calvin picks up the phone receiver and calls Penny. No answer. Calvin replaces the black receiver in its cradle. "Damn it."

"Nobody love you?" the sheriff mocks.

"Go to hell."

The sheriff laughs.

When Sheriff Woodburn is gone, Calvin paces. His cell contains a steel-framed cot, a cold-water sink and a foul lidless toilet. The only light comes from a bare bulb hanging over the sheriff's desk, plus the distant light of another bare bulb down at the other end of the cellar. Calvin's shadow, blurry against the block wall, paces the small cage with him. His head throbs under the bandage. The air is damp and stale. Overhead he can hear the shuffling of feet and the pounding of pool cues on the wooden floor. In the other cell the old black man snores.

Calvin sits on the cot, wraps the wool blanket around himself and shivers. He wants some food, so he sheds the blanket, stands up and grabs the fencing. "I'm hungry!" he shouts, rattling the fence. No one comes, of course. Where does he think he is, the men's grille at the Country Club?

Calvin sits down, re-wraps himself in the blanket, sweats, shivers, thinks about this morning out in the Old Reservoir. It all comes down to one question: Where is Karl's truck? Someone had to move it before Dr. George got there. Or did Dr. George move it himself? Was he in with Charlie Stanfull and Karl and maybe the whole damned Hunt Club plotting to kill Calvin and make it look like an accident? He pictures them all sitting around the motel room with Karl, laughing. Long live the Louisville Hunt Club.

No, that's absolutely crazy.

Calvin wishes he had a deck of cards so he could play some Klondike while he tries to figure this whole mess out. Maybe Karl will turn up. Calvin won't even file charges. He just wants the hell out of this place. He lies back on the cot and wishes he had some whiskey. Ace comes down a few minutes later, bangs open the outer door, unlocks Calvin's cage, tosses in a sandwich wrapped in wax paper. "Supper," he says, locking the door back.

"Hey," the old black man says weakly, not even turning over on his cot.

"Don't *hey* me," Ace says.

"When'm I gon' have supper? I wants a hamburger."

"You ain't gittin no free meal outta *this* town, you old drunk."

On the way out, Ace turns off the lights. Calvin has never experienced such absolute blackness, no light whatsoever, no possibility of light. He eats the sandwich, peanut butter and jelly, and tries to talk to the old man.

"Hello?"

Nothing.

"Sure is dark in here."

Nothing.

Calvin flops back on the mildewy mattress, eyes open, seeing absolutely nothing. After a time, he doesn't know how long, the noise in the pool hall overhead subsides, then dies away altogether. The old man isn't snoring anymore. All Calvin can hear is his own breath rushing in, blowing out, rushing in, blowing out. He lets his hand drop and feels the cold hard dirty floor. Though he does not want it to, his body shivers. The blanket does not help. In the timeless darkness the walls of his mind fall away.

"Hey."

There is someone in the cell with Calvin. He sits up, sees nothing.

"Hey, wake up, Mistah Calvin."

Calvin knows that voice. It's Eli, from the airport.

"Les play cards," Eli says.

"There's no light."

"Cards make they own light."

Calvin feels Eli's weight settle on the bed. Eli lays out seven glowing Turtle Cards, face-down, creating a neat row of seven smiling turtles perched on seven sun-drenched logs out in the Old Reservoir. Calvin can see only the shadows of Eli's hands in the faint cardlight.

"What's the game? Klondike?"

"Fortune."

"How do you play that?"

"Turn over dat first card."

Calvin flips it over. It's Grandma Calvin, Ginny, in her living room crying, her pure white china hands in pieces on the floor.

"I don't wanna play any more."

"Nex card."

There's Grandpa Calvin, Roy, in his kitchen, apron on, washing dishes, an empty bottle of whiskey nearby.

Five cards left. "What's my fortune?"

"Nex card."

It's a faded black-and-white portrait of Calvin's Grandmother, Oola Turtle.

"I never knew her."

"Nex one."

This is Grandpa Turtle, Ishmael, Turtle Company founder. That makes four grandparents, two pairs, two Kings, two Queens.

"How does this tell my fortune?"

"It tells yo' fortune, but it don't tell yo' future."

"What's the difference?"

"Fortune's what you git give to you. Future's what you do wid it."

"You mean the Turtle Company?"

"Nex card," the old man says.

It's an aerial view of the forested diamond with the Primal Soup at its center, the Old Wilson Place.

"I own that," Calvin says proudly.

"Turn them las' two cards."

Calvin expects to see his mother and father, but the last two cards are blank, milky white, no pictures at all.

"Where are they?"

"You killed 'em."

"I did not!"

Eli's shadowy hand passes over all seven cards, picking them up, their faint light disappearing, leaving things totally dark again. Calvin feels Eli get up off the bed.

"Hey," Calvin says. "Where ya goin'?"

Silence.

Calvin tries to get out of bed and follow Eli, but when he puts his foot down he feels cold water instead of cold concrete.

"Hey, Eli!"

Silence.

Calvin dives into the frigid water. Heavy strands of duck moss coil around him, pulling him down, down, down like a high-compression golf ball shanked into a water hazard, sinking out of sight forever. He finally comes to a damp, shadowy room aglow with faint, reddish phosphorescence. He gropes his way along a wet, stony wall. It's warm down here, too warm. A thin puddle of slimy water covers the floor and the smell is awful, like burning flesh.

Calvin lets go of the wall and, as he moves toward the darkened far end of the room, his foot touches something soft, a small body clad in yellow pajamas lying on a white, sparkly blanket. "Oh God," he says.

"Find her okay?" Eli says.

Calvin looks around but he still cannot see Eli. "Where are we?"

"In de Cave."

"The cemetery Cave?"

"Sho."

"Where are you, Eli?"

"I gotta be goin'. Mo planes comin'."

"Eli!"

Silence.

Calvin looks down at his sister. She is lying on her stomach, head turned to the side. Her eyes are open. He bends down and takes the outstretched little hand, cold and hard as fine china, and rubs it with both of his own. "Hey, Jewel," he says, "what are *you* doing down here?"

She does not speak. She does not move. Calvin cuddles her stiff body until his back aches and his heart feels dry and cold and hard.

When he stands, there are two serpents dressed in full royal garments, one all black, one all red, standing together, holding hands before him. A glittering crown sits atop the dark one's diamond-shaped, slanty-eyed head: the King of Snakes. From the other one's weirdly oval head flows a feathered cape, and from the scaly red face protrudes a snouty beak, cracked open in a knowing smile: the Queen of Turtles.

Calvin glances down at Jewel, then raises his eyes and points a finger at the King and Queen. "You killed her."

The King and Queen are calm, their eyes downcast and sad. Still holding hands, they move forward and reach out to Calvin with their free hands. He feels like a charred, spent skybomb, no *BLAM* left. He must be dead now, too.

The three of them form a royal circle around little Jewel – the King of Snakes, the Jack of Skybombs, the Queen of Turtles – and together they begin a slow, sensuous dance, swaying first to the right, then to the left, casting languid, twisting, drifting shadows on the glistening walls of the Cave. *This is nice*, Calvin thinks. *It's all I've ever wanted.*

To the measured rhythm of the dance, the King and Queen chant: "A'hunting we will go, a'hunting we will go, hi ho the dairy-oh a'hunting we will go." Calvin closes his eyes and sings along, low and shy at first, then bolder, until the three of them fill the chamber with the chanting halting swaying expanding undulating contracting movement and sound of their cozy little circle. Calvin is loose and free. Nothing can hurt him now. *This is Love*, he thinks. *We are a family.*

But there's one last thing. He squeezes each of their hands and says softly, "I didn't kill you."

The King and Queen do not look at him and do not squeeze back. Instead they drop his hands, move away and gaze at each other lovingly, as if they didn't hear him.

"I didn't kill you," Calvin repeats.

The King and Queen are smiling seductively at one another now, and it's starting to piss Calvin off. "Listen to me!" he says, taking a step or two toward them. "I did not kill you. You killed yourselves."

The King turns his head and shows his fangs, then the Queen disengages from the King and comes toward Calvin. She stops only a couple of inches away and locks eyes with him. Her face is hideous, scaly red skin, horrible beak, but those eyes, so sweet, so sad, so full of need. Calvin is getting an erection. The King rises up behind the Queen and hisses at Calvin over her shoulder. "Get out," he says, his breath pungent and foul.

The Queen sniffs, says coldly to the King over her shoulder, "He's bigger than you are."

Calvin asks the King, "Wanna play hearts?"

The King's face is a horrible mask. "Out!" he yells, striking Calvin on the temple. Calvin's flesh burns.

"Kill you in two minutes," the King of Snakes boasts, but the

Queen is crying, *down up, down, down, down,* and Calvin is puking the King's hot poison out like bad, bad whiskey until there is a flood of tears and puke filling the cave. The King of Snakes and the Queen of Turtles yell and scream and slap at each other until, at last, they tire, and together sink out of sight.

Calvin swims in desperate circles until he finds Jewel's little hand and, oh, thank God, it is warm now, not cold as you might expect, and her face begins to glow like the Fourth of July parachute. Together, hands joined, Calvin and Jewel ride the foul flood out of the Cave and bob up in the clean waters of the lake, two free, just like that.

Light streams through the opening in the tree canopy as Calvin and Jewel rise, hands still joined, drifting eastward over Louisville along Highway 42 until they hover above the practice tee where Calvin withdraws his hand and Jewel begins to rotate, a dimpled golf ball spinning faster and faster until there is a gentle and brilliant burst of color and little Jewel is gone.

SUNDAY, NOVEMBER 26ᵀᴴ, 1972

Calvin wakes. Someone is standing near the cot. "You're free," he says.

It's Mr. Stanfull, khaki pants, green polo shirt. Calvin sits up and rubs his face. His muscles are stiff and blood pounds the inside of his head. The old black man is gone from the other cell.

"What does 'free' mean?" Calvin mumbles.

Mr. Stanfull explains in a low voice that Sheriff Woodburn claims to have spent the whole night out at the Old Wilson Place looking for Karl. They supposedly boated all over the Old Reservoir, poking in the duck moss for a body. He even claims they got a dog from the Arkansas State Police, but the dog couldn't find Karl either. According to the sheriff, no one in Gaheena has seen Karl or his truck since Saturday afternoon, and his girlfriend has disappeared too.

"Money," Calvin says.

"Beg your pardon?"

"That's his girlfriend."

"Oh." Mr. Stanfull sounds surprised and a little suspicious.

"And you don't believe the sheriff?" Calvin says.

"They might have searched for Karl, but I think it's all a sham. This is Gaheena. The sheriff knows good and goddamn well where Karl and his girlfriend are and he's not about to arrest them. He's just putting on a show. It looks to me like Karl's girlfriend is the one who took Karl's truck. I think she was waiting in the truck with the engine running and the heater on, waiting for Karl to come back after he got you lost in the Old Reservoir, then she had to take off when she saw Jim's headlights coming in the fog. She picked Karl up later somewhere, and the two of them are hiding until this blows over. The sheriff knows it, too."

"Yes," Calvin says, and just like that he knows it's true, not just what Mr. Stanfull is saying, but something deeper, something he has known in the back of his mind all along but hasn't been willing to believe until this moment. The two of them were in it together. He doesn't quite understand why they lured him to Arkansas, seduced him (*He beats me,* Money said), then threw his clothes on the porch and hopped into bed together, nor why they wanted him back in Arkansas *(He beat me again,* she said) just to throw him off the trail with that Revival and baptism. Were they trying to drive Calvin crazy? Make him want to kill himself? But he does understand why they wanted him dead: He threatened Karl's dominion over the Old Wilson Place.

"Jesus, I can't believe that son of a bitch tried to kill you," Mr. Stanfull says. His face is red and puffy, and he won't quite look Calvin in the eye. "But the question is, why did he want to kill you?"

Calvin sees that Mr. Stanfull is embarrassed by what happened at the motel last night. "There were two crimes yesterday," Calvin says, touching his throbbing temple. "Karl tried to kill me and so did you."

"Nonsense."

"You tried to kill me in the motel last night."

Mr. Stanfull sighs. "Okay, if you say so, Calvin. Everyone is out to kill you."

"I thought you'd be happy to see me in jail."

Mr. Stanfull sounds weary and small. "It's over, Calvin. You win." He turns and steps out of Calvin's cell.

IT'S NOT OVER

At the small metal desk Sheriff Woodburn takes down Calvin's phone number and address. "This isn't over," he says, casting Calvin a threatening look.

"No, it's *not* over," Calvin replies. "Karl Bunting-strife tried to kill me yesterday, and you need to find out where the hell he is and his girlfriend accomplice too and arrest them both."

The sheriff is taken aback by Calvin's tone. "Yeah, well...." He glances at Mr. Stanfull. "Don't neither one of you think I'm gonna quit on this."

Calvin follows Mr. Stanfull up the stairs toward the pool hall, then stops. The sheriff has to halt below him while Mr. Stanfull continues on to the top and disappears through the door. Calvin tries to appear casual: "What do you know about Karl's girlfriend?" he asks the sheriff.

The sheriff raises his eyebrows in that threatening way again: "I suggest you get the hell out of this town, Mr. Turtle."

LONG LIVE THE HUNT CLUB

Calvin has invited Mr. Stanfull, Dr. George, Mr. Kentlinger, and Mr. Headmore to follow him out to the Old Wilson Place before they all head back to Louisville. The five of them squat on the dock and watch ducks funnel into the Old Reservoir.

"He's out here," Mr. Stanfull says.

"Karl?" Dr. George says.

"No, Sonny. He's out here, I can feel it."

Calvin understands that he will never see Karl and Money again, but in his mind a two-headed monster remains, his father and his mother, two parts of the same creature that will always exist somewhere out here underneath all the duck moss until the Old Reservoir itself is gone, an ending that seems all too real a possibility with the few remaining tree trunks nearly disintegrated into the Soup and the duck moss choking everything out. Maybe someone will come up with a way to restore the Old Reservoir, but it seems unlikely. Oxygen gets used up. Everything dies.

Mr. Stanfull produces a flask of whiskey, takes a pull, passes it along the row of men until Dr. George offers it to Calvin.

"No thanks," he says. What he wants now is the solace of Klondike in his living room at home.

A flight of mallard drakes banks and soars down to the Old Reservoir, their green heads brilliant in the cold sunlight, the purest color Calvin has ever seen.

"God, would you look at that," Mr. Headmore says.

"Beautiful," Mr. Stanfull agrees.

"We'll hunt next year," Calvin says.

"Forget it, Calvin. The Hunt Club is dead," Mr. Stanfull says.

"Don't be stupid, Charlie," Dr. George says.

"Fuck you," Mr. Stanfull says.

Mr. Kentlinger bellows, "That's what I like to hear. Long live the Hunt Club."

The flask moves back down the row.

FRIDAY, DECEMBER 1ˢᵀ, 1972

Calvin hasn't played much Klondike since he came back from Arkansas; there's been no time. He thinks he might even be done with solitaire, anyway. Why keep playing a game you can't win? Why not spend your life doing something more productive? He thinks of that song that Johnnie sings all the time: *Sweet Surrender.*

It's true: surrender is sweet. Just quit fighting and let go. Life takes you downstream and you can relax and enjoy the ride instead of struggling against God all the time. Either way you end up dead.

Calvin has been working twelve hours a day, seven days a week. Every night he comes home, has a quick bite of one of Johnnie's casseroles or roasts in front of the TV, then hits the sack. Morale at Turtle Manufacturing is up. Business is booming and Nelle is turning out to be a fine superintendent. Calvin calls her into his office this morning to tell her so.

"Thanks," she says, turning to leave. "I gotta get back."

"Wait." There is something Calvin wants to say to her, something about life and how doing the right thing is tough, but the words are not coming.

"Yes?" With one hand she fiddles with her curly black hair.

What Calvin really wants, he decides, is to hear Nelle tell *him* that things are going to be all right. "Are we going to be all right?" he says, suddenly feeling like a child.

She is suspicious. "Meaning what?"

Calvin shakes his head and produces a weak smile. "Never mind.

After work, Calvin drives over to Our Lady of Peace. Aunt Virgie is dozing, her head nearly buried in a cloud of pillows, an uneaten plate of supper on the little plastic table hooked to her bed railing. She is so thin and pale and sad tonight. Calvin understands that she will not live much longer. Everything dies. He touches her shoulder and the eyes pop open, find him, and her face comes to life.

"Hey, sonny boy," she says.

"Merry Christmas."

For a moment hers is the shy, beaming face of a little girl. "Christmas," she says quietly.

"I'm back from Arkansas."

Virgie sits up and straightens her nightgown. She yawns, looks down at herself, her fingers fluttering around the buttons at her neck, then she looks up at him. "I dreamt you were dead."

"What?"

"I dreamt you went down to Arkansas and got yourself killed, and that godawful man Charlie Stanfull was the one who shot you."

"That's crazy, you sicko."

Aunt Virgie looks up at him and the color is back in her face. "Ha!" she says. "You're the sicko, sonny boy. So, what'd you do, kiss up to the boys in the Hunt Club? You let 'em hunt, didn't you? Ha! I knew it."

"They did not hunt. I am in charge now and they did not hunt."

She cackles, looking and sounding for all the world just like the Wicked Witch of the West. "Joined the Hunt Club fat asses, didn't you? Well, now you'll live a long fat happy life."

This pisses Calvin off, because he *will* live a long fat happy life now, and why shouldn't he? He went down to Arkansas and came back alive, so damn right he's going to have a long fat happy life. He decides to whip his smart-ass Aunt Virgie at cards tonight. Jumping up from his chair, he clears the plate and utensils from the little plastic table, fetches the playing cards from a drawer and starts dealing out a hand of gin. "I'm gonna beat you so bad," he says.

Aunt Virgie leans forward and catches his hands, halts the deal. For a few moments those bony hands remain still, cupped around his like a warm bowl, while her sad old eyes hold him too. "It's all right, sonny boy," she says. "It's gonna be all right."

"Yes," Penny says when he asks her to marry him.

Calvin kisses her urgently and holds her against him as they shuffle awkwardly back to her immaculate bedroom where they make hungry love.

Spent, his arm draped over her breasts, Calvin says, "Let's wait and announce it on Christmas Eve? We still have a date, don't we?"

"Well, I guess so, but may I at least tell my parents?"

"Please wait just a few more days. I am NOT going to change my mind this time, I promise, I'm down for the count, hooked on love, can't live without you." The image of Money's naked breasts with the finger-sausage nipples steals into Calvin's mind, so real he can almost taste them, and he can almost smell that dangerous musky odor of hers, too. *No*, he tells himself. *That's crazyland.*

"Penelope George," he says, nuzzling her neck, inhaling her Shalimar, "you've always been the one for me. I've just been too stupid to figure that out until now. I love you. You are the finest girl in the universe and I want to spend the rest of my life with you, okay my little sweetie pie with ice cream and cherries on top?"

"Okay, okay, don't get carried away, Calvin. I do believe you this time. Something's different. I trust you now, but you sound... I don't know, you sound sad about it. Are you sad?

"No, honey, I'm not sad, I'm happy to have you in my future. It's just that I've been through a lot in the last six months and I'm tired, so goddamned tired, but I'm okay. I just need a little more time to think things through and get ready to have you in my life, okay? I swear, I promise on a forty-foot stack of Bibles, I am not going to run away or push you away this time, I swear."

She touches his face. "Calvin?"

"Yes."

"Relax, honey." She kisses him gently. "I think, maybe just a little bit, I am starting to understand what you have been going through. Dad told me what happened down in Arkansas. He's really upset about it. I've never seen him like this." She pulls the sheet over her breasts and turns onto her side, her gaze right on him now. "What really happened down there, Calvin? Did Karl what's-his-name really try to kill you?"

"Yes, he did, but the story goes way further than that."

"It goes all the way back to your sister Jewel, doesn't it?"

Calvin is shocked; how does she know this? He wraps his arms around her, pulls her close so he doesn't have to look at her. "Dear Penny," he whispers, "I will tell you everything some day, but not today. Okay, babycakes? Okay?"

"I love you, Calvin Turtle."

"Christmas Eve, then?"

"Yes, my love."

MONDAY, DECEMBER 18TH, 1972

Anxiety is up and hope is down in America. Nixon is bombing the hell out of Vietnam, and under his wage and price freeze the economy is worsening. People are buying playing cards in record volume. All of the layoffs at Turtle have been rescinded and extra workers have been hired for the holiday push.

Calvin calls Donte Miller down in the West End. "Merry Christmas," he chirps.

"Whaddayou want?"

"Why haven't you come back to work? We'd like to have you back."

"You already got my wife's mama cleaning your damn house and washing your dirty underwear, and her father serving you cocktails at the Pendennis Club. You won't never get me again."

"Donte, I can't help how the world is and neither can you."

"I can and I will."

"Do you remember when you said, 'I know who you are, motherfucker?'"

"Naw, I don't. What about it?"

"Well, here's who I am. I'm the owner and you're the employee, world without end, amen, but it doesn't mean I'm any better than you. It's just the way it is. We have to accept it the way Johnnie accepts it and the way Johnnie's husband, what's his name...."

"Lucius."

"The way Lucius is proud of working at the Pendennis Club. Hell, Johnnie and Lucius are the upper class, as far as I'm concerned. Having money doesn't mean shit."

"You ever go without eatin'?"

"No, you're right, money does mean shit, but you know what I mean. What really counts is how you treat people. Jesus didn't have any money, right?"

"Man, don't be layin' that shit on me. If you're gonna talk that talk, first you give away all your money, *then* you tell me about Jesus."

Calvin forces a little laugh. "Guess I'd make a lousy preacher."

Donte is silent. This thought pops into Calvin's head: *Weather always moves in from the West.*

"So, will you come back to work for us?" Calvin finally says.

"Hell, no." Donte hangs up.

CHRISTMAS EVE, 1972

Johnnie is fixing a chicken casserole while Calvin reads the paper. Nixon has approved a short halt in the bombing for the holidays, the Governor of Mississippi has released a Ku Klux Klansman who murdered a black leader in 1966, Harry Truman is dying, and the Apollo 17 astronauts have sent back breathtaking color pictures of a beautiful blue-brown-white earthball. In a little box at the bottom of the front page is printed verbatim a letter sent to the North Pole by a fourth grader in Mrs. Walt Henry's 4th grade class at Layne Elementary School down in the West End:

Dear Santa,
    This is my frist letter so I would like for you to read it carefully. So hear is what I would like, I would like to have peace in this world and the diferint colored people come together and be friends.   *Lisa Jenkins*

When Johnnie is done in the kitchen, she disappears into the basement to change back into her street clothes. When she emerges, Calvin hands her an envelope with a big Christmas bonus inside. She shoves the envelope in her purse and gives him a warm hug. "Just put that casserole in at 350 for 30 minutes when you are ready to eat it," she says into his shoulder. Calvin holds her a second too long. When he pushes back, she looks worried.
    "You okay?"

"Fine and dandy."

"Okay, then. I gotta get home to my babies." She starts to leave, turns back and says, "Donte's a fool."

Calvin smiles. "Tell him I said Merry Christmas."

Johnnie smiles too. She grabs the doorknob and says with her back to him, "*You* the one needs a Merry Christmas."

ROUND AND ROUND WE GO

The cemetery is full of people, even though the sky is heavy grey, the air bitterly cold and damp. An endless parade of cars creeps around the lake like a slow merry-go-round. *Christmas Eve,* Calvin thinks. *Birth and death. Death and Birth. Round and round we go.*

Every now and then a car stops and the people get out with flowers, buttoning their coats one-handed against the chill, their foggy breath swirling and mingling and disappearing as they troupe up or down a slope to lay the flowers on a grave. Calvin is sitting next to Jewel's flat stone:

JEWEL ANN TURTLE
Born November 20, 1950
Died December 24, 1957

On the far side of Jewel, patches of mud and scraggly dead grass mark the recent graves of his mother and father. Calvin chastises them: "Is that all you could think of to put on her tombstone?"

Their answer is cold still silence.

He closes his eyes and pictures the accident, his car pushing them toward the high rock wall. Bitterness floods his throat. He opens his eyes, coughs up a little slime, spits it toward the lake, then looks down and tells his mother and father once and for all, "All right, I'm guilty. I killed you. I'm not sorry. I forgive you. Goodbye."

Some kids in bright jackets and caps are feeding the ducks down at the lake. There is no decorum, of course.

The little boys and girls fight over the bread, and when they hurl jagged white chunks into the water the ducks flap and splash and climb over each other to get at it.

"Over the river and through the woods, to grandmother's house we go," Calvin sings quietly. Down at the far end of the clean, sparkling lake near the mouth of the Cave, a couple of swans drift among dead leaves, apparently indifferent to the feeding orgy going on across the way.

"How do you do that?" Calvin asks the regal swans. "How do you refrain?"

Just above him on the hill, a peacock squawks as he begins to cross the road in front of Calvin's parked car, then as if to seduce the car, he fans out his magnificent tail while he struts before the unseeing headlights. On this cold, miserable day, that brilliant mandala of blues and greens is too much and Calvin begins to cry. He stands up, brushes off his pants, gazes down at Jewel's small headstone: "You're free," he blubbers, then he turns and trudges back up the hill where that goddamned peacock is still in full bloom.

SAIL A CARD FOR JESUS

Calvin nibbles on Johnnie's delicious chicken casserole, drinks some whiskey and watches *The Wizard of Oz* on television. They show it every Christmas Eve.

Near midnight he pours more whiskey in a flask and drives over to St. Mark's Episcopal. By the time he gets to the door, the midnight service is underway, muffled organ music floating on the freezing air.

Calvin understands that his future is inside that church. Penny, Dr. and Mrs. George, the Stanfulls, the Kentlingers, No-Knees Headmore, they're all in there. All he has to do is pull open the dark oaken door and step forward, but he hesitates, as if this is a game of Sharks and Minnows and he is last to dive into the deep end. *Come on, Calvin. Go!* he tells himself. How he wants to just dive in and spend the rest of his life in Penny's sweet Shalimar embrace. She will be a good wife, she really will, and her parents are good parents too, but he can't make himself open that door. He backs away, sits on a cold concrete step, takes out the flask, downs a gulp of hot whiskey. *What is the problem?* he asks himself.

A little snow is falling now. Large flakes drift through shafts of stained-glass light turning yellow, then blue, then red, then dead black and gone like sparks from a Fourth of July colorburst. Calvin sees that over in the dry fountain the concrete statue of Mary is still smiling down at Her concrete Son. In Her arms the haloed Baby Jesus beams rapturously back at His loving Mother.

What a life, Calvin thinks.

He notices too that Baby Jesus, cradled at his Mother's breast, makes a little shelf on which the fat snowflakes are beginning to accumulate, a shelf you could land a playing card on if you were good. There is a deck of Turtle Cards in his car. *Just a quick little game*, he tells himself, then he will dive into the future.

Sail a card for Jesus, he dubs it. Land a card in His little Lap, go to heaven. Calvin makes it to heaven maybe a dozen times this dark night before he picks up all the cards, heaves open the heavy door and steps inside the warm, dark sanctuary.

ABOUT THE AUTHOR

SQUIRE BABCOCK has taken a long and fascinating path to becoming a novelist. He grew up in an abusive Louisville home and was eventually arrested and jailed for possession of heroin. In the ensuing years, he worked as a ballroom dance instructor, farm hand, weigh-man in a cotton gin, hunting guide, pool table repair mechanic, small business owner, carpenter, freelance journalist and blues drummer. At the age of 30, he sold his Nashville pool table business and registered as a freshman English major at the University of Massachusetts. After graduating with his B.A., he taught English at a Massachusetts boarding school for three years before returning to UMass for his MFA. In 1996 Kentucky Governor Brereton Jones pardoned Babcock's heroin conviction. He is currently Associate Professor of English at Murray State University, where he has taught English and creative writing for 16 years and heads up the Low-Residency MFA Program in Creative Writing.